ROGU

By John R. Monteith

Stealth Books

Table of Contents

CHAPTER 1

Captain Second Rank Dmitry Volkov raised his head and pressed his palms into the navigation table. His back straightening, he felt cloud's lifting from his mind's haze.

"Say that again."

"Sir, the dolphins report a submerged contact," the sonar operator said.

He stretched his hands to the overhead piping to squeeze blood through his cramping muscles. He absorbed the absurdity that a dozen sonar systems, twice as many radars, and lasers scouring the Sea of Azov had failed where two mammals had succeeded in discovering Ukrainian saboteurs.

"Summon the trainer."

He watched the young sailor raise a sound-powered phone to his cheek as he rousted his shipmates to the manhunt.

"I've got a few people looking for him, sir. Are you sure you don't want to page him on the open circuit?"

"You heard the dolphins," Volkov said. "There's a submerged contact out there. I'm not risking the noise."

His wait proved short when the trainer stepped through the room's forward watertight door. Lithe, the dolphins' master slipped into the compartment with the dexterous ease of the animals he commanded. Eager eyes glared back at him.

"What did they say?" the trainer asked.

"Submerged contact," Volkov said. "I want you to discern the details."

The trainer bumped the sonar operator's shoulder as he sat at the console beside him.

"Let me hear the recording."

Volkov watched the trainer slip headphones over his ears and listen as the sonar operator pressed his capacitive touchscreen to replay the transmission.

"That's Andrei," the trainer said. "He's reporting a submerged contact."

"I know that much," Volkov said. "What else?"

The trainer shook his head and frowned.

"There won't be anything else because he's awaiting your command before sending more data."

At the onset of his submerged anti-saboteur patrol, Volkov had foreseen a negligible probability of needing to communicate with the dolphins. His failure to memorize the proper response to their report embarrassed him.

"I see," he said. "And how should I respond?"

"If you'll allow, sir, I'll handle it."

"Let me know your intent before you transmit each message."

"Of course, of course. Just let me talk to him. He's probably worried since you haven't responded yet."

"Very well," Volkov said. "Shift control of the underwater communications to the trainer."

"Shifting control of the underwater communications to the trainer, sir," the sonar operator said. "Control is shifted."

"Tell me what you're saying," Volkov said.

"I'm sending him the basic acknowledgement message. Even if Andrei is managing to remain calm, Mikhail must be terrified. He's fragile, emotionally. He must think I've abandoned them."

"I can think of worse fates for dolphins."

The trainer glared at him.

"They're not made of steel. They're made of flesh like us. They'd be saddened by the loss of a friend like me."

"Emotional or not, I'll give them credit for their tactical value–provided this supposed submerged contact proves real."

"It will. May I transmit?"

"Very well, transmit the acknowledgement message."

Volkov twisted a knob above his head to pipe sound through the compartment's loudspeakers. He listened as his submarine, the Improved *Kilo Project 636*-class *Krasnodar,* simulated an aquatic animal by broadcasting a recorded dolphin's message.

The series of whistles meant nothing to him, but the relaxed features on the trainer's face affirmed their intended significance.

"That should calm them," the trainer said.

"Very well," Volkov said. "Now I want information. Start with bearing and range to the contact. Can they do that?"

"They can determine all the information you could want as a holographic image in their minds. Their challenge is trying to tell us about it. We seem quite limited to them compared to their understanding of the undersea world."

"Spare me the sermon and tell them to locate the target."

The trainer tapped his screen, and a new series of recorded whistles from the *Krasnodar's* hydrophones filled the room. Moments later, Volkov heard a dolphin's high-pitched response.

"They've echolocated the contact," the trainer said.

Volkov forced himself to incorporate the bottlenose dolphins' perspectives into his tactics to identify, and possibly destroy, the submerged contact. He accepted their view of the undersea world as a sonic painting, but their mental pictures eluded his grasp. He sought the limited, discrete information they could share.

"If I remember correctly," he said, "the next step is to determine their position."

"Yes," the trainer said. "I taught them to respond immediately to a certain click which gives the range. You already know the bearing of their incoming responses. I'll do it three times to get an average. May I?"

"Go ahead."

Three series of outgoing recordings followed by mammalian responses filled the control room.

"Based upon round-trip timing and the sound-velocity profile in these waters, the distance to the lead dolphin is nine thousand yards," the sonar operator said.

"Very well," Volkov said. "Plot it on the chart."

Below his chin, the icon of a thick black cetacean appeared. He scowled.

"That's a whale," he said.

"It's the closest thing to a dolphin we have in the system, sir."

"So be it. Now tell me where the submerged contact is relative to my dolphin-whale."

"I'll query for the bearing next," the trainer said.

"Go ahead."

Another exchange of chirps and whistles.

"I taught them to understand bearings like the hours of a clock. Our submarine is twelve o'clock to their reference. Andrei says the submerged contact is at three o'clock."

"Very well," Volkov said. "What about range?"

"That's unfortunately the least accurate parameter. The best I could teach them was near, far away, or in between. They roughly understand near as within a nautical mile, far as beyond ten."

"So be it. Go ahead and ask."

More chirps.

"In between," the trainer said.

"Call it five nautical miles and plot it," Volkov said. "Give it a radius of uncertainty of five nautical miles."

An icon of a submarine surrounded by a translucent circle of uncertainty appeared near a pipeline and utility cables that supplied natural gas, electricity, and telecommunications between mainland Russia and Crimea.

"Sons of bitches," Volkov said. "Man battle stations. Ready tube one to attack this new submerged contact."

The senior enlisted sailor on watch, a veteran with a tight face, crow's feet, and a graying beard, orchestrated the actions of the half dozen men in the control room and the newcomers who responded to the battle stations command.

"Now, order the dolphins to approach the target," Volkov said.

A frown cast a shadow over the trainer's eyes.

"Is there a problem?" Volkov asked.

The trainer's shoulders rose and slumped with his sigh. Perplexed, Volkov stared at him and pondered the man's hesitance. Resentment gave way to curiosity, which succumbed to understanding. Feeling the crew's eyes upon him, he measured his words as he dismantled the impasse.

"I see," he said. "Can you give them the order, or would you prefer that I spare you from this burden?"

"You can't do this. Why would you risk them?"

"You know why. You trained them to deploy explosives. Now is not the time to protest capitalizing upon their abilities."

"Why did you bother getting a torpedo ready if you're going to use my babies?"

"Contingency. Backup in case my tactical assets–and let's be clear that they're my assets and not your babies–fail."

The trainer said nothing.

"I can do this without you. The basic commands to the dolphins are mapped into my tactical system, and my operators recognize them even if I don't. I'll use them if you don't comply within the next ten seconds."

"Yes! Yes! Better that I do this, if they are to survive."

"Very well, order the approach"

Recorded whistles. Mammalian response.

"They've confirmed," the trainer said. "They're accelerating towards the target."

Volkov locked eyes with his sonar operator, who nodded his overheard concurrence of the communications exchange.

As the animals' usefulness unfolded, so did Volkov's memory of their abilities. He recalled that cameras atop their body harnesses could capture images of the target to confirm its identity.

"Very well. I want a dark photograph first, without a flash to alert the target. Then I will assess."

"A dark photograph first," the trainer said. "Got it. I will send the order."

After the dolphins confirmed, the trainer tapped his fingers on the console.

"Why so nervous?" Volkov asked. "You trained them for this exact activity."

"I don't like it. The explosives may trigger early. The Ukrainians may have weapons to use against them. God knows what fate you're making me send them towards."

"Instead of fretting, you should expect to soon be proud of

8

your achievement. Their explosives will protect the lifeline to Crimea from our adversary with little to no trace of our involvement."

"Perhaps, but I still worry."

Volkov turned and walked to the elevated conning platform at the compartment's rear. He sank into his foldout captain's chair.

"Get a report of their location."

Three series of transmitted recordings spurred mammalian responses.

"The distance to the lead dolphin is ten thousand yards," the sonar operator said. "Bearing is three-four-two. Updating the chart."

Volkov watched the whale icon shift on the liquid crystal display beside his forearm. Velocity data appeared above it.

"They're moving at eleven knots," he said.

"Any faster, and you risk muscle cramps while they're fully loaded," the trainer said. "They can't sprint the distance. So they're pacing themselves at optimum speed."

"Very well."

"They'll be in camera range in twenty minutes, ignoring the uncertainty of the distance."

"How can you most quickly remove that uncertainty?"

"I trained them to announce when they pass a distance boundary, either from long range to medium range or medium range to short. They'll tell us when they've closed within a mile."

Periodic solicited dolphin chirps updated their icon on the chart. Volkov's anxiety grew as the animals passed over the expected location of the target, but he exercised restraint to avoid stating his concern about the positional inaccuracy.

Then the unsolicited chirp arrived.

"They're within a mile of the target," the trainer said. "Four minutes until dark photograph range."

Four minutes later, Volkov ordered the image. The ship's recorded chirp told the lead dolphin to point its nose at the target for three seconds while the camera atop its head snapped a picture of the dark depths.

He recognized the new sound of crackling shrimp, the camera's signal that simulated the sea's biological noises, pulsing through the loudspeakers. Given the low baud rate, he expected five minutes to form the full image.

"Order the dolphins to hold their position," he said.

The trainer complied.

As the synthetic shrimp symphony sounded, a grainy picture took form on Volkov's display. He noticed the trainer glaring at the same image evolving at his console.

"Doesn't that bright narrow triangular area appear to be artificial lighting?" Volkov asked.

"It's too soon to tell," the trainer said.

"I don't share your pessimism. I've determined that the target has a light source and is conducting illegal sabotage activity. Since we used no flash and kept the photograph dark, the target is not alerted. The dolphins will have an uncontested approach. Prepare them for explosives deployment."

The heightened anticipation kindled Volkov's memory of the dolphins' capabilities. He envisioned one sliding its snout into the carrying strap of the bomb attached forward of the dorsal fin of its partner.

A chirp announced the completion of each animal's arming.

"They're ready to lay explosives," the trainer said.

"Very well, deploy the explosives."

As the trainer reached to relay the order, a new pattern of mammalian sounds filled the room.

"What's that?" Volkov asked.

"The new threat signal," the trainer said.

"Belay my last order. Hold the dolphins."

The trainer tapped a command and then suspended his hands above the console.

"I've stopped them."

"What sort of threat?" Volkov asked.

"Submerged, of course. That's the only type they report unsolicited."

"I need data. Bearing and range, just as before. Gather the data, and don't wait for me to approve each message. The timing is too critical due to the threat to the pipeline."

The trainer began the exchange with the animals.

"Sir," the sonar operator said, "I hear the new threat now. High-speed screws, but very faint."

"Faint?" Volkov asked. "Meaning at great distance?"

"No, sir. More like very small with minimal shaft torque."

"Could it be another submersible?"

"I don't think so. It's more like small craft. Two of them. In fact, I just lost the signal."

The dolphins' data revealed a twin threat. Two small, mechanized, and hostile targets to the south materialized. When the icon appeared on his screen, Volkov surmised the coordination of the sabotage.

"They're attacking the bridge, too," he said. "Split the dolphins. Send one to the south to assess the threat to the bridge. Have one continue with the attack on the submersible near the pipeline."

"Splitting is impossible," the trainer said. "There's no such order or concept. They're a team, and you may as well ask me to order this submarine split in half."

"Very well. Have them take out the submersible with just one detonator. I want to save the other for the threat to the bridge."

"Again, I can't order one to act without the other. They either plant explosives together or they do not."

"Damn it, then. Have them plant the explosives on the submersible near the pipeline."

As the trainer set the dolphins into their attack, Volkov ordered the *Krasnodar* to periscope depth. The deck rocked in the shallow sea's swells.

"Raise the radio mast," he said.

An enlisted man seated at a control console at the front of the compartment tapped a screen, and Volkov heard hydraulic valves clunk over his head.

A red light from a transceiver box mounted over his head signaled his connectivity with a nearby ship that relayed his voice to the Black Sea Fleet headquarters. He yanked a handset down towards his mouth.

"Wolf Den, this is Wolf One. Over."

An amplified voice issued from the transceiver.

"Wolf One, this is Wolf Den. Over."

"Wolf Den, Wolf One. I've found a submersible with artificial lighting near our pipeline. I need verification that we have no authorized work being done on the pipeline. Over."

"Wolf One, Wolf Den, there's no authorized work. That's a hostile. You're weapons free."

"Wolf Den, Wolf One. I understand weapons free on the submersible. I also need a minimum distance to a main caisson of the Kerch Strait Bridge at which I can detonate a heavyweight torpedo without damaging the caisson. Over."

An uncomfortable silence told him he had stymied the watchman who manned the phones. The replacement voice carried the authority of the senior officer on watch at headquarters.

"Wolf One, Wolf Den. That information doesn't exist here. I'll need to send an urgent message to the Highway Authority to gather that information. How soon to you need it? Over."

Volkov glared at the sailor seated at the weapons control console.

"How long will it take the weapon to reach the closest caisson at maximum speed?"

The sailor looked to his screen.

"Sixteen minutes, sir."

"Wolf Den, Wolf One. I need an answer in fifteen minutes–and not a second later. I've discovered another submerged threat that I believe is preparing to sabotage the bridge, and I will detonate a weapon in the vicinity in sixteen minutes. Over."

"Wolf One, Wolf Den. Understood. Out."

He secured the handset.

"Shift the weapon in tube one to coordinates one hundred

yards distance from the closest caisson, bearing zero-four-five from the caisson."

The weapons operator obeyed and announced the readiness of tube one.

"Shoot tube one," Volkov said.

The pneumatic torpedo impulsion system beyond sight in the ship's forward compartment thrust a weapon into the ocean while sucking air into its piping. The rapid pressure change popped his ears.

"Tube one away, normal launch," the weapons operator said.

Whistles and chirps filled the room.

"The explosives are applied to the target at the pipeline," the trainer said. "The dolphins have swum to a safe distance for detonation."

Volkov studied the image of the submersible. The synthetic shrimp crackles had continued building the resolution, and his target's form had become clear.

"That's a mini-submersible," he said. "Minimal yield on each detonator will be sufficient. Set both detonators to minimum yield. We may yet be able to make this look like an accident."

The trainer appeared relieved with the lessened risk of collateral damage to his animals.

"I've set the settings to minimal," he said.

"Detonate."

The two pops reminded Volkov of an assassin's bullets.

"The submersible has flooded," the sonar operator said. "It was almost instantaneous."

"Very well. Give me an update on our torpedo."

"Twelve minutes to detonation, sir," the weapons operator said. "Running at full speed."

"Send the dolphins to the caisson."

"Why?" the trainer asked. "Haven't they done their jobs?"

Volkov wearied of the civilian's questions but accepted them as an annoying necessity.

"For battle damage assessment. I'll want their cameras telling me what I shot and making sure I killed it."

"Okay. I'll send them."

Volkov reached for the radio handset.

"Wolf Den, Wolf One. I've used the explosives from the dolphins to sink the submersible near the pipeline. I'll send an image and coordinates. Over."

"Wolf One, Wolf Den. Roger. Over."

"Where's my engineering assessment? Over?"

"It's still coming. Don't do the saboteurs' work for them with an over-aggressive torpedo shot. Over."

"Then get me my damned assessment. Out."

During the next ten minutes, he watched the icon of his weapon race toward the caisson.

"Wolf One, Wolf Den. The engineering assessment is one nautical mile. Over."

"That's ludicrous, Wolf Den. That's cowardice–not an engineering assessment. Tell the engineers to reassess."

"There's no data on this, and there's no time to run an accurate simulation. You demand a rapid answer, you get a rapid response. Over."

Volkov lowered the handset to avoid cursing into it. He then returned it to his mouth.

"I'll detonate my weapon one hundred yards from the caisson. I assume responsibility for the outcome. Have our ships stay out of the way. Out."

He drove the handset back into its cradle and looked at the weapons operator.

"You heard me. One hundred yards."

"Yes, sir. It's almost there."

"Then you'd better hurry and send the signal to the warhead."

The sailor tapped icons and announced the detonation. The sonar operator nodded.

"I heard the explosion, sir. Our weapon has detonated."

"You don't hear concrete shattering, do you? I didn't destroy the caisson, did I?"

"No, sir. I can't attest to hidden structural damage, though."

"Neither can I," Volkov said. "I'll leave that to our engineers to resolve."

He took the *Krasnodar* deep to avoid the chastising radio chatter he expected from headquarters.

"Where are the dolphins?" he asked.

"Half way there," the trainer said. "I can get you pictures in about fifteen minutes."

After waiting for the mammals to reach the caisson, Volkov ordered multiple images of his torpedo's aftermath. The dolphins found a pair of lifeless divers' bodies and two scuba scooters suspended in the shallows beside the concrete pillar.

"Move them closer to the caisson," he said. "Get close ups of the full circumference of the concrete."

Fifteen minutes later, he viewed a still life of explosives attached to the caisson. He could only wonder how close the divers had come to completing their work and bringing down the bridge, but he was certain he had discovered and defeated an enemy with the resolve to challenge Russia's annexation of Crimea

"Load that image into the radio system," he said. "Whatever whining the engineers may have about my torpedo, let them compare it to this."

CHAPTER 2

Jake Slate glanced across the waiting room at Pierre Renard.

"She's making us wait even longer than last time."

"Miss McDonald is reminding us how important she is," Renard said.

"She's pegged to be the next DCIA, right?" Jake asked

"Not quite yet, but close. I suspect she needs one more feather in her cap, so to speak."

Jake watched the Frenchman's steel blue eyes shimmer as he passed a gold-plated Zippo lighter under a Marlboro.

"I thought you only smoked now when you were feeling the pressure. You're not afraid of Olivia, are you?"

"You've known me too long for me to deceive you, and I must admit that I'm suffering a good deal of anxiety."

"Do tell. The great Pierre Renard, anxious about talking to Olivia McDonald? She was just a young CIA agent when you let her nab us. Don't tell me she's got you quaking in your boots ten years later."

"Don't fool yourself, my friend. She may have erred in falling in love with you back then, but that was her solitary mistake. She's well armed in the battle of wits. She all but had you captured in Avignon."

"But not you. You were already out of France before she could have pulled the trigger."

"Indeed I was, but if she had taken you into custody, she would have had me as well."

Jake watched gray clouds rise from the amber butt.

"You would have come out of hiding to help me?"

"You know I would have."

"Yeah, I suppose so. That aside, why would her wits scare you now? She's never outsmarted us completely, and DCIA or not, she's just one of many powerbrokers in your network."

"Therein lies the rub, my friend. She's not yet the Director of the Central Intelligence Agency. Just a deputy thereof, though one of the most powerful in recent history and topping my list of noteworthy rainmakers."

"You sound like you wish she'd just stay a deputy."

"Perhaps. Her ambition is the only thing that's growing faster than her influence. I'm sure she's concocting a final chess move to assure herself her next promotion."

"So what's the problem? She's an ally growing in power. Isn't that a good thing?"

He felt like an idiot for asking as he predicted his mentor's response.

"It's good until she grows too powerful to respect our free will. After our Spratly Island campaign, I sensed the balance of power shifting to her. She was beginning to need us less than we need her. The South Korean campaign, however, was more my doing. I developed the relationship with our new clients. But she was involved in the background, and she continues to be my only conduit to satellite data and other kinds of important information."

"How involved was she in Korea?"

"I don't know. That's one reason I'm anxious. I fear that she understands our full capabilities and is calling upon us for that final resounding success she needs for her advancement."

"That's normal. She always calls on us for shit like that."

"What's irking me is the stakes," Renard said. "I don't know how much goodwill she believes we owe her from Korea. Nor do I know how she values her own growing power against our last ten years of working together. She may perceive that what I considered an even scorecard has evolved into a debt I owe her."

"You're walking into a negotiation without the facts. You don't know where you stand."

The Frenchman exhaled smoke and placed his cigarette into an ashtray.

"Precisely. And worse, I don't know what she wants, nor do I fully understand my own desired outcomes since there are several scenarios for which she may have summoned us."

"I never thought the day would come where you'd walk into a negotiation working uphill."

"It has. But I sense enough power on her end to warrant our presence, compromised as it is. From her brief invitation, I predict a weighty endeavor."

Jake pondered his mentor's assets. He knew the Frenchman's network had grown strong, and his mercenary fleet of two *Scorpène*-class submarines and one custom, armed submarine transport ship was in top condition. For every nation that loathed him, two nations stood ready to purchase his services.

"Let me guess," he said. "You're here for the usual, but you're not sure if you're going to get it."

"The usual?"

"A mission you can't refuse, supported with intelligence from Her Majesty of the CIA, for a cash payout that gives you more clout to grow your enterprise."

"You know me well."

"If she'd ever open the flipping door, we might find out what she's offering. Any idea what it could be?"

"Several. The world is a mess, and that's part of my quandary. My mind is overworked with scenarios, payouts, and risks, on top of my ignorance of the goodwill accounting she's tallied."

A middle-aged lady in a dark suit behind a desk, flanked by an American flag and a CIA banner, lifted her nose and announced that Olivia McDonald was ready to receive them. Jake stood and watched his friend extinguish his cigarette before following him.

"Well, shit, Pierre. He we go."

Sexy with a curve-hugging suit, Olivia McDonald stood and walked around her desk to greet Jake. As she embraced him, he sensed her coldness, and her words sounded sterile. He thought for a moment that she sounded lonely.

"It's good to see you again, Jake."

Lines forming on her face showed age catching up with her, but in a world led by old men, she shone as a beacon of bright, young energy. As she kissed Renard's cheeks and then slinked back to her desk, her movement suggested that her arrogance had grown in lockstep with her prestige.

He waited for her to sit before lowering himself into her leather guest chair.

"It's great to see you both again."

"It's our pleasure to be with you," Renard said. "Seeing you is something I always look forward to."

"You're always too kind, Pierre. How are you?"

"Splendid. My business and network are thriving, and I owe much of it to your support."

"Yes, you do," she said. "I'm glad you're willing to acknowledge it. I'm also doing well. You probably know where I stand in the hierarchy. So I won't bore you with bragging. What you probably don't know is what stands between me and the next level."

"I just might," Renard said. "People have short memories, and I suspect that your superiors have forgotten much of your past accomplishments. I believe that you need something attention-grabbing to secure your next promotion, and that's why we're here."

She gave the Frenchman an inquisitive stare. As her features softened, Jake realized that she lived in a world surrounded by underlings who feared rendering frank feedback. She appeared to like Renard's candor.

"I can't remember the last time someone spoke to me so directly, except my boss. But the difference between you and him is that you're right. He rarely is. I'll be doing the intelligence world a favor by taking his place. And yes, you can be a part of making that happen."

"How can we help?"

"I haven't thought through any elaborate plans, but I need you to inflict a little damage on a tyrant."

"What sort of damage?" Renard asked.

"Interrupt cross-straits commerce between two major land masses. You'll cripple a bridge, a pipeline, and a few ships."

Jake noticed a change in his friend's demeanor to a mood he failed to identify. The Frenchman appeared plasticized.

"You're turning my team into saboteurs?" Renard asked.

"Call it what you want. But this is a calculated move, and I'll spare you the speculation. It's a message to the Kremlin."

"A message? Not the taking of an asset? No oil field? No land grab? No armaments pilfered? Nothing to be gained?"

She smirked.

"A later phase of this operation, after your involvement, may lead to lasting changes of sea-based asset ownership in the region. But that's secondary."

"That's what I was afraid of."

"Afraid? You?"

"Messages are only heard if they catch the attention of the listener, and to catch someone's attention, one must do something splashy. From the parameters you've mentioned, I surmise that you want me to enter the Black Sea–perhaps as deeply as the Sea of Azov–and challenge the annexation of Crimea."

"I expected you to guess it by now, but it always impresses me when I watch you piece the puzzle together."

Jake found the silence uncomfortable as his mentor slowed the conversation to heighten the effect of the compliment. He held his breath until the Frenchman spoke.

"I think you fail to realize how difficult a battle within a closed sea can be," Renard said, "especially when the adversary owns the sky, has the dominant fleet within it, and a Muslim state owns the only sea route in or out."

"You'll have the element of surprise. You sneak in, attack, and get out. I'm not asking you to take on the entire Black Sea Fleet. Just do what you do best and pull back."

"At great peril to my assets. What reward merits this risk?"

"Nobody's been willing to stand up to Russia on this, but now's the time. It's been just over four years since they took Crimea, and it's the inflection point. Crimea is fully dependent on their connection to the mainland through the lifelines you're going to destroy, and the original outrage for the annexation is still recent enough to be remembered."

"There's a groundswell movement to return the land to the

Ukrainians? My network has heard of such uprisings, but nothing has ever taken root."

"And it may or may not. It depends who you ask, and the results could vary anywhere from Crimea becoming an independent state to backfiring and bringing stronger Russian dominance."

Renard leaned back, revealing an uncertainty so honest that Jake believed it.

"So you really don't care about the results–just the message. You undermine the Russian president in his new term, you secure your position within the CIA, and you declare America's willingness to stand up to Russia."

"Close," she said. "You're not representing the United States. You're representing the United Nations."

"You gest."

"Nope."

"That explains it then. That's how you expect me to pass the Bosporus and Dardanelles unchallenged. You've already negotiated Turkey's involvement through channels in the United Nations."

She cleared her throat.

"Yes, but don't ask me the terms or who knows about them. And don't expect that the passage will be trivial, but I will introduce you to a Turkish admiral who can help you manage it."

"Understood."

Jake capitalized on a moment of silence.

"Hold on," he said. "Have either of you considered that Pierre's fleet doesn't have any weapons designed to attack pipelines or bridges? I mean, maybe the *Goliath's* railguns could pound away at a bridge, but what would happen is just a guess."

"I can get the weapons," Renard said. "Let's assume this is possible. What I don't understand is why you don't just send in a team of clandestine divers. You could use Navy Seals and commandoes from a few other nations to claim it as a United Nations action. That would accomplish your message."

She shook her head.

"The Ukrainians tried this unilaterally, and the Russians caught them red-handed. A submarine torpedo blew up close to the bridge, and the shock wave killed a pair of divers. There was also a submersible that was lost while trying to break the pipeline."

"A submersible was lost?" Renard asked. "Taken out by the same submarine?"

"We don't know. The Ukrainians don't know. It could've been an accident, but we have to assume it was the Russians."

"The Russians? Using divers of their own? Those waters are shallow enough for diver operations all the way to the bottom."

"Maybe. Or maybe trained animals. The Russians use them for defense, just like we do."

"Well, shit," Jake said. "You want to send me in against the Black Sea Fleet, which includes frontline *Kilo* submarines operated by arguably the best diesel submariners in the world. They're actively guarding the targets you want me to attack, and they've got Flipper on their side, too?"

"Jake has a point," Renard said. "Of course, I foresaw this as one scenario you might propose, and I have considered tactical options. But I must be candid that this is the most troublesome mission I've ever considered. We face a long road to reach agreement on this."

Her face darkened, and Jake feared that she prepared a tirade to remind them that she held the trump card of having them both executed for past crimes. Past verbal assurances of debts paid in full felt fleeting. She grabbed a pen and a sticky pad, upon which she wrote before extending it to Renard.

"I assumed it would come to this," she said.

As the Frenchman reached for the note, Jake expected his friend's face to turn ashen with a silent threat of imprisonment or worse. Instead, his mentor blushed, folded the paper, and stuffed it into his breast pocket.

"Do you have a timeline?" Renard asked.

"I don't have any deadlines other than the patience of those who will support me, and I'll tell them how long they need to be patient. You tell me how much time you need, and I'll let you know if it works for me."

Jake sensed Renard stiffening his back moments before Olivia stood.

"Wait," he said. "That's it? We're done?"

Olivia blushed while pursing her lips.

"I'll explain in private, Jake," Renard said. "Trust me for now."

"I always have."

He followed Renard's silent example and remained quiet as they walked to their limousine. He slid into the seat and burst with curiosity as the car started moving.

"Well?" he asked.

"She wrote down a dollar figure I couldn't refuse."

"You sold me to the Russian's for money?"

"No. You know me better than that. I have a plan that will succeed. You, Terry, and your crews will be fine."

"You're sending two ships? A submarine and the *Goliath*?"

"Yes."

"You're risking a lot of money worth of your fleet–not to mention your people."

"I always fear for my people because I care about them. The war machines are insured."

"Is that what she wrote?"

"Part of it, yes. She insured the hardware. She also offered to cover all expenses plus a generous fee."

Jake considered the politeness of asking.

"Well, are you going to at least give me a hint?"

"You recall what she's paid in the past."

"Yeah, a few hundred million was the most, right?"

"Correct. It's much more this time. Enough to complete the purchase of the second transport ship I wanted."

"Damn! Nice."

"And then some."

"Shit. What? Nine figures?"

Renard raised his palm.

"No. Don't be silly. It's not that much."

"Oh."

He stared at the Frenchman, who failed to suppress a childish grin.

"But it's really, really close."

CHAPTER 3

A gust tilted the helicopter, and Terrance Cahill cursed. "Bloody hell."

The aircraft recovered and touched down on the dirt.

"Welcome to Pengjia Islet," Renard said. "There's no easy way to get here."

"Worst landing I've ever had."

"That was indeed rough. But in all fairness, when Jake first arrived here, he did so with a tandem jump that nearly killed his companion. Your arrival is luxurious by comparison."

Cahill tossed his helmet to a crewmember of the Taiwanese helicopter, ducked, and followed Renard into the night.

Moist air rising from the island's cliffs caressed his cheeks as he escaped the rotor wash. A blast of wind made him crouch, and a look over his shoulder revealed the lights of the fleeing aircraft climbing into the darkness.

Laboring against soft earth, he saw the elder Frenchman outpacing him. He stifled a complaint and vowed to improve his physical conditioning.

When he joined Renard at the lighthouse, the islet's solitary habitable edifice, a motion sensor illuminated a bulb and revealed a keypad. The Frenchman tapped a code and pushed open the door.

Cahill followed him into the circular structure. A Taiwanese sentry approached, exchanged words in Mandarin and nods with the Frenchman, and gestured the men forward.

"You understand Chinese?" he asked.

"Enough."

The sentry helped Renard slide a desk, kick back a carpet, and pull open a trap door. The Frenchman started down steep stairs, and Cahill followed his silvery hair into the stone tunnel.

Florescent lights revealed a crude, jagged ceiling, and Cahill's legs ached as he stooped.

"Pace yourself," Renard said. "It's a long way to the submarine pen."

"Slow is good. Me thighs are burning already."

"We shall take our time and rest as needed."

Five minutes later, Cahill slowed and lowered his knees to the rocky floor.

"Pierre."

"Yes, of course. We shall rest for a moment."

Fifteen minutes later, Cahill rose from his third stop, and his next steps revealed metal plates blocking his view of the leveling ground.

"What's that metal all about?"

"It's a design based upon the South Koreans' treatment of infiltration tunnels in the demilitarized zone. The barriers force a zigzagging path to slow assailants."

After wiggling through the plates, Cahill watched Renard punch a code into a console by a steel door. His French boss shouldered the door open to reveal a control room no bigger than a suburban living room.

He entered and latched the door behind him. Windows at the far wall revealed a cave hewn by nature, with fingers of stalactites, expanded and reshaped by explosives.

Halogen lights bathed a concrete dock beside which rose a black conning tower. He recognized the *Specter*, the *Scorpène*-class submarine like the one he had helped Renard steal from the Malaysian Navy. The sight triggered his memory of commanding the Australian submarine, *Rankin*, to bring the *Wraith* into Jake Slate's trap.

He pointed at the submarine.

"What's all that?" he asked.

"I assume you mean the mine belts strapped to the *Specter*. They're staggered laterally to avoid interfering with the hydraulic rams that hold the ship within the *Goliath's* bed."

"I was afraid you'd say that. I don't envy meself or Jake carrying mine belts."

"They're completely safe. Mine laying is normal operations for the submarines of many navies. They're also positively buoyant, which means Jake can deploy them while in your cargo bed."

"I still don't like it, mate.

"You need them. You'll have the entirety of the Russian Black Sea Fleet pursuing you during your escape. You'll want Jake to leave a trail of speed bumps, so to speak."

"Speed bumps? More like Armageddon."

"They're all set to low yields. I'm in business to protect my assets and deter you being chased, but I don't need to crack the keel of every ship that pursues you. That would create angrier lifelong enemies."

The former Australian submarine commander had never deployed mines, and they worried him.

"Still, we're talking about blowing big holes in ships. Men will die, and smaller ships may be lost."

"Only if your pursuers are brave or foolish enough to chase you through your minefields. I expect instead that after the first mine detonates under a Russian ship, the rest will honor the coordinates of the minefield I will announce."

"You'll announce it? How? You may not know where we are or where we've laid the mines."

"I'll make a conservative estimate and invite the Russians to skirt the outer edge. At the very least, I will have done my duty by announcing the hazard to all vessels. Jake will set the mines to disarm within twenty-four hours of deployment, which will give you more than enough time to reach the Bosporus while keeping my reputation clean of minimizing unnecessary damage."

Cahill decided to digest the need and future use of the mines during the long transit to the operations area, and he let his gaze shift down the dock to the larger vessel–the one he commanded.

Like an enormous catamaran, the *Goliath* and its rakish bows extended toward the cavern's walls. The illuminated domed bridge on the transport ship's starboard hull cast checkered radiance against the hewn ceiling. The forward sections, produced for Taiwanese frigates, appeared capable of slicing waves.

The sterns of the *Goliath's* tapered upwards towards fantails to allow for elevated surface-combat weaponry. He recognized the railguns and the radar system's panels on each raised aft section.

Submerged cylinders of equal girth to the *Specter* connected the customized bows and sterns of each hull. Fuel lines reached from the subterranean pier to the *Goliath's* black arcs jutting above the still water.

He felt proud ownership as he remembered being the ship's solitary occupant when a North Korean torpedo had transformed the *Goliath's* port bow into twisted shards.

"Hardly looks like it's been scratched," he said.

"Repairs have been complete for some time," Renard said. "But I did have to pay overtime for the structural tests to get them completed before the latest modifications."

"Latest mods? I thought you had all the mods being worked in parallel with repairs."

"Most but not all. The latest modifications are customizations for the immediate mission."

"What more could I need? You're already giving me all the goodies I asked for."

Cahill ran through his mental checklist. He had demanded and received a Phalanx close-in weapon system to replace his near-impotent laser cannon, a network of blue-green laser transceivers to give him secure communications with the *Specter*, and an anti-torpedo weapon system.

"After my latest audience with Miss McDonald, I've taken some liberties. When I explain the full mission, you'll understand."

"It's still Miss McDonald? Not Misses Argentina?"

"The tabloids say she's engaged, but my intelligence network says the marriage will wait until her promotion to the DCIA."

"Call me romantic, but doesn't love matter?"

"Not with her."

"She's driven only by power, is she?"

"Right. And based upon our latest audience, I believe that she finally needs us more than we need her."

"Why so, mate?"

"She needs a navy to stand up to Russia while offering her plausible denial of America's involvement. That's us, my friend."

"Maybe being kicked out of the Aussie Navy wasn't such a bad deal after all. I get more confident that I've joined a winning team each time you describe it."

"As it should be."

"I know where we're going and that we're going to attack static targets, but what are the targets?"

"I can tell you now. The primary target is a bridge. The secondary is a shallow undersea pipeline."

Cahill envisioned the possibilities.

"I'm not sure where to begin asking me next questions."

"The targets connect Russia to the Crimean Peninsula. You're going to exploit Crimea's dependence upon mainland Russia. Most commerce runs through the bridge, including rail, auto, fossil fuels, and utilities."

"Got it. You also said I'm taking out an undersea pipeline. But you're also suggesting that there are pipelines on the bridge."

"Yes. The pipelines on the bridge deliver fuel and utilities. The undersea pipeline preceded the bridge in construction, but it remains an important secondary means of supply. If you take out both targets, you'll beget Crimea's decay by atrophy."

Trying to remember his knowledge of the former Ukrainian landmass, he imagined the implications of his mission.

"The best I can tell, you're having me ruin a tourist destination. I'm not seeing the big picture."

"Try to see it from the Russian perspective. You want to be a superpower, and you grab a jewel from your neighbor to demonstrate your might. When nobody stops you, you've proven that you are a superpower. China did nothing. Europe did nothing. America did nothing. Ergo, you've made your political statement. But Crimea is starving for resources, and it must be fed."

"And I'm breaking the feeding tube."

"Indeed. Crimea will begin a slow death, and the Russian president will face the harsh decision of either launching a costly crisis response campaign or the embarrassing walk to a negotiations table."

"I see why you're talking about new upgrades. I can't see me railguns taking down a bridge, at least not efficiently. Maybe if I pounded it with half me arsenal."

"Quite unnecessary. I've equipped you with externally-mounted tubes that have the coordinates of a main caisson programmed into them."

"You sure that's going to work? I can't see a torpedo taking down a concrete structure of any appreciable size."

Renard tapped a screen to invoke a map, and then he pointed at the bridge.

"The weapons will target the middle section to the west of the Tuzla Spit where the bridge reaches its highest point. I'm assured that the detonations will at least crack the concrete and make the caisson unusable, if not crumble a section of the bridge altogether."

"Detonations? Plural?"

The Frenchman furrowed his brow and appeared to calculate his response while lighting a Marlboro.

"You'll need to detonate a warhead on either side of the caisson simultaneously. The weapons will be staggered in location in order to apply a torqueing tensile stress and create a brittle fracture of the concrete. The explosions will be shallow to minimize backpressure from the water."

"Sounds optimistic."

"No need to take my word for it. See the video. A team of Taiwanese engineers ran a test and recorded the results on underwater cameras."

He crouched while Renard tapped icons on a screen and nothing happened. The Frenchman stood and spoke Mandarin, and a watchman hurried to his side. After a curt conversation, gestures, and assistance navigating the screens, his French boss invoked a video as the Taiwanese sailor returned to his post.

Progressing in slow motion, four frames moved forward with a different camera's view in each quadrant of the display. Two overhead vantages and two nose-on shots showed a pair of torpedoes moving through shallow, clear water.

The first weapon detonated, and the second followed it within ten milliseconds.

"Separated by ten meters laterally," Renard said. "Separated by seven meters axially. The locations and timings were well within specification. This is the only test I had run with actual warheads, but there were twenty non-explosive runs that showed comparable positions and timing."

"How's that possible?"

"The seekers. Since the coordinates of the detonations are already known, there's no need to use them to chase moving targets. So they've been modified to allow the weapons to track each other and to hold a prescribed relative geometry."

"Still, you can't reach good terminal accuracy with just inertial gyros. You'll be off by meters, which could mean the difference between success and failure."

The Frenchman exhaled smoke, making Cahill appreciate the control room's ventilation system. He glanced at the two Taiwanese sailors who sat behind monitoring panels and reminded him of chain-smoking chimneys.

"Not to worry," Renard said. "The seekers will still be used for terminal targeting to assure a proper distance from the caisson. In fact, the flatness of the concrete makes for an excellent acoustic return and precise locating."

"So if I get close enough to launch a pair of weapons, I'll cripple the bridge. Period."

"Indeed. The construction of the bridge is well-understood, given its public visibility. This allowed accurate modeling of the simulation. The weapons will succeed. I even gifted you the ability to launch from outside the strait. You can remain in the Black Sea while shooting."

"Really? How?"

"The weapons have a pre-programmed waypoint algorithm,

mapped to the turns of the strait. Fortunately, there are only two turns, but mapped they are. I don't want you getting trapped in the strait."

"Nice. How many chances do I get?"

Renard stared at him and raised an eyebrow.

"Do you mean how many pairs of anti-bridge weapons are in your arsenal?"

"Yes."

"An excellent question. Four pairs, in addition to two weapons dedicated to the pipeline, which is a much simpler target to cripple. That's ten total weapons, five per side, mounted on your hull."

"Four pairs for the bridge. That's overkill for weapons you just told me are guaranteed to work. It suggests risks I don't yet see."

"Perceptive. We're undertaking this mission after a failed attempt by the Ukrainians. I'll share the details during the mission brief, but beware that the Russians are watching and defending the bridge. You may need more than one shot to hit the target."

"That leaves only six weapons in me internal tubes for other purposes like self-defense."

"Jake will be handling that for you with the *Specter*."

Cahill envisioned the world map in his head and added up a challenging distance.

"Provided we can get there. There's a lot of ocean between here and the Black Sea."

"That's a good opportunity for me to show you the liberties I've taken with the *Goliath* for your mission."

"I can't wait."

He followed Renard down a staircase to the chiseled ledge of rock serving as a wharf and marveled at the brutal elegance of the waterfront.

The Taiwanese had packed spare weapons, fuel tanks, and electronic cables into carved recesses. Fed by fuel and lubricant lines, a diesel generator whirred with air ducts running into the rock ceiling.

"How'd they get all this down here?"

"The cutting took two years," Renard said. "Once the rocks were carved, the concrete, wood, and machinery arrived aboard submarines. It was a high-priority exercise when the Taiwanese were responding to the invasion by China. I've kept the place running as the new home port of the *Goliath* and *Specter*."

Cahill's boots tapped concrete as he trailed Renard onto the dock. A huge pile of a disassembled ship's hull sections caught his attention.

"What ship was that?" he asked. "And why's it down here?"

"That's your camouflage."

"Say again?"

"Camouflage. I'm not sending you over thousands of miles without camouflage, especially since you need to traverse no less than five intensely watched chokepoints."

Unsure how his boss planned to make his ship and its elevated cargo submarine invisible with black hull sections, he glanced at the *Goliath*. Beyond the hull-mounted torpedo tubes, he saw the stanchions and rigging that Taiwanese sailors were attaching to his deck.

"You mean for me to appear like what? A tanker?"

"A freighter. A freighter allows for piling empty shipping containers into a shaped fit over the *Specter*, and it creates a multi-colored illusion to onlookers."

"You expect me to operate at top speed surfaced and submerged with whatever coverage scheme you're concocting?"

"Quite near top speeds, minus the extra weight and drag. You'll obviously be more hindered underwater. But note that the material is light–fiberglass-reinforced plastic, and the drag is minimized by having the bulkheads extend only two meters below your waterline."

"What about me weapons? Radar? Sonar? The laser communications? What the bloody hell, Pierre?"

"All usable. Trust me. I've thought this through."

"How'd you get all this custom stuff down here?"

"I had an underwater barge built. Picture a barge with ballast tanks, pulled by a semi-retired Taiwanese submarine. It's rather simple and cheap in the grand scheme."

As Cahill pondered the inconvenience of a makeshift freighter shell wrapped around his ship, a Taiwanese naval officer marched down the steps. Shadows covered the man's stern face.

"I dislike his demeanor," Renard said.

"He doesn't look happy."

The officer spoke English with a thick Mandarin accent.

"Mister Renard, I have an urgent message for you."

He extended an envelope.

"What does it say?"

"I am sorry. It's above my security clearance, but I will wait here in case you need my assistance with a response."

"Thank you," Renard said.

Cahill watched the Frenchman balance a Marlboro between his fingers while he tore open the envelope and then read the sealed paper's contents. His respect for Renard grew as he watched his mind digest weighty news in a fleeting instant.

"This changes our timing," Renard said.

"What's going on?" Cahill asked.

"An update from Miss McDonald. Apparently, the United States Navy has been kind enough to keep an eye, or an ear rather, on our latest adversary. An *Akula*-class submarine deployed from Avacha Bay and is heading in our direction at flank speed."

"Shit."

"There's no indication of its mission, but I would bet that it's to track the *Goliath*."

Cahill felt his adrenaline rising.

"Why track me? Why not just blow me out of the water outright? Who the hell would avenge me?"

"Don't be so certain that Jake and I wouldn't, even against the Russians. But you're right that this is a grave risk. You must deploy sooner than I'd planned, carrying the *Specter*."

"How the hell did they know about us?"

"I'm afraid that a side effect of success is that people start watching my moves with increased scrutiny. The home porting of the *Goliath* and *Specter* at this location is a general secret, but it's not to the Chinese."

"But even if the Chinese shared that information with the Russians, how do they know that we're going to attack them in Crimea? How could they guess that we're intending to attack them at all?"

"They can't, unless Miss McDonald suffers from a traitor in her midst. My suspicions are that the Russians have instead enjoyed intelligence from the Chinese, who watch this islet like hawks. They're aware that we're gearing up for a mission, and they're going to watch us with paranoid curiosity."

"I can barely outrun an *Akula*. What's me speed advantage surfaced? A knot or two? Parity? Bloody hell, Pierre, I can't afford to submerge at all, or I'll lose the tail chase."

"That's why you'll have to trust your camouflage."

Cahill looked again at the piles of external hull sections.

"If the Chinese are watching this islet, how do you expect me to escape without me cover being blown?"

The glint in the Frenchman's eye instilled Cahill's confidence.

"I said they watch this islet like a hawk. What I didn't tell you is that we have countermeasures to spring you free."

"I can't wait to hear more. But with all this Chinese and Russian attention and Jake being far away, are you going to trust Henri to command the *Specter*?"

"He has been learning tactics over the years. But, no. All new information considered, I think it best that an expert commander handle the *Specter* on this egress."

"Me? I'm still learning about the class of ship, although I'm sure I could handle it and trust Liam with the *Goliath*."

"No need," Renard said. "I've commanded a few submarines during my career. I'm sure I remember how. Until we can clear prying Chinese eyes and make you look like an average freighter of no interest to the *Akula*, the *Specter* is mine."

CHAPTER 4

Cahill pressed his tennis shoe into the last temporary external tube.

"Feels stable," he said. "They're all mounted rock solid. But that's forty holes you've drilled into me ship for extra weapons, and I've lost count of how many you've drilled for your camouflage."

"Two-hundred and forty-two," Renard said. "I estimate thirty minutes for an eight-man crew to remove them all. But you can sever each stanchion and each weapons tube mount with the explosives that are mated to them. The stanchions and weapons are on different circuits for severing their mounts independently."

"I can blow them all with a command from the bridge?"

"Yes. I needed to equip you with a rapid method of shedding your baggage and exoskeleton, so to speak. But you'll need to remove each bolt manually to rid yourself of the stanchions completely."

He knew the Frenchman had considered the structural integrity of the modifications. So he jumped to his next concern as he waved his hand at the scaffolding.

"Do you know what all this has done to me acoustic signature?"

"I regret that I do not. You'll have to use the *Specter* to take sound cuts when you're at sea."

"I figured. Are you sure you don't want me to just use the *Goliath* the way you designed it? Let me sprint away from danger while I can and submerge when I can't."

"You'd be too vulnerable in the Suez, and you may need the camouflage while you traverse the other chokepoints."

"Okay," Cahill said. "I have to agree with you, but I don't have to like it. I know it's weird coming from a submariner, but I feel claustrophobic."

As he traced stanchions from bolts drilled into the *Goliath* to a section of scaffolded hull, the suspended bulkheads surrounded him like bath tub.

"I believe that you should keep the facade as long as you can, possibly until you're within torpedo range of the bridge," Renard said. "Of course, if your cover is blown prior to then, the rules change."

"Agreed, mate."

The Frenchman exhaled smoke.

"Let me be more clear. If your cover is blown prior to the Suez, I'm aborting the mission. You must pass through the Suez Canal in disguise. If you cannot, then the Russians would have no question about your destination, and they would sink you while you're trapped in its tight channel."

"Then let get me out of here before that *Akula* arrives."

"Right. The facade hull is complete except for the crossing sections that will join the containers in covering the *Specter*. You'll have to submerge the *Goliath* in the center of the basin and then drive under me for the loading procedure."

"The basin is deep enough?"

"I had it dredged."

"Okay, mate. But once that's done, is the egress tunnel tall enough to squeeze through with all the containers?"

"I had it expanded higher and wider. All is ready. We only need to execute."

Cahill stood at the corner of the bridge that jutted from the *Goliath's* starboard bow. Through the polycarbonate windows that interlaced steel bars backed and reinforced, he glanced at the Phalanx system on the left half of the ship.

"Lowering the Phalanx," he said.

He tapped an icon, and the white-domed close-in weapon system sank into the ship's port bow. Hatches rolled shut for a watertight seal.

Liam Walker, his executive officer and a former sailor from an *Anzac*-class frigate, kept his eyes on a status screen.

"The Phalanx is stowed," he said.

"Very well," Cahill said.

He flipped through camera angles that looked beyond the exterior of the facade.

"I don't see any lines. I assume we're cast off from the pier."

"I assume so, too," Walker said. "Best to confirm, though."

Cahill tapped an icon to connect via radio to the submarine behind him.

"*Specter, Goliath*. Over," he said.

"*Goliath, Specter*. Go ahead. Over," Renard said.

"Am I free from the pier? Over."

"Yes. You may submerge when ready. Over."

"I'm ready. Stand by. Out."

Cahill tapped icons and then stepped to the aft of the bridge. Behind and below his window, bubbles rose from the *Goliath's* submerged ballast tank vents under the starboard hull.

"Ten meters," Walker said. "Eleven. Twelve."

As the *Goliath* sank, bubbles burst from cargo tanks under the centerline bed that would cradle the *Specter*.

Placid water lapped the bridge windows, refracting artificial light across the consoles. A look over his shoulder revealed the port and starboard weapons bays at the sterns of his ship remaining visible above the submerging transport vessel.

"Fifteen meters," Walker said.

As he shortened the distance of his gaze, Cahill watched the water creep up the bridge windows.

"The ship is submerged and is stopping its descent," Walker said. "We're steady at twenty meters."

"Very well. We've still got a few meters below us. Lowering the outboards."

"It's tight, but I agree," Walker said. "We need them."

"Outboards are lowered. Energizing side-scan sonar."

Cahill tapped an icon that brought the *Goliath's* extensive side-scan acoustic search system to life. Selecting the rearward-looking perspective to his monitor, he set his ship crawling backwards.

"Energizing outboards on course three-three-five, speed one-half knot."

Minutes later, the rounded form of the *Specter's* hull, floating in the underground basin, appeared on his monitor.

"I see it," Cahill said.

"Me too. Care to let the automated system handle it from here?"

"Let's give it a go."

He tapped an image and then folded his arms. As the *Goliath* continued its reverse crawl under the *Specter*, the submarine's oblong shape appeared over the transport ship's centerline cradle. He turned and watched his cargo's dark form glide forward between his hulls.

"It's left of center, Terry. Its stern is too far to our port side."

"Let's see how the system handles it."

"Right. Agreed."

The *Specter's* shape walked forward on the sonar display, and the four icons of the outboard motors, one under each corner of the *Goliath*, indicated a quick reversal followed by a burst to stop the ship.

Then two diagonal outboards flipped ninety degrees, spun their propellers to twist the twin hulls, and then hit rapid reverses to return the ship to motionlessness.

"That aligned us," Walker said. "System-calculated distance from the bed to the cargo's keel is two meters."

"Very well. Keep an eye on our trim. No need to snap pieces off either ship before we begin our trip."

"Trim control is in automatic loading mode, set at one meter per minute rise rate."

Cahill shot periodic glances at the display to double-check Walker's double-checking of the automated loading. Instead of seeing the errors he feared, he admired the *Goliath's* delicate computerized dance of shuffling water fore and aft between its trim tanks to stay level while shedding water overboard to gain levity.

He absorbed the reversed illusion of the *Specter* falling through translucent liquid into the *Goliath's* waiting cradle.

"Per protocol, the system is stopping the ascent to allow us to assess for manual adjustments," Walker said.

"No need. Continue loading."

Cahill watched the *Goliath's* retracted hydraulic presses climb up the cargo's side like mechanical fingers.

"Slowing to half a meter per minute."

"Very well."

"Contact!"

"Verify bed pressure."

"Bed pressure is verified. We're bearing the cargo's weight."

"Engage the presses!" Cahill said.

"Done. Presses are engaged."

The presses rotated and pinned down the submarine.

"Let's try our laser communications," Cahill said.

He tapped an icon.

"*Specter, Goliath*, test of laser communications system. Over."

"*Goliath, Specter*, test is satisfactory."

"It works!"

"Of course, it works," Renard said. "Would I ever steer you wrongly? This is a highly secure line. Once our connection is verified, there's no need for radio protocols. You can speak as if talking within your own ship."

"Okay, mate. Got it. What's next?"

"I'll order the final covering of the facade. It will take several hours. I recommend you get some rest."

Cahill checked the clock and realized that the local time was approaching ten o'clock at night.

"Right," he said. "We'll all get some sleep except for a minimal watch section. Call me when we're ready."

"I'll take the watch, Terry," Walker said. "You need to be in top form for the egress. I'll catch up on sleep later."

"Thanks, Liam."

Cahill passed through a door, latched it behind him, and descended a steep stairway to a tight, odd-shaped compartment under which welds held the rakish bow module to the cylindrical, submarine-based section.

As he reached for a watertight door, a peek in the bilge

revealed the inverted triangular keel section, which provided stability and added buoyancy, continuing underneath the ship. Swinging the door open, he stepped through its machined frame into the familiar, circular-ribbed world of a submarine.

Lacking a torpedo room, the *Goliath* presented Cahill its tactical control room as its first cylindrical compartment. Four men staffed the space, with three seated in front of consoles and a supervisor hovering over them.

"Good evening, sir," the supervisor said.

The young leader had been an officer aboard Cahill's submarine prior to quitting the Australian Navy for lucrative mercenary adventures. He had also joined him in the *Goliath's* maiden mission near the Korean Peninsula.

"Get some sleep," Cahill said. "We've got a few hours."

"This fake ship that's surrounding us. I don't like it. None of us do. It's going to create flow noise."

"I know. But if it works, we'll be hiding in plain sight. Nobody will give us a second look."

He continued his sternward walk, passing electronic cabinets that appeared where he would have expected a conning platform and a periscope on a *Scorpène*-class submarine.

As he passed into the elongated berthing area, he thought about going into his stateroom, but he opted to explore the starboard hull, which held the bulk of his crew. He crept into the ghost-silent scullery and then continued to the mess hall.

As he entered the next compartment, he tested his memory to recall the term MESMA as an acronym for the French-designed Module-Energy, Sub-Marine, Autonomous ethanol-liquid-oxygen propulsion plant. Unlike the *Specter*, with one MESMA plant, the *Goliath's* design of three per each catamaran-inspired hull impressed him. They provided his ship much of its cylindrical length, and with half the battery capacity and twice the mass of the *Specter*, the *Goliath* relied upon the plants for undersea power.

The hiss of steam filled the section, and he felt heat waft over him. With his jumpsuit unzipped and flopped over his waist, a technician Cahill had recruited from a civilian power plant exposed a sweat-marked tee-shirt. He was examining gauges on a control station as his partner, an Australian Navy recruit, climbed up from the lower deck and joined him.

"Terry, what's your opinion about this fake shell of a ship?"

"It's fine, as long as it works."

"What if it fails?"

"Then, we'll take it off and fight our way out of whatever mess we're in. But let's give it a chance, shall we, mate?"

"Sure. I don't see why not."

"Secure all the MESMA plants except for plant one. Tell the rest to shut down in the next fifteen minutes. Let the guys get some sleep."

Twenty-five meters and two MESMA plants later, Cahill bid farewell to his third MESMA team and ducked through another watertight door. He walked under the wide air ducts that supplied a large gas turbine engine.

A man in coveralls seated before a control panel turned and looked up. Cahill nodded, kept walking, and glanced at the top of the electric motor, which the Taiwanese builders had sunk into a custom recess for the *Goliath*. The motor drove the starboard shaft, which stretched below his view through the tapered keel and through the stern bearing at the ship's tail.

He then opened a hatch above him that Renard had retrofitted onto the engine room's slope, reached upward to handles, and pulled himself through.

Closing the hatch, he noticed the quietness of the weapons bay. He climbed a ladder and entered his ship's aft space.

The railgun was unimposing, deceptive in its lethality. With its barrel aiming forward, the weapon system impressed him with its compact size.

A smallish man who reclined in a cot reading a book under a recessed curve in the hull looked to him.

"Hi, Terry."

"Good evening, mate."

"At least that fake ship doesn't block the view back here."

"Right. Pierre made the windows and the radar elements flush with the fake bulkheads."

"True enough, but I hate to think what happens if we need the cannons."

"You'd just blow holes in the plastic, wouldn't you?"

"Roger that. That's what you pay me to do–blow holes in things. I'm up for it."

"Great. Everything's in order. I guess I'll hit me rack. Are you going to stay here and sleep?"

"It's the quietest place on the ship when I'm not blowing things up."

"I guess you're right."

"Night, Terry."

Four hours later, Cahill's alarm rousted him from a forgotten dream. After freshening up, he joined Walker on the bridge. The facade surrounding his ship enshrouded him with an artificial blackness.

"Now I'm really feeling claustrophobic."

"It was weird watching the cranes pile the containers over me," Walker said.

"We're in a coffin."

"Want to see a picture from above?"

"Sure."

Walker nodded and pointed at Cahill's screen.

"Pierre sent it. Call it up."

From above, the *Goliath-Specter* tandem appeared like a freighter with its bridge covering the *Specter's* hidden conning tower and multi-colored containers spread over the decks.

"Impressive," Cahill said. "Pierre's outdone himself."

"Give him a call. It's time."

Cahill opened the channel to the *Specter*.

"Pierre?" he said.

"Good morning," Renard said.

"You've done an impressive job with the camouflage."

"Thank you. Are you ready to deploy?"

"I am. I don't like that this facade blinds me, but I suppose a submarine commander can't complain about it."

"You have cameras mounted to cover your every angle. I suggest you use them to avoid jagged rocks on the way out. And stay as deep as possible to avoid embedding my conning tower into the roof."

"Good point. We'll use the outboards."

He sank the transport ship within a meter of the rocky bottom.

"Depth is twenty-two meters," he said. "Engaging the outboards to drive us toward the exit. Coming to one and a half knots."

As the ship crept forward, he pointed it at the black hole of the submerged egress tunnel. Shadows engulfed his fake freighter's centerline bow.

"How big of a head start do we have?" Cahill asked.

"You mean over the *Akula*?"

"Yes."

"A day and a half, roughly, by the time we break out of here."

"Break out?"

"What else would you call it?"

Cahill pondered the actions he would take in escaping the island free of Chinese submarine, shipping, and satellite detection.

"It's a perfect description. I just didn't think I'd hear you call it that."

"Believe me," Renard said. "If I could come up with a better description, I would. But I'm afraid that breaking out is the best explanation of what we're about to do."

CHAPTER 5

Jake entered the Keelung command center and felt a dozen eyes rise from an electronic navigation chart. The Taiwanese military's chief of staff stood straight.

"Welcome, Mister Slate," Admiral Danzhao Ye said. "For once, we're meeting free of a crisis."

Ye nodded, and the officer who had escorted Jake into the command center departed.

"Maybe not a crisis," Jake said. "But one false move and we'll end up in one."

"Let's avoid that. Come see the chart."

Jake traversed the floor, stopped beside Ye, and shook his hand. Ye ran his thumb across a controller, and bright icons representing shipping dimmed. A baby blue line marking an undersea hydrophone system rose to connect Taiwan to the nearest Japanese island.

"The sound surveillance arrays have remained operational since you were last here," Ye said. "They'll provide a line of protection for the *Goliath-Specter* tandem during its egress from the Pengjia islet."

"How's the Chinese mainland naval activity?"

As the admiral wiggled his thumb across the controller's touchpad, red outlines of hostile surface combatants appeared.

"Calm relative to what you're used to. We see the usual surface patrols in the straits, but we believe that they stopped dedicating a submarine to monitoring Pengjia two years ago."

"Well, that's good."

"The concern is that they may have reversed that policy when we leased the space to Mister Renard."

"So, there's a submarine watching Pengjia?"

"Unknown. Our patrol craft haven't detected anything, but a *Yuan*-class submarine has been added to their order of battle and remains unaccounted for."

"It could be anywhere."

"True, but we take precautions. Your operations off the Korean Peninsula weren't unnoticed by the mainland."

"What sort of precautions?"

"Just one, really. The hydrazine system at Pengjia has been modified to create diversions. Pipes have been run in a pattern fanning out from the egress tunnel. A submerged vessel can choose a corridor to depart the islet while surrounded by a wall of concealing bubbles."

Jake recalled the chart around the islet.

"But the water gets too deep too fast to mount piping out to any useful distance."

"We addressed that by using a light and flexile carbon polymer that's neutrally buoyant. The piping floats and drifts slightly with the ocean current, and each corridor extends two miles."

"That's impressive, but isn't it counter-productive to use the system? Doesn't its use announce when a submarine is leaving?"

"It would, except that we exercise the system three times a day at random intervals."

"Now I'm impressed."

"Let's see how you feel once the *Goliath-Specter* tandem is free. The egress should start in twelve minutes. If you need to freshen up after your travels, now is a good time."

Jake left the main floor and made a quick pass through a rest room. He stopped in a kitchenette to gulp black coffee and inhale a bagel before returning to Ye's side.

The tactical view held new images that attracted his attention. White lines like the spokes of half a wheel fanned out southward from the islet, and a red submarine appeared to the north with Mandarin characters beside it.

He pointed.

"The *Akula*?" he asked.

"It's three hours old, but that's the latest location information we have on it."

"There's nothing else submerged in the vicinity?"

"Nothing known."

"Let's keep it that way."

A captain announced something in Mandarin, and Ye answered.

"I've given permission for Mister Renard to begin."

"Do we have communications with him?"

"Yes. Hold on."

The admiral wiggled his thumb over his controller, and Renard's voice entered the command center.

"We're passing through the tightest section of the tunnel now. Damn!"

"What's wrong?" Ye asked.

Jake heard harsh metallic groans.

"Pierre?" Ye asked.

"Yes. Sorry. It's fine. The container atop my conning tower hit the roof, but we're through it now."

"We'll lose laser communications soon. Are you through the tunnel yet?"

"Yes. We just cleared."

"Excellent," Ye said. "We'll be watching from here."

The radio line fell silent, and Jake pointed at the white lines that fanned from the islet.

"Which path are they taking?" he asked.

"It's up to Mister Renard. The intent is to preserve randomness in case our communications are intercepted."

"So, we just wait?"

"There's nothing more we can do. He'll raise a mast and call if he needs help."

"I suppose he will."

Jake pointed again.

"What are those ships?" he asked.

"Each one is a *Tai Chiang*-class stealth patrol craft."

"Good to hear you've got some firepower out there guarding their backs."

"They're searching in passive mode only, though. I don't want them announcing the egress."

As Jake exercised patience during the *Goliath-Specter* tandem's slow and uneventful escape, his head slumped deeper below his shoulder blades. After two hours had passed, he sat in front of a console and watched the navigation chart.

Four hours later, a captain's report spurred him to life. Ye sprang from his seat at a console and moved to the captain's side. Jake let the officers analyze the data before requesting a translation.

After a minute, the admiral volunteered it.

"Submerged contact, moving at seven knots. We picked it up on active return from the hydrophone array."

"That's them, right?"

"It should be, but I've vectored a stealth patrol craft to intercept as a precaution."

Moments later, another officer made an announcement in Mandarin, and Jake noticed levity in the room. The Frenchman's voice then issued from the loudspeakers.

"We've passed the array," Renard said.

"Send your coordinates," Ye said.

"One moment."

The captain monitoring the hydrophone array's input nodded.

"We have you on the hydrophone array," Ye said.

"I assumed so. That's quite a powerful system. I hardly need my sonar system to hear it."

"Let's wait before celebrating. I want to make sure you weren't followed. Continue to do the rendezvous point."

Fifteen minutes later, the icon representing Renard's movement reached a predetermined dot in the ocean. The admiral stretched his arms and yawned.

"That's a successful egress," he said. "The helicopter is waiting to take you and your colleague to the *Specter*."

Jake had forgotten about his traveling companion, who he had allowed to sleep during the night. One of the officers gave the admiral an update.

"Correction," Ye said. "Your colleague is in the helicopter with all your baggage. Whenever you're ready, you may join him."

An hour later, Jake watched the color fall from the priest's face as the aircraft lurched.

"Father Andrew?" he asked.

The helicopter dipped, shook, and recovered, and the Iraqi Chaldean holy man cringed.

"Father Andrew!"

"Yeah?"

"You look terrible. Are you nauseous?"

The priest nodded.

"Give me your hand. I know an old acupuncture trick. Acupressure, in this case."

Jake grabbed the wrist with one hand and then pressed his other hand's thumb into the crease over the priest's vein. He released and repeated the pressure ten times before shifting to the holy man's other hand.

"It's a little better," Andrew said. "What are you doing?"

"Stimulating your pericardium to combat nausea. You have motion sickness."

"I'm starting to think I should have stayed home."

"No. I wanted you here for a reason."

"Bishop Francis told me you made a huge donation to our charitable fund for the Iraqi refugees."

"I wasn't trying to rent a priest for three months, if that's what you mean."

Andrew stared at him, measuring an appropriate response.

"Well, okay, that's exactly what I was doing," Jake said. "But it was for a good cause."

"Two good causes, if God will allow me to count what we're doing now."

"If God will allow? The Vatican renounces the annexation of Crimea, right? I see no question that we're doing the right thing."

"I wouldn't be here if I didn't personally think it was the right thing. But how you do it will be important."

"Right. That's exactly why I brought you. You're the sheriff of my conscience."

The Taiwanese officer seated beside Jake pointed at the horizon.

"Do you see those lights?"

"Yeah. It looks like a merchant ship."

"It's a freighter–one of ours. The *Goliath-Specter* tandem is surfaced near it. I must now give you a message from Mister Renard. He wants you to search for him within a radius of one nautical mile around the freighter as a test of a camouflage system."

"Seriously?"

The officer handed him a pair of night vision binoculars.

"Seriously."

Jake centered the optics on the freighter as filters ratcheted down the incoming light from the ship's running lights. He then worked the lens in a circle around the vessel, seeking the familiar form of the *Specter* aboard the *Goliath*. Widening the circle, he sought his target again, and then a third time.

He lowered the binoculars and shook his head.

"There's nothing out there but that freighter."

The Taiwanese officer reached for a dial to channel Renard's voice into the cabin.

"Good morning, Jake. Can you hear me?"

"Hear you, yes. I'm starting to think you told the pilot to fly to the wrong place, though."

"Look again, only much closer to the freighter."

He raised the optics and sought signs of his mentor's presence within the wake of the cargo vessel.

"I still don't see anything. We're on the east side of the freighter. Are you sure you're visible from my angle?"

"I assure you that I am."

"And you're completely surfaced?"

"Indeed."

"Forget it, Pierre. I'm not in the mood for games. I just want to get on board and relieve you."

"Jake?" Andrew asked.

"Hold on, Pierre," Jake said.

He looked at the priest.

"What?"

"If you trust your friend's wisdom, trust that there's a reason for his game."

"That doesn't mean I need to let him make me look like a fool."

"A trusted friend wouldn't make you look like a fool, unless he had a reason. You may want to be patient and entertain his request."

Jake sighed to calm himself.

"Fine. What would you like me to do, Pierre?"

"Let's try a different test. See if you can guess the loaded tonnage of the freighter."

While scanning the optics across the vessel's length, Jake made his best calculations.

"It doesn't look too heavy. Freeboard looks high for its length. I don't see that many containers. I don't know. Eighteen thousand tons?"

"Good guess," Renard said. "How about the beam length?"

"Fourteen to fifteen meters. It looks like about a meter on either side of the containers, and the containers are normally twelve meters."

"Good. And how about the overall length?"

Jake scanned the containers that, except for the bridge, covered the vessel from bow to stern.

"A hundred meters."

"That's an excellent guess," Renard said. "Would you care to join me on its bridge?"

"What?"

Jake whipped the lenses towards the bow and stopped at the vessel's superstructure. The white light from the bridge backlit a human form. As the silhouette's arm waved, Jake surveyed the room's floor and noticed it was void of equipment.

Pointing at the pilot, he grabbed the Taiwanese officer's arm.

"Have him circle the freighter."

The officer translated, and the helicopter rose and then

dipped towards the vessel's stern. As Jake digested the ruse, the lack of detail became evident.

"You don't have an anchor," he said.

"That would have been too difficult to fake," Renard said.

"I'm passing the stern. I see that you gave the fake ship a name. The 'Marie Lucille.'"

"Named after my wife."

The helicopter's spotlight moved up the stern.

"What flag is that? Panama?"

"Yes," Renard said. "Hiding in plain sight requires a flag of convenience. Your manifest, bill of lading, and all documents will reflect your registration in Panama."

"What cargo from where to where?"

"Transistors from Kaohsiung, Taiwan to Berdyansk, Ukraine."

"Your wake tells me that your propellers are too deep for the ship you're trying to imitate."

"Perceptive. There's no faking that."

"You don't have any lights on your supposed deck."

"It's best to keep the ship dark, and I wasn't going to risk running the additional electrical wires."

"What about your running lights?"

"Waterproof, battery powered. They'll last for months."

"Can I turn them off?"

"Yes, wirelessly from the bridge."

"Are the *Goliath's* radar elements usable?"

"They're flush with the camouflage and are fully functional."

The helicopter flew up the vessel's starboard side.

"I see the *Specter's* radio mast."

"All the *Specter's* masts can be raised through a gap in the covering. That's your way of communicating with the outside world."

"How do you power the bridge?"

"I run a cord from the *Specter*."

"Holy cow. I see it now. You've got the fake bridge resting around the fairwater planes."

"Most of the weight of the bridge is transferred to the top of the tower. To fit through the tunnel, I could leave no margin there. So access to the bridge is from a ladder behind the conning tower."

The aircraft rounded the bow.

"I think I'm looking at your most amazing work now," Jake said. "The bow looks real, but I know it's not resting on anything."

"The material's light weight places minimal rotational stress on the *Goliath*, even with long scaffolding arms. The greatest stress is longitudinal as the bow pushes through the water, and that's transferred to each hull of the *Goliath* through pole arms."

Pressing the optics into the chest of the Taiwanese officer, Jake absorbed the dark shape of the cargo vessel with his naked eyes. He accepted the simple brilliance of his mentor's plan.

"You were right, Father Andrew."

"About what?"

"My friend making me look like a fool for a reason."

"I'm not following you."

"Pierre toyed with me to give me the confidence in the camouflage. Thanks to his game, I have no doubts."

CHAPTER 6

Jake banged his ankle against the top of the bridge.

"Damn it!"

The pendulum his body formed with the helicopter swung him over the apex of the faux-ship's exoskeleton. Dragging his throbbing limb over metal, he slowed himself. He pulled the release that freed him from the harness and landed.

Twisting, he reached for a strap and then waved his free arm to signal for extra cable slack. After yanking the harness to his side, he knelt, pressed his chest to the bridge's roof, and then banged on a window below.

Renard's muffled voice commanded him.

"Port side! Port side!"

He crawled to the edge of the roof and looked down. His mentor passed through a door and presented his rotor-whipped silver-haired head under the aircraft's spotlight. The Frenchman craned his neck to welcome Jake with familiar steel blue eyes.

Responding to Renard's inviting wave, he dangled his boots over the edge, slid his rump forward, and fell to the deck. He landed with a thud and a whispered a curse for the agitation of his ankle.

As he steadied himself and stood, he felt Renard's hands clasp his shoulders. The Frenchman followed rapid air kisses beside his cheeks with a yelled command.

"Your harness!"

He extended the webbing and watched his mentor wiggle his way into it.

"That's it?" Jake asked. "Hello and good-bye?"

"I would wish you luck, but it's pointless because there's no doubt that you're still charmed."

Renard waved his arm and ascended into the night.

Alone as the rotor wash subsided, Jake walked through the doorway, and the priest's lean frame appeared ghastly in front of the compartment's overhead lighting.

"I knew he'd want to get off this thing fast," Jake said. "That's why I sent you down first."

"He didn't seem surprised at my presence."

"I'm sure his Taiwanese buddies warned him."

Jake rapped his knuckle against a window and scanned his surroundings. The *Specter's* conning tower dominated the space, which struck him with its emptiness.

"There's practically nothing up here," he said.

"He showed me the binoculars and a bridge-to-bridge radio," Andrew said. "He also explained that communications with the crew are managed with this laptop computer. He told me to remind you to bring them down with us so that they don't get wet if we have to submerge."

As Jake walked towards the starboard side, he saw that the fairwater planes blocked his path. He changed direction and traveled behind the conning tower.

A glimmer caught his eye, and he looked down. Holes bored low in the compartment suggested that Renard had allowed for flooding and draining of the space if the ship submerged. Reaching the far side, he passed through the starboard door and found it a replica of the port side.

He returned to the priest's side.

"Spartan but functional," he said.

"I'll take your word for it."

He admired a final panorama of the empty seas and then led the clergyman down a ladder.

The *Specter* felt familiar as memory guided his walk to the control room. He passed through a doorway and positioned himself behind the shiny railing of the elevated conning platform.

The metal casing that housed the consoles and monitors of the Subtics tactical system shone with the polish that Renard had paid the Taiwanese maintenance crew to administer.

Key familiar faces greeted him. To his left, before one of six dual-stacked Subtics panels, sat his sonar systems expert, Antoine Remy. To his right, seated in front of panels and gauges that controlled the ship's skeletal and cardiovascular systems, the white-haired, sharp-featured Henri Lanier epitomized dignity in stature, appearance, and knowledge of any moving part of a submarine.

A few younger French-trained mercenaries, familiar from past missions spanning from the recapture of an Israeli submarine to the undersea rescue of a stranded South Korean vessel, sat by consoles.

"Reunited once again," Henri said.

Before Jake could answer, the Frenchman crossed the deck, grabbed his shoulders, and kissed the air beside his jaw. Then Remy, his toad-like head appearing oversized for his body, joined Henri.

"It's good to see you, Jake," Remy said.

The younger sailors then greeted their commander.

"It's great to see you guys," Jake said. "Is anyone else feeling creepy about this fake ship around us?"

"I think we're all still getting used to it," Henri said. "But I must admit that I'm more concerned about your new friend, whom you have failed to introduce."

"Sorry," Jake said. "Father Andrew Seba, from the Saint Thomas Chaldean Church of West Bloomfield, Michigan."

"A priest?"

"Pierre didn't tell you?"

"No," Henri said. "And quite frankly, it's odd. An unannounced guest is a first, and so is a priest. The combination of the two novelties is alarming."

"Many ships carry chaplains," Jake said.

"Ours never have."

"I wanted him here to make sure I did the right thing."

Henri glared at him, and Jake found the silence uncomfortable until the Frenchman's face relaxed.

"I understand," Henri said. "May we speak in private?"

"Of course. But have someone show Father Andrew to his berthing area. He'll be bunking with me in the commanding officer's stateroom."

"If you insist," Henri said. "But I also invite him to bunk with me. It's only proper that a special guest ride with the executive officer. Shame on me if I were to violate etiquette."

"Thanks, but I want him with me."

In the wardroom, Jake sat opposite Henri.

"I guess I should have warned you I was bringing him, but it was a spur of the moment decision. I can't believe Pierre didn't tell you."

"Pierre is wise. Perhaps he meant for the surprise to spur this very conversation."

"Possibly. What's on your mind?"

"I think I understand why you brought him, but I didn't want to say it in front of the others. "

"Okay. Go ahead."

"You want him to prevent another rampage like the one you inflicted during our sprint out of North Korean waters."

Jake admired that Henri's habitual laser-guided insight reduced the priest's presence to its simplest element.

"Yeah, I guess you're right. It may be more complex than just that, but you're spot on with that example."

"As your friend, I cannot reiterate enough how concerned I was about that rampage. It was frightening to live through it."

"I know. But it's been over for months now."

"You'll need your priest in the control room frequently, if he is to make a difference. Are you sure he can handle the stress?"

"He did a six-month tour in Kurdish territory tending to displaced Iraqis around the clock. This will be easy for him in comparison."

Seeming appeased with the explanation, the Frenchman leaned back in his seat.

"On to business, then," Jake said. "We're in protected waters until we reach the hydrophone array on the Philippine side south of Taiwan. I'm going to use the transit time to get some sleep."

"You look like you were up all night like the rest of us. I'll set a watch section so that we can all get some rest."

"Okay, have someone wake me when we're twenty miles from the hydrophone line."

Noise from his stateroom door rousted Jake from his slumber. The enthusiastic beating of palms against the door annoyed him.

"That's enough. You can stop now."

"Where would be the fun in that, mate?" Cahill said.

"How the hell'd you get on my ship?"

"There's a walkway mounted between two of the temporary weapons tubes. I can extend it to your ship and visit whenever I want, as long as you're in me cargo bed."

"No shit?"

"No shit. What's this I hear about you bringing a priest with you? It gives me the willies."

Jake looked to the empty rack below his. Seeing no sign of Andrew, he rolled to the deck and talked while relieving himself in the toilet. From the corner of his eye, he saw Cahill sit at his desk.

"I thought he'd be sleeping now."

"No, mate. He's up and about exploring the ship. I assume he's never been on a submarine."

"Probably not. But I didn't ask him if he's been underwater before. I just wanted him here."

"But in God's name, why?"

Jake moved to the sink and washed his hands.

"In God's name, just because."

"Perhaps you consider him a good luck charm?"

"Sure. Let's go with that."

"Bullshit. You're our good luck charm. At least that's what Pierre would have me believe."

"Then why'd you ask?"

"Because you're not giving me an answer."

Jake lifted a tablet from the table beside Cahill's arm and glanced at the *Goliath-Specter* tandem's place in the seas. It approached the hydrophone line that marked the boundary of his Taiwanese protection from submerged threats.

He stepped towards the shower as he yanked off his tee-shirt and dropped his underwear to the deck. Aiming his bare buttocks at Cahill for effect, he ended the query.

"I've given you the best answer I can. Stop prying."

"I can take a hint, mate. You didn't need to show me your bare hairy arse to make the point."

Jake allowed himself a full-water shower. The warmth energized him. When finished, he stepped into his stateroom and found the air cool as he reached for a towel.

Cahill had vanished.

Dressed, he reached the control room and found his Australian colleague seated in the captain's chair.

"Just keeping it warm for you."

"Thanks."

As Jake sat, the *Goliath's* commanding officer faced him while leaning his lower back into the railing.

"We'll have radar support from aircraft most of the way," Cahill said. "But time to blend in now."

Jake glanced at the display on a console.

"There's a ton of shipping out there," he said. "We'll blend in just fine."

"Hide in plain sight, right?"

"Right. Don't you have a ship of your own to command?"

"Liam's got it. I just wanted to see you in person before things get too intense."

"I appreciate it. But it's going to stay boring long before it gets intense. We've got a lot of time for social calls."

"Four days to the Strait of Malacca, assuming we can sustain this speed and don't have to submerge."

"How fast is our top speed with this exoskeleton?"

"I took it to twenty knots with the engines at eighty percent. Pierre didn't want me to push it further for fear of ripping off our camouflage, but I think we could get twenty-two, maybe twenty-three knots if needed."

"Shit, that's slow."

"For the *Goliath*, yes. For the freighter we're supposed to be, it's admirable. Anyway, we can make about only nine knots submerged while this fake ship is covering us"

"Sounds like we can average our charted speed of seventeen knots. That's four days to Singapore, then twelve days to the Suez. You'll have plenty of time to visit me."

"Are you trying to get rid of me?"

"I'd feel better knowing the *Goliath* is in your hands."

"Well, let me finish updating you, and then I'll leave. We can blow the exoskeleton off at any time, but we'll have shards of scaffolding attached until we can unscrew them all."

"How many to unscrew?"

"Nearly three hundred."

"So, we'll look like a pin cushion for a while if it comes down to it. What else?"

"I can fire all me externally mounted weapons with the exoskeleton still in place. Pierre assures me they'll hit the water and dive below the bulkheads. But if we need any of me other torpedoes, I need to blow the scaffolding."

Jake envisioned an exception.

"What about your railguns?" he asked.

"I can shoot them through the bulkheads without blowing the scaffolding, but it would be messy."

"What about sonar?"

"Just need to consider that the hull-mounted systems are a bit degraded by the exoskeleton being in the way and by its flow noise."

"Our improved communications?"

"The laser system will shift frequency within the blue-green spectrum if the signal fades, to try to penetrate whatever color of water we're dealing with. It's got great bandwidth and is undetectable, but we need to be within fifty meters of each other for it to work. Otherwise, we're stuck with the acoustic phone like the old days."

"The laser communications work when we're surfaced, too, right?"

"Of course. We're as good as being on the same ship as far as sharing data goes."

One of Jake's displays showed the innards of the *Goliath's* bridge. Walker stood at its far end.

"Can you hear me, Liam?" he asked.

The former Australian frigate officer raised his thumb, and Jake looked back to Cahill.

"What languages do you have covered with translators?"

"I've got two translators covering Korean, Chinese, English, Russian, and Arabic."

"Why Korean?"

"By accident. Dr. Tan speaks it, but he's our Chinese translator, and he also speaks pretty good Russian. I wanted him because he handled the pressure well in Korea."

"You have a super-fluent Russian translator, I hope."

"That's the other academic type. He also speaks the right dialect of Arabic to cover us around the Saudi Peninsula."

"That's all I can think to ask," Jake said.

"I won't be far if you think of something else. I'll get back to me own ship now."

Cahill turned his head to the display as he stood. The icon marking the *Goliath-Specter* tandem crossed the hydrophone array and entered the South China Sea.

"We're outside of Taiwan's protective naval reach now," he said. "The *Goliath* needs its leader."

CHAPTER 7

The announcement sent a spike of adrenaline up Jake's spine.

"Chinese warship approaching," Cahill said.

With the *Akula* having returned to the Russian Far East for lack of a mercenary submerged target, Jake calculated that his freedom from a foreign threat had lasted less than two days. But he registered the tension level in the Australian's voice as below an immediate crisis. He tapped an icon and shifted his screen from raw sonar data to an overhead view of shipping.

A red icon of a surface combatant appeared outside the fifty-mile ring surrounding the *Goliath-Specter* tandem.

Nothing seemed suspicious until he tapped another icon to add speed leaders to his picture. The warship barreled towards him at twenty-seven knots.

"I see it. Is this information coming from the Hawkeye?"

"That's right," Cahill said. "From our eye in the sky."

Jake reflected that Taiwanese E-2 Hawkeye patrols were offering him coverage to the Straits of Malacca, after which he expected support from other nations friendly to Renard.

Knowing that the exoskeleton covered the *Goliath's* masts, he looked to the *Specter's* sensors. Since he wanted to avoid drawing attention, he kept the submarine in listening mode with darkened radar, but his electronic support measures suite sniffed a Chinese long-range Type-517 detection system.

"It could be any sort of Chinese warship," he said.

"Wait," Cahill said. "There's separation on radar. Make it two Chinese warships."

"Their course and speed don't mean they have any interest in us. They could just be heading to a patrol area in the Paracels or the Spratlys."

"Right, mate. What should we do, if anything?"

Jake glared at his screen.

"First, stay calm," he said. "We've got so many options with this camouflage that it's mind-boggling. We may be able to mind our own business and avoid them, but get your translator to the bridge just in case."

"He's on his way."

Jake brooded in silence as minutes ticked away, and the Chinese combatants continued on an intercept course.

"Terry?" he asked.

"Still here."

"Am I being paranoid if I think that this intercept geometry is no accident?"

"No idea, mate. But here's the rub. Our radar is dark. So as far as they're concerned, we have no way of knowing where they are. If we react to them by changing course or speed, they'll know we're getting radar information from somewhere else."

"We could submerge and just confuse them."

"You know better than that."

"I do. It would draw attention and probably turn us into easy prey for a helicopter or two. I'm just thinking out loud."

When the dubious threat reached thirty miles away, Jake heard an authoritative voice in Mandarin over his loud speaker.

"Shit," he said. "Is that them? Can your translator tell?"

His display showed a short man with thick glasses on the *Goliath's* bridge.

"We are being hailed," Doctor Tan said. "At least I believe it's us. He's giving coordinates to identify who he's talking to."

"Write them down," Jake said. "Let's be sure it's us."

"I didn't hear them all."

"I'll replay it for you."

Jake looked to Henri, who nodded and tapped a screen to replay the message. Murmurs from the *Goliath* revealed that Tan and Cahill translated the coordinates.

"It's us, Jake," Cahill said.

Angrier, the same Chinese spokesman hailed again.

"We need to answer," Cahill said.

"I know. Patch Doctor Tan through the radio."

"He's patched through," Cahill said.

A glance to the nodding Henri confirmed the link.

"Terry, write down what I say for Doctor Tan. Doctor Tan,

take your time to listen to my words and read Terry's writing as you speak to make sure you get it right. There's no room for error."

"I understand," Tan said.

"How did they identify themselves?" Jake asked.

"They didn't," Tan said. "They just demanded a response."

"How did they identify us?"

"They called us the vessel at our coordinates, heading on our course and at our speed."

"Okay, tell them this is the vessel at our coordinates, course, and speed. We acknowledge their hailing, and we request to know their location and intent in hailing us."

As Cahill scribbled notes and whispered to Tan, Jake looked to his sonar expert.

"Antoine," he said.

"Yes?" Remy said.

"Assign the slow-kill weapon in tube five to the closest Chinese warship. Assign the slow-kill weapon in tube six to the other warship."

"I'm assigning the weapons," Remy said. "Tubes five and six are assigned."

Jake confirmed the targeting on his monitor as he heard Doctor Tan speak his response.

"You're not planning to shoot, are you?" Cahill asked.

"No, but I need to be ready. The slow-kill weapons would cause enough damage to slow them down so we could get away."

"Or just piss them off."

"I'm not firing unless they're already pissed off."

"You sure the weapons will work if you launch from your height in me bed?"

"I can only guess," Jake said. "They'd fall about five meters, hit the water, and hopefully dive below our exoskeleton. But they're the only weapons we have that don't ruin our camouflage."

"Me cannons will work with just a few holes in our shell."

"Sure. Get them warmed up, too. Target their propulsion."

The Chinese warship responded, the angst having ebbed but the voice's authority strong.

"He's asking us to identify ourselves, our cargo, and our destination," Tan said.

"Did he identify himself?"

"No."

"Did he at least state his location?"

"No."

"Tell him we will identify ourselves after he states his location. Tell him we are concerned about collision and want to verify his location for safety."

As Tan obeyed, Jake noticed that the warships approached his horizon.

"Terry, send Liam over to man my bridge. They'll expect someone to be able to confirm visual on them. I want eyes up there."

"Right. He's on his way."

The warships' spokesman answered the translator.

"He identified his location," Tan said. "He said that he can see some sort of green light and demands that we identify ourselves."

"That's our starboard running light," Jake said. "They can already see us. Go ahead and give him our name, and tell him we're transporting electronics to the Black Sea."

Tan translated Jake's message, and then Cahill reported that his railguns were ready.

"What the heck do you think he wants, Terry?"

"No idea. He has no reason to suspect us unless he's been tipped off."

"That's what I'm afraid of. But let's resolve this with a conversation, if possible."

He looked to Andrew, who sat at a console. The priest met his stare with an expression that Jake deemed approving.

The warships' verbal response came, and Tan translated.

"He identified himself as representing two warships from the People's Republic of China and demands to know why we are not using our surface search radar."

"Well, shit. It's because I don't want to be found."

"That's the wrong answer," Cahill said.

"No shit, but I suck at lying. How about you?"

"Not too bad. Let me see. Uh, let's say that our third mate is on watch, he's an idiot, and he forgot to turn it on?"

"What the heck? Go with it. Tell him we'll have it on soon."

As Tan translated, Jake ordered Henri to raise and energize the *Specter's* commercial Furuno surface search radar.

The spokesman for the Chinese warships reminded the occupants of the *Goliath-Specter* tandem to respect international safety rules of navigation, and then they changed course.

Heaving for breath, Walker entered the control room.

"What did I miss?"

"Sorry, Liam," Jake said. "Technically, you missed nothing. False alarm."

Two weeks later, Jake watched the display show the *Goliath-Specter* tandem in the western end of the Gulf of Aden. The Pakistani corvette that had escorted him across the Indian Ocean bid him farewell as the narrow Bab al-Mandab Strait between Djibouti and Yemen compelled the warship back.

As he entered the Red Sea, he hailed his mentor over a satellite link.

"I appreciate your old friends covering me for so long."

"Admiral Khan may be retired, but he still has enough clout to loan me a small warship from time to time," Renard said. "But the attention of a Pakistani warship in the Red Sea would defeat any further support it might offer you."

Walker stopped at the elevated conning platform and interrupted.

"I'm heading up to the bridge, Jake. Okay?"

"Yeah, go ahead. Keep us from hitting islands or anything else, for that matter."

The *Goliath's* executive officer disappeared.

"You're on your own until you reach the Suez," Renard said.

"You should be fine, but make sure you're there before Thursday's four o'clock departure time. I've assured your place in the convoy."

"Are any of the other ships in the convoy yours?"

"The yachts ahead and behind you will be my agents, as will your pilots before and after the Great Bitter Lake. Visas, crew list, certificate of registration, fees, and bribes are all handled."

"Bribes? Really?"

"Yes. I've spared you the culture shock, and to avoid any discomfort or risk, I've been quite generous."

Half a week later, Jake stood on the bridge with Walker and the Russian-Arabic translator. Darkness covered the calm waters as he heard the former surface warfare officer navigate the *Goliath-Specter* tandem behind the stern lights of a two-hundred and fifty foot yacht facing the channel.

He stepped to the port bridge wing and looked at the running lights of the yacht behind him. The door clicked open.

"I can't wait to see what that beauty looks like in daylight," Walker said. "Do you know what one of those costs?"

"No idea," Jake said. "Somewhere in the fifty to a hundred million dollar range, I guess."

"I'm sure they'll look impressive in a few hours when we can see them. They look lovely now just with their deck lighting."

"Maybe that's the point. If I know Pierre, they're going to be gorgeous and serve as distractions to prevent anyone from giving us a second look as we pass by."

"That bloke's thought of everything."

Ten hours later, Jake woke from a nap and climbed to the bridge. The sun shone through the windows as he reached the deck, and the priest's tennis shoes tapped the metal rungs below him.

"You didn't have to join me up here," Jake said. "The chance of me going on a weapon-shooting rampage in the Suez is slim."

"I'm sure you're right," Andrew said. "But I thought I'd enjoy the nice weather."

On his way to the port bridge wing, Jake walked by the rifles he had stashed on the deck for contingencies. The warm breeze relaxed him, and he raised binoculars from his chest to his face.

"Holy shit," he said. "You may want to avert your eyes."

The priest's voice issued from the doorway.

"Why?"

"You'll lose your religion if you see what I see."

Through his optics, he gazed at the trailing craft where a trio of young women flattered bright bikinis of pornographic skimpiness. The yacht's graceful majesty served as a mere backdrop for serving up the three glistening, oiled female forms from which Jake failed to avert his eyes.

"If you have a prayer to erase my mind of what I'm thinking about, please hurry. God help me."

"I see what you mean. Temptation is easiest to resist by avoidance. Perhaps it's best if we look at something else."

Jake looked ahead.

"Dang, Liam wasn't kidding. That yacht's even bigger than the one behind us, and it looks brand spanking new. I'm sure it's an absolute beauty from any angle other than its stern, which isn't a bad view at all."

"It's easier to hide in plain sight with distractions."

"Pierre's a genius. Nobody's looking at us."

He allowed himself a parting lustful glance at the bikinis before leading Andrew back inside.

"And I mean–nobody."

Lacking air conditioning, the bridge felt stifling, but Andrew's spirits seemed strong.

"Pierre showed a lot of foresight when he surrounded us with these yachts and all their splendor."

"Splendor's a good description. Leather, bells, whistles, and the full lap of luxury. Throw in the girls with all the sex you could want, and it sounds great. But if you think about it, what does all the wealth mean? I have all the money I could want, and look at me. I have to pay a priest to make sure I don't throw temper tantrums and commit genocide. Why has it always been so tempting for me to lash out?"

"C.S. Lewis described temptation as an ever increasing appetite for an ever decreasing pleasure. You must get some sort of relief from your anger, but it's never complete. That's the nature of this fallen world that tries to pull you away from doing what you know is right."

"So what's right, and how do I know it? I mean, is this mission right? You've said that the Vatican approves it, at least hypothetically based upon its position on Crimea. But nobody's tapped my shoulders with a sword and knighted me for this crusade."

Andrew frowned in thought.

"Once you step outside obvious doctrine, the definition of what's right or wrong comes down to the moral law imprinted upon your heart and your ability to tap into it. I can only guide you, but God is the ultimate authority, and even He will let you stumble from time to time to learn."

"But am I doing the right thing now? You must have an opinion. This mission is big enough to warrant knowing."

"Yes, you're doing the right thing," Andrew said. "Consider me the sword against your shoulder."

As the sun yielded to the lights of Port Said behind him, Jake bid farewell to Walker and the Russian-Arabic translator, who descended to find rest. Cahill's face moved within the borders of the laptop's screen.

"Turn us northwest, Terry."

As the Australian obeyed, the lights of Northern Africa slid up the ship's port side.

"Henri says we're being hailed in English," Cahill said.

"Right on time. It's the Israelis, right?"

"It's coming over a secure data channel, and they say they're the Israeli corvette, *Hanit*. So I sure hope so."

"Well, they've either discovered our plans and have broken our encryption, or we've found our escort to the Dardanelles.

That's the biggest ship in the Israeli surface fleet."

"Our identity may remain a secret all the way to Turkey," Cahill said. "With a little luck, it may remain a secret forever."

Two days later, Jake watched the icon on the laptop display representing the Israeli warship turn back from the entrance to the Dardanelles.

"I rather enjoyed their company, quiet as they were," Walker said. "We never had them within visual range, did we?"

"They may have been on our horizon once or twice, but I'm glad they just shadowed us. Their proximity would only have raised suspicions."

"And now we're alone again. There's no way to have an escort from now into the Black Sea without drawing suspicion."

"Agreed," Jake said. "But look at this strait. I suspect it has more four-legged observers than people. I'm not concerned about the Dardanelles. It's the Bosporus where we may need a little help."

Ten hours later, the setting sun cast long shadows into the waters as Jake watched the underside of the aging First Bosporus Bridge pass over him.

"Get a couple guys up here with binoculars," he said. "This strait is tough and filled with moving and hidden dangers, especially at night."

"Right," Walker said. "I'm on it."

Thirty minutes later, artificial lights of all colors danced from the European and Asian shores over the shimmering water.

"I'm tempted to take advantage of a solid fix to feed corrections into our satellite navigation," Jake said. "We've got the Istanbul Sapphire over there, the western spire of the Blue Mosque, and I think I can see the dome spire of Hagia Sophia."

"How can you tell which is which?" Walker asked. "There's a mosque on every hill."

"I should remember. I took Linda here on our honeymoon

tour of Europe. But you're right, I could be wrong."

"A visual fix sounds good, though. I'm sure we could figure out which mosque is which on the chart."

"Don't bother. I said I was tempted, but I'm not going to. All fixes on this ship are relative to the periscope, which I won't raise."

"Well then, you'd be best to keep your eyes on the water."

As the Australian finished his sentence, the starboard lookout yelled through the open door that a small boat was about to hit.

As Jake raced after Walker to the bridge wing, he heard an ugly scraping and crushing sound. He looked down and stared at a fishing boat embedded in his exoskeleton.

The boat's driver stared at the puncture wound his small vessel had inflicted upon the freighter, incredulous that his hull remained intact. Jake screamed and waved his arm for the man to reverse engines. Shock or chemical abuse prevented the man from responding. Walker and the lookout yelled as well, to no avail.

Jake stormed inside, grabbed a rifle, and returned.

"Don't hurt him, Jake," Walker said.

"Just motivating the proper behavior."

He aimed at the vessel's bow and fired. The ricochet caught the man's attention, and he turned his head over his shoulder while shifting his vehicle into reverse. Clearing the fake ship, the boat drove away, leaving a three-meter gap at the waterline.

"What now?" Walker asked.

"We reduce our freeboard to hide as much of that as we can, and we pray that nobody sees it."

Ten minutes passed, and the fake ship *Marie Lucille* settled into the Bosporus, leaving a small but visible chink in its camouflage.

"Any deeper, and we may as well just submerge," Jake said.

"I hope you have your priest friend praying," Walker said.

"I wouldn't worry. We're more than half way through this messy passage."

Ten minutes later, Jake saw a spotlight illuminate a ship several hundred yards behind him, and red and blue lights pulsated atop the watercraft.

"Damn! Police," Walker said. "You summoned them with your rifle. They're investigating the noise."

Jake's heart sank.

"They may not come to us," he said.

"That's wishful thinking. Look, they've already progressed forward a ship."

"Sound echoes violently on the water. They have no way of pinpointing the shot to us."

"That doesn't matter if they're thorough, and they're looking like a pretty damned thorough set of water cops."

Jake stepped to the laptop mounted beside the *Specter's* conning tower.

"Terry!" he said.

"I'm here, mate. How do we look? Did lowering our freeboard hide the damage?"

"No, not enough. And there's a high-speed police boat working its way to us to investigate my rifle shot."

"Shit," Cahill said. "Can you attract them to the port side? Maybe they wouldn't see the damage that way?"

"I don't know how to do that other than shooting the rifle from that side and hoping the sound pulls them that way. But that would just make things worse."

"How could they get any worse?"

"No need for such extreme measures," Renard said.

The authoritative interrupting voice soothed Jake's nerves.

"I hope that means you have a plan?" he asked.

"Call it my final gift before you enter the Black Sea. Look down a bearing of roughly two-three-zero."

"I'd need to walk away from the laptop."

"Then have your lookout look for you. It may take a minute or two."

"I don't have a minute or two, Pierre. What's your point?"

"Not to worry," Renard said. "Whether or not the act has yet begun, it's already been reported to the authorities."

"Okay," Jake said. "Julien!"

A young Frenchman stuck his head in the window.

"Let me know if you see anything interesting on bearing two-three-zero, plus or minus ten degrees, over the next minute or two."

The youngster acknowledged and stepped away.

"You're not even going to tell us?" Jake asked.

"Let me enjoy my dramatic moment, will you? Just trust me and don't do anything rash."

Walker entered the bridge and approached Jake.

"The police craft ran off. I can't believe it. We got lucky."

"Maybe not lucky, unless you count Pierre's planning as luck. He's got a surprise for us on bearing two-three-zero."

"I can't wait."

Walker stepped away to join the young Frenchman. Seconds later, he returned to Jake's view, animated.

"You won't believe it," he said. "A fire broke out on a ferry."

"Pierre, you didn't risk a ferry full of people! Not innocent people. Not for this."

"I wouldn't have unless I'd first commissioned Paris' finest firefighters to handle it. They'll make it look dangerous, but they'll have it under control the whole time."

"The flames are already dying!" Walker said. "And now they're gone. That was fast. There must be an amazing automated suppression system or something miraculous on that ship."

"No," Jake said. "The only miracle is the seeming infiniteness of Pierre's foresight–and his balls to act on it."

A day later, Jake saw his target on the horizon. He had slowed his trek across the Black Sea to launch his attack at night, and he approached his target during darkness. The pulsating warning lights on the horizon matched the tops of the Kerch Strait Bridge on his chart.

"We made it," he said.

"The Ukrainian helicopter coverage has been spotty," Cahill said. "It's a wonder we didn't run into anything."

"Don't you trust our Furuno? I've kept it on to prevent Chinese warships from getting curious."

"Chinese, Indian, Greek, Turkish, Russian, whatever. It still doesn't reach beyond our horizon."

"Be thankful we had periodic helicopter air views for that. We owe them for not allowing anyone close enough to see the hole in our shell. For barely having a standing navy, the Ukrainians did a pretty good job alerting us to cross traffic."

"I hope they're as friendly once we've done the dirty work to help their cause. Shall I warm up the weapons?"

"Yes. Liam and I will be down, and we'll be ready to submerge and flee if needed."

"If needed? You don't expect to escape otherwise, do you?"

"We believe a deployed *Kilo* is around here, but we can't be sure. If there's no sign of trouble, we'll stay on course until the explosion, and then we'll behave like a freighter would and turn tail."

"Shall I slow us, now? We're within weapons range of both the bridge and the undersea pipeline."

"Come to all stop. Send Doctor Tan to my ship so that I have a Russian translator in case this attack separates us."

"He was already standing by, and now he's on his way."

"Now warn Pierre so that he can warn the authorities. We'll be right down to finish this and head home."

CHAPTER 8

Captain Second Rank Dmitry Volkov raised his head and pressed his palms into the navigation table. He felt that nothing could chase away his mind's haziness.

"I should have already been promoted," he said.

"I'm sorry, sir," the sonar operator said. "I couldn't hear you."

"It's I who should be sorry. I'm lamenting my fate out loud."

"You're not alone, sir. Everyone's getting tired of protecting the bridge and pipeline. We already foiled the Ukrainians, and we were all looking forward to something new when we got back to Novorossiysk. But they just sent us back out to do the same thing."

"I wish I could change our tasking, but we have our duty. We must respect it as part of the frustrations of military service."

"I know, sir. But these waters once held so much excitement, and now that we've scared our enemy back to shore, boredom is our punishment for success. Even the dolphins are bored."

Volkov snorted.

"How could you possibly know that?"

"The trainer has said as much."

"Damn it, then. I cannot refute that man and his sixth sense about his babies."

"It's spooky, isn't it, sir?"

"Sometimes it is. I cannot alleviate the fate of the dolphins, but I can share with you a secret that I was going to withhold for another few days. But you've forced my hand by playing to my pity."

"I'll take any good news you have."

"We're nine days from our estimated midway point of this patrol. I've arranged for rations of beer and vodka for the crew on that night, three drinks per man. Go ahead and spread the news as you wish."

The young sailor's eyes sparkled.

"Thank you, sir! I'll be hailed as the saving messenger!"

"I know."

A shadow crept over the sonar operator's face, and he pressed his earpieces to his head. Volkov read the man's reaction and recognized potential danger. He also knew to exercise patience and wait for the sailor to complete his assessment.

"Torpedo in the water."

"Are you sure? You don't seem alarmed."

"Yes, sir. It's very far away."

"Is it coming at us?"

"Doubtful. It has a bearing rate and should pass well ahead. But it should get closer before it gets farther away again. Wait! Now I hear another."

"On the same bearing?"

"Yes. Probably from the same launch platform."

"You're sure they're not heading for us?"

"Positive now, sir."

"Then update the system with your best solutions."

As the torpedo icons and the image of their possible launching ship materialized on the chart, Volkov ordered battle stations, and he took the *Krasnodar* to periscope depth. The deck rocked in the shallow sea's swells.

"Raise the radio mast," he said.

An enlisted man seated at a control console touched a screen, and Volkov heard hydraulic valves clunk over his head. A red light from the transceiver box signaled his connectivity with a nearby ship that relayed his voice to the Black Sea Fleet headquarters.

"Wolf Den, this is Wolf One. Over."

An amplified voice issued from the transceiver.

"Wolf One, this is Wolf Den. Over."

"Wolf Den, Wolf One. I detect two hostile torpedoes heading towards the Kerch Strait Bridge. I'm sending my position and my best solution to the weapons and the launching ship. I also recommend abandoning the bridge. Over."

"Make that four torpedoes, sir!" the sonar operator said.

"Wolf Den, Wolf One. Correction. Four, I repeat, four torpedoes are heading for the bridge. Over."

"Wolf One, Wolf Den. I understand four torpedoes are heading towards the Kerch Strait Bridge. We just received a bomb threat for the bridge. It's already being abandoned. Over."

An uncomfortable silence told Volkov that he and the watchman on the phone felt like helpless bystanders to an orchestrated attack. The replacement voice carried the authority of the senior watch officer at headquarters, as well as concern for being surprised.

"Wolf One, Wolf Den. Are you sure the torpedoes are heading towards the bridge? Did you detect any submerged contacts? Over."

"Wolf Den, Wolf One. No submerged contacts. Nothing submerged could have passed the Bosporus without being detected by our hydrophone field at the exit, and I have no evidence of a submerged vessel here. Over."

"Wolf One, Wolf Den. I'm correlating your data to a ship in the area. This suggests illegal arming of a merchant vessel. I'm vectoring in our patrol aircraft for visual and the *Muromets* to board the assailing vessel. Stay out of the way so you don't get shot. Over."

"Are you sure you don't want me to send a torpedo at the bastard and just end this?"

"Yes, damn it, I'm sure. We haven't confirmed the shooter or a target yet either. You could sink an innocent ship or ruin the evidence of the attack. Out."

Volkov secured the handset and glared at the sailor seated at the weapons control console.

"Prepare tube one anyway, for the hostile weapons launch platform. But don't you dare launch it without making eye contact with me if and when I give the order."

As the weapons operator obeyed and announced the readiness of tube one, the sonar operator waved to Volkov.

"Yes, man. What is it?"

"Loud, distant explosion, bearing two-five-five."

"Mother of God, what's going on?"

He reached for the handset.

"Wolf Den, Wolf One. Loud, distant explosion, bearing two-five-five. Please correlate with sonar systems from other nearby naval vessels. Over."

"Wolf One, Wolf Den. Wait. Over."

"Waiting. Over."

Volkov's executive officer, a handsome but uncaring man with political connections, moved to his side. He found it odd that the man showed interest, given that he had secured the future command of a submarine through his family's name.

"Captain, since we can't head that way ourselves, maybe we can use the dolphins. They could be close enough to take a look."

"That's actually not a bad idea."

As Volkov drew breath to summon the dolphin trainer, the lithe master of the mammals slipped into the compartment with the dexterous ease of his animals.

"The rumor has already spread throughout the ship. Someone is attacking the bridge with torpedoes?"

"An armed merchant ship, if you can believe it," Volkov said. "It's a suicide attack. They must know there's no way out of this."

"No. There isn't," the trainer said.

"As it stands, I can't get any closer with my ship due to the risk of friendly fire. So I want the dolphins to discern the details."

The trainer brushed the sonar operator's shoulder as he sat at the console beside him.

"Let me find my babies. Do I have your permission to talk to them?"

"As usual, let me know your intent before you transmit each message. But yes. You have control of the underwater communications sonar."

"Since there's so much activity, I'll just start by asking for their location. They need to know I'm thinking about them."

Volkov twisted a knob above his head to pipe sound through the compartment's loudspeakers. He listened as the *Krasnodar* simulated an aquatic animal. Three series of outgoing recordings followed by mammalian responses filled the control room.

"Based upon round-trip timing and the sound-velocity profile in these waters, the distance to the lead dolphin is ten thousand yards," the sonar operator said. "Bearing is two-six-three."

"Very well," Volkov said. "Plot it on the chart."

Below his chin, the black whale icon appeared. He frowned.

"That's still a whale," he said. "Nobody changed it? Never mind. Tell me what bearing, or hour on the clock, rather, they need to swim to find the origin of these torpedoes?"

"Four o'clock, sir," the sonar operator said.

"I'll send them," the trainer said.

Volkov nodded, and another exchange of chirps and whistles filled the room.

"They're swimming in the correct direction," the trainer said. "I sent them at eleven knots."

"That's twenty-two minutes of swimming," the sonar operator said.

"They'll be fine," the trainer said. "They're my athletes."

The amplified voice garnered Volkov's ear.

"Wolf One, Wolf Den. I'm sending you data about the explosion. It's near a section of our undersea pipeline, and we've lost system pressure. So we know it has taken damage. I'm also sending data of the ship that's been identified as the hostile torpedo launch platform."

Volkov analyzed the data as it fed his tactical system. The explosion had been triangulated to a section of the pipeline, and the freighter, *Marie Lucille*, appeared at the likely origins of the torpedoes that raced towards the bridge.

His sonar operator mentioned that the alleged assailant freighter was slowing.

"Wolf Den, Wolf One. The *Marie Lucille* is slowing. Over."

"We've used the bomb threat as a reason to order every ship within twenty-five miles of the bridge and heading towards it to come to all stop. Over."

"It's not trying to run or fight. It's not behaving like it has any knowledge of the weapons. How did you identify it as the culprit? Over."

"By your information and a visual from our aircraft. Over."

"My information is long-range passive sonar. It might correlate to other ships. What did your aircraft see? Over."

"Nothing unusual. Just running lights. The admiral didn't send any aircraft closer in case of anti-air missiles. The *Muromets* will intercept it in twenty-four minutes, and fighter jets have been scrambled as back up. They will be caught. Stop trying to run this from under the water. Out."

Volkov turned and walked to the elevated conning platform at the compartment's rear. As he sank into his foldout captain's chair, he studied his monitor. The update of the target, *Marie Lucille*, shortened the dolphins' estimated swim time.

He waited for the trainer to lift his head and make eye contact, and then he gestured him to the conning platform.

"Yes, sir?"

"You're not at all concerned that I'm sending the dolphins to investigate a surfaced contact?"

"I've trained them to work against surfaced vessels below the water line, and they can plant their explosives on any ship."

The confidence made Volkov question if he had misjudged the man earlier.

"That would hardly damage a ship of that size," he said. "And I must admit I expected resistance from you on this."

"Not after seeing the faces of your crew last time. They were elated to be a part of our last deployment's success. And so were Mikhail and Andrei. They know when they're part of something important. They can tell."

"And you would have them help now, even when there's little they can do?"

"They need to do something to make this crew feel useful. I can't take any more of this negativity. We all need to believe that we're doing something important, and if pictures and possibly explosive detonations from Andrei and Mikhail can help, then I want to help."

"They'll be in camera range in fifteen minutes. They'll be able to plant explosives in sixteen, which beats the arrival of the *Muromets* by almost five minutes."

"What's your angle on this, sir?"

"Can they place explosives on the shafts?"

"Impossible. That's too dangerous. In fact, I've trained them to avoid the propellers."

"Understandable. Can they surface and get photos of the deck?"

"That they can do. What are they looking for?"

"Guns. Torpedoes. Missile launchers. Before the dolphins get there, the torpedoes will have run their courses. Depending what sort of fate those weapons meet, the intensity factor may skyrocket. It will be worth knowing if that ship is trying to hide weapons."

"Time will tell a lot. My babies can help."

Fourteen minutes later, the sonar operator's face became ashen.

"Multiple heavyweight explosions. I can hear concrete hitting the water. The caisson is crumbling. The bridge is coming down."

"Mother of God," Volkov said.

He contacted the fleet headquarters senior watch officer, who confirmed the explosions and the loss of the bridge.

Somberness engulfed the room, except for the trainer, who tapped his screen to send recorded whistles from the *Krasnodar*. Moments later, Volkov heard a dolphin's high-pitched response.

"They've echolocated the contact," the trainer said.

"A surfaced contact? The *Marie Lucille*?"

"Yes. I trained them for it, since it's necessary for harbor attacks. So I can command it."

"Very well, order the approach"

Recorded whistles. Mammalian response.

"They've confirmed," the trainer said. "They're accelerating towards the target."

"Very well. I want a surfaced but dark photograph first, without a flash to alert the target."

"They're within a quarter mile of the target," the trainer said. "I'm ordering the dark photograph."

Volkov recognized the new sound of crackling shrimp, the camera's signal, pulsing through the loudspeakers. Given the low baud rate, he expected five minutes to render the full image.

"Order the dolphins in closer," he said.

The trainer complied, and the dolphins acknowledged as one's camera sent its synthetic shrimp symphony to form a grainy picture on Volkov's display. He noticed the trainer glaring at the same image forming at his console.

"It's hard to tell with the weak backlighting of the stars," Volkov said. "But nothing looks like weapons. There should be something mounted on the deck to allow it to shoot torpedoes."

"I see nothing unusual either," the trainer said. "But what about that dark spot near the water line?"

"That's interesting and suspicious. I am curious to get a closer look at this ship."

Chirps.

"The dolphins are within lighting range of the ship."

"Have them take a picture of the bow from underwater," Volkov said. "Perhaps these torpedoes issued from phantom tubes below the waterline. Have them use the flash this time."

A chirp announced completion of each animal's positioning.

"They're ready for the picture," the trainer said.

"Very well, take the picture."

After the trainer relayed the order, more incoming shrimp crackling filled the room. The image formed, and acid began eating away at Volkov's stomach. As the trainer watched the same picture come to life, he requested the dolphins to arm their explosives. Volkov shouted his permission.

"Prepare the dolphins to lay their explosives."

He reached for the handset.

"Wolf Den, Wolf One. It's a trap! Get the *Muromets* out of there! Over."

"Wolf One, Wolf Den, the *Muromets* is tying up to the *Marie Lucille* right now. What sort of trap? Over."

"I'll send you the picture as it forms, but suffice it to say that the rumors of an armed submarine transport ship are true."

CHAPTER 9

Cahill's trembling finger hovered over the icon to detonate the scaffolding. He had blown the temporary tubes overboard after taking down his targets, and he wanted to remove his ship of all its facades and burdens.

"Not yet," Jake said.

"How much longer? Liam and I both saw the flash. There's something out there dead ahead."

He watched a night vision camera's view of a *Grisha* class corvette slowing in preparation to tie to his fake ship's port side.

"I know our cover's blown," Jake said. "I know there's something out there under the surface. Antoine says there's a surge in dolphin and shrimp noise, which means something is spooking the fish. But we have a few seconds to agree upon the order of things before we start shooting."

"I need to take out the main cannon on the *Grisha* with me cannons."

"Before or after you blow the scaffolding?"

"After. Me gunners can't see with this blasted exoskeleton in the way."

"But you could hit the engine room through the exoskeleton, right? Their propulsion equipment is a big enough target at this range shooting semi-blind. Take a few free shots."

Cahill looked to the display that showed the innards of the *Grisha*-class corvette. Comparing the return of the warship from the *Specter's* Furuno radar to the angle of his raised railguns' barrels, he believed he could aim the rounds into the twin diesel engines and the solitary gas turbine.

"I can do that," he said. "Take out the engine room, then drop the scaffolding, then take out the main cannon."

"Then the thirty-millimeter gun, then the Gecko surface-to-air launcher. Then torpedoes. Ignore the depth charges."

"We'll need to take out both torpedo nests. I can't get a clear shot to the port side nest from here."

"We'll go around and deal with it on the other side."

"Understood. May I begin now, mate?"

"Shoot straight," Jake said. "Commence fire."

"Aim both cannons at the engine room," Cahill said. "Set the rounds to splinter. Target the diesels and the gas turbine."

"They're aimed, Terry. The splintering may not reach the full effect damage radius at this range."

"I know, but we'll do the damage we need. You have control of the cannons, Liam. When you think you've disabled propulsion, shift fire to the main cannon, then the thirty-millimeter gun. I'll be dropping the scaffolding for you soon."

"I'm ready," Walker said.

"Fire."

The boom from the starboard railgun preceded the super-sonic crack from the port hull's weapon. Infrared imagery showed the supersonic rounds slicing hot puncture wounds in the rear quarter of the corvette.

"Good shooting," Jake said. "Keep it up."

Requiring five seconds for each round, the railguns punched eight holes through the *Grisha's* engine room, turning the space into a white-hot vision of friction wounds and a secondary fire.

But the Russian crew fought back, and Cahill saw flashes erupt on his display from the cannon and the thirty-millimeter gun. He tapped the icon that blew the scaffolding to the exoskeleton, and thumps echoed around him as the fake bulkheads splashed.

"Take out that cannon!" he said.

"I've ordered it," Walker said. "We're aiming."

Three rounds from each railgun walked toward the Russian cannon until a round punctured it and silenced it. But Cahill felt a shudder across the catamaran's hull.

"What's been hit?" Jake asked.

"Damage report, Liam!" Cahill said.

"No response from the port cannon. The port induction mast is offline. The port gas turbine intake system has automatically shifted to a cross-connected feed from the starboard induction mast."

"Shit," Cahill said. "A round hit the port weapons bay. Use the starboard cannon to take out the thirty-millimeter gun."

"Hurry!" Jake said. "They're pummeling my conning tower."

As the starboard railgun found its way to the thirty-milli-meter gun, Cahill watched the last active threat fall silent. He exhaled a sigh of relief that he knew would be short-lived.

"Continue to the Gecko surface-to-air launcher," he said. "We don't want them coming at us in slam mode."

"Continuing to the Gecko," Walker said. "We have them now, you know. That's it for the short-range weapons."

"I know. Coming to ahead two-thirds. Right full rudder."

"Why?" Jake asked. "I think I know what you're doing, but explain."

"I'm going to circle around this *Grisha* with me starboard can-non and take out its surface-to-air missiles and torpedoes."

"Agreed," Jake said.

"How's the damage report?" Cahill asked.

"The port engine room is sealed," Walker said. "Damage is re-stricted to the compartment above it. It appears that the round hit the port cannon's magazine."

"No communication from the port weapons bay?"

"No. I'm sorry, Terry."

His heart sank.

"Take the bridge, Liam. I'll head back there."

"No, Terry. Damage control is an executive officer's job. The ship needs its captain here."

Walker darted down the stairs, and Cahill slid a headset over his ear.

"Starboard weapons bay, come in," he said.

"Starboard weapons bay, here, sir."

"Send two more rounds into the surface-to-air launcher, then put three into the starboard torpedoes. Do it while we're turn-ing. I'll get you a clear shot of the port torpedoes as we head out of here."

As the *Goliath-Specter* tandem doubled back behind the si-lenced *Grisha*, the starboard railgun disabled the corvette's starboard torpedoes. Passing its stern, Cahill opened range to give his functional cannon a line of sight to the port torpedo nest.

Noting that Walker had illuminated the *Goliath's* phased array radar system, Cahill looked at the influx of tactical information. Two high-speed jet fighters raced towards him, as did several surface combatants.

"I think we need to submerge," he said.

"Agreed," Jake said. "Time to hide."

"Let me make sure I have no holes in me people tank first."

He tapped a key to send his voice throughout the *Goliath*.

"Liam, contact the bridge."

"Liam, here," Walker said. "I'm in the port engine room."

"What do you have?"

"That round hit the port weapons magazine."

"What about Daniels? The port weapons bay watch?"

The delay in Walker's answer concerned Cahill.

"He's hurt bad. His legs are shattered, and I'm not sure he's going to keep them both. I've got him being moved to the port hull berthing area, and the corpsman will do what he can for him."

"What else can we do for him?"

"Let the corpsman determine that. For now, he'll just stop the bleeding and give him sedatives."

"What about the port cannon?"

"The round took out communications, electronics, and hydraulics. The cannon might be operational again in manual mode after clearing out the magazine."

"That's good news about the gun. I'll be submerging us. Stay there to watch for leaks."

"I heard the mixed news," Jake said. "Sorry about your man. *Specter* is ready to submerge."

Cahill narrated as he tapped icons.

"Shifting propulsion to the MESMA systems. Securing the gas turbines. All six MESMA systems are running normally, bearing the electric strain. Propulsion is running on air-independent power. Maintaining five knots. Shutting the head valves and recirculating internal air."

He then tapped icons to flood his ballast tanks. Cargo containers blocked his habitual views of the diving process, but patience and the laws of physics brought dark, lapping crests to the bridge windows. He anticipated the creaking of the cargo containers that had refused to topple away with his exoskeleton, but the noise was subtle as the crates floated away on the sea's surface.

The *Goliath* settled at twenty meters with the *Specter* scant meters below the surface.

"Twenty meters," he said. "I'm giving Liam a few minutes to check for leaks before we go deeper."

"Fine, but bring us to ten knots. Let's create distance and start becoming harder to find."

As Cahill accelerated his ship, an overhead silhouette startled him. He looked up, and the primal fear of being shark food turned his skin into needles. Then a pair of thuds reverberated throughout the bridge, and two sleek aquatic forms absconded into the darkness.

His mind registered that two explosive devices had latched onto his windows. Flat metal surfaces under each device appeared to be electromagnets seeking ferrous metal, while the suction cups in each corner explained how the attackers had planted the devices on the glass a meter from his head.

He turned and jumped down the stairs, guiding his crash-landing by sliding his palms over the railing. His ankle turned over as he hit, but he hopped to the watertight door, yanked it open, and ducked through.

"Help me close this! Now!"

Standing on his good foot, he pulled the door shut and felt a pair of helping hands finish the job.

The sonar supervisor released the latch and frowned.

"What's wrong, Terry?"

Scanning the tactical control room, Cahill sought a monitor, limped to it, and sat.

"Patch me through to Jake."

"Done," the sonar supervisor said.

"What's going on, Terry?" Jake asked.

"I think I was just attacked by dolphins."

Jake frowned.

"You think, or you're sure?"

"I'm sure I was just attacked by something. There are two explosive detonators attached to me bridge windows. God knows what else is attached where."

"We need to surface, then," Jake said. "In case we're facing a loss of watertight integrity."

Loud cracks preempted Cahill's response.

"Never mind," Jake said. "Take a look. Unless you've got flooding somewhere else in your ship, it's over."

Jake's face disappeared, and a camera view of the *Goliath's* bridge appeared. Water poured in, and within seconds, the compartment flooded. Cahill had power to the bridge secured to avoid an electrical short.

"Well, shit," Jake said. "Russian dolphins one, *Goliath* zero. I hope they're out of ammo, because we have no way to stop them."

"Can you replay the bridge video when they laid their weapons?" Cahill asked.

"Good idea."

The video ran, showing shadows above his head approaching from outboard, laying the detonators, and turning back the way they had come.

"I don't know the proper tactical response to that," Jake said. "They're silent, armed, and under the control of God knows who."

"I think I know who."

Cahill recognized Remy's voice and his toad-like head as he leaned beside Jake on the *Specter's* conning platform.

"All that dolphin noise had been bothering me even before they attacked. I've been rerunning the tapes, and there's definitely a master dolphin giving orders."

"A master dolphin?" Cahill asked.

"Yes. Whatever it is, it's definitely a dolphin's sound. It may be pre-recorded sounds, but it's not manmade."

"Do you have a bearing to this master dolphin?"

"I have a series of bearings, yes. I'm tracking the master dolphin at eight knots."

"What range at that speed?"

"Far. Eighteen thousand yards."

Cahill checked the tactical display.

"There's nothing on the surface out there."

"Right," Jake said. "It could be some small ship that's got a sonar system for communication with dolphins. That's how I'd manage it, if I had attack dolphins."

"But you don't have attack dolphins," Cahill said. "And you don't have, or didn't have, a bridge to protect. I'm going to be more pessimistic and say our master dolphin is a Russian *Kilo* submarine."

"Yeah, we have to assume that. At least we're heading in the right direction to get away from it."

As Cahill allowed himself a glimpse of optimism that he may escape the Black Sea alive, he heard a report from a young sonar operator within the *Specter*.

"Torpedo in the water!"

Remy disappeared, and Jake's face became stern.

"Is it an immediate threat to our ship?" Jake asked.

"No, it's far. But it appears well aimed. On our left, drawing right. It looks like a perfect intercept shot."

"I don't have it," the sonar supervisor said. "Our towed array sonar is still stowed."

"That's why we use the *Specter's*," Cahill said.

Remy reappeared next to Jake.

"I've confirmed it," he said. "It's a dangerous shot. I assume it's being wire-guided, too."

"Of course, it's wire-guided," Jake said. "That doesn't bother me when the guiding ship is nine miles away. Even with these annoying scaffold shards still attached to us, they can't possibly hear us. Are you claiming otherwise?"

"Sort of. I'm listening to the dolphins now. They're pinging on us, and I'm sure they know where we are."

Cahill watched Jake rub his forehead.

"Dolphins are pinging on us?" Jake asked.

"As nature intended," Remy said. "It's only a small challenge to notice them doing it. I just set the active sonar intercept alerts to the frequencies they use, and *voila*."

"So what?" Cahill asked. "How do they tell a human on a submarine our exact coordinates, speed, and bearing?"

"I have no idea," Remy said.

"Jake," Cahill said. "Let's get some insight from Pierre. Let him research what dolphins can do as far as such tactics are concerned. Maybe we can learn something useful."

"Go ahead and take me shallow so I can link to Pierre," Jake said. "No need to fear radar when Flipper's already ratting us out."

CHAPTER 10

Jake flagged the dolphins for future consideration and focused on the threat he understood.

"Prepare tubes one and two for the *Kilo* submarine. Prepare
tube three for the *Grisha.*"

"Tubes one and two are assigned to the *Kilo*," Remy said.
"Tube three is assigned to the *Grisha.*"

"I want passive search while I have wire control. If I lose a
wire, I want the torpedoes to shift to active."

"That's tricky, but possible. I'll need a minute to work
through the menus."

"You've got a minute while I turn."

He looked to his display and needed a second to reconcile
Cahill's face against the background of the *Goliath's* tactical control room.

"Terry, point us at the *Kilo*. I don't want my torpedoes running into your hulls during their wake up and wire clearance
routines."

"Got it, mate. I'm pointing us at the *Kilo.*"

Jake grabbed a railing as the deck tilted hard left.

"Easy," he said.

"I got you. Me hydraulic arms are holding you in place."

"Sometimes I wonder."

"We're facing the *Kilo*. I recommend you shoot now so we can
get back on our evasion course."

"Shoot tube one," Jake said.

The torpedo tube's pneumatic whine filled the *Specter's* control room, and the rapid pressure change popped his ears.

"Tube one, normal launch," Henri said.

"Shoot tube two."

"Tube two, normal launch."

"Shoot tube three."

"Tube three, normal launch."

The final whine decayed as Jake cleared his inner ear.

"Get us back on the evasion course," he said.

"With pleasure," Cahill said.

As the deck tilted hard the other way, Jake ordered the tubes reloaded. Then Renard's voice came through weak and fuzzy.

"Can you hear me?" the Frenchman asked.

"Barely," Jake said. "What's going on?"

"I'm sending you as much data as I can on the tactical feed. The Russians are already attempting to jam our satellite connection."

"Obviously. You're cutting in an out. Pierre?"

Static and hissing overcame the Frenchman's response.

"Pierre?"

"He's gone, mate," Cahill said.

"Yeah, I see. Take us back to the surface."

"We'll be exposed to aircraft and anti-ship missiles."

"I know, but we need to get away from these dolphins and the torpedo. We'll deal with the air threats as they come."

"Right, then. Taking us to the surface."

The rise felt imperceptible, but the rhythmic bouncing over the waves confirmed Jake's desires. The *Goliath* had surfaced and pushed ahead at maximum speed.

"Thirty-three knots and change," Cahill said. "Almost thirty-four. The broken stanchions don't slow us when we're surfaced, but I'm sure they'll add drag when we're below."

"That's a problem we'll deal with later. There's no time to send anyone topside to clear them."

"I agree. Take a look at what me phased array sees, and also what Renard's data feed gave us. His feed identified which ship is which. This is lining up pretty much like we expected."

Jake's overhead display showed the entire Black Sea Fleet readying to race towards him.

"This was going to be a narrow escape fighting our way out with both cannons," he said. "Now we have just one, and that pair of Fencer fighters needs to be knocked out of the sky."

"They're less agile than modern fighters," Cahill said. "We can take them with one cannon."

"Good. Start shooting."

The hypersonic crack filled the *Specter's* control room.

"The jets are close enough for me to use the phased array to guide me rounds. But I'm facing heavy jamming."

"They're close enough that a ballistic shot should be good enough. Just aim and take them down!"

Jake's blood pressure rose as the cracks echoed, the dolphins pinged him, and the torpedo chased him.

"Got one!" Cahill said. "One Fencer is turning back. I must have winged it."

"Keep shooting! Take down the other one."

"I'm on it."

Rays of horror leapt to life on his display.

"Vampires!" he said. "Coming from the port at Novorossiysk, both Fencers, and land-based launchers from Crimea."

"Saturation attack," Cahill said. "We'll have to dive."

"But we have anti-submarine helicopters inbound from Crimea."

"They're seven minutes away. The vampires are the problem we need to solve first."

The dooming lines showing incoming missiles became clearer as the *Goliath's* tactical system calculated their geometries.

"Hold on," Jake said. "It's not a saturation attack. It's more like suppressing fire. Those vampires are staggered. Some are heading towards waypoints. They're going to blanket us and make us stay submerged."

"To protect their helicopters."

Jake rested his mind from the airborne threats and looked at Remy, who announced that the weapon from tube three had detonated under the *Grisha*. With the target dead in the water, most of the twenty-four undersea limpet bombs had attached, scattering holes across the corvette's length. Remy also informed him that the *Kilo's* inbound torpedo held its deadly course.

Preparing to hide under the water's surface, he lowered the *Specter's* periscope.

"Jake, we need to submerge. Now!" Cahill said.

"Slow to thirteen knots and submerge," Jake said.

The display of the *Goliath's* internal tanks showed the inundation of seawater as the transport vessel's centrifugal pumps sucked liquid into the beast.

"We're under," Remy said. "We're slow, but I can hear better now. The inbound torpedo is eight thousand yards away. Time to impact has shifted from twenty minutes at our surfaced speed to seven and a half minutes at our evasion speed of thirteen knots."

"Very well, Antoine," Jake said.

He looked into his monitor.

"Let's review our threats, ignoring the vampires. We've got three inbound helicopters that we know of, and we're still in a tail chase with the *Kilo's* torpedo seven and a half minutes behind us."

"The torpedo is still the least of our worries," Cahill said. "If a helicopter gets one whiff of us, we won't have seven and a half seconds before it drops a weapon on our heads."

"They've got us in a squeeze play. Damned if we surface, damned if we stay under."

"We've been through this before."

"But it wasn't this bad. We need a new tactic. Fast. Something that allows us to be in between states–surfaced enough to fight the helicopters but submerged enough to avoid the vampires."

A glint in Cahill's eye told Jake he had spurred the right thought in his Australian colleague.

"I know what to do, mate. We'll toggle between states like you said."

"Are you thinking about porpoising?" Jake asked.

"Damned right I am. Now get your submarine off me back. I can't do it with your radar cross section exposed above the water."

"Got it," Jake said. "Before we disconnect, I'm sending you coordinates for our reunion."

He tapped the navigation plot at a random point to the southwest.

"I have the coordinates," Cahill said. "I'll meet you there. Make yourself light, and I'll make meself heavy. You'll need to veer to the south and head deep. I'm driving us deeper now to give you room to maneuver without broaching."

The deck angled downward.

"I'm going to bottom myself and hope that the torpedo and the damned dolphins stay on you."

"That should work," Cahill said. "We're crossing the three-hundred-meter curve, and the floor angles down steeply from here. That should help hide you from active torpedo returns."

"There's nothing active. Antoine can barely hear the high-speed screws. They must be guiding the weapon to us."

"Even better," Cahill said. "Stay quiet, and they'll definitely key on me."

The deck leveled as the *Goliath-Specter* tandem settled at one hundred meters. Jake looked to Henri, who nodded. He then glanced at his internal tanks and saw that the Frenchman pumped water overboard to make the *Specter* light.

"I'm light," he said.

"I'm heavy," Cahill said. "You're about to break free of me presses on your own. Let's do it."

"Shoot straight."

"Hide well. Disengaging!"

Jake shut down the laser communication system, and the screen went dark.

"We're rising," Henri said.

"I know. Give Terry time to clear under us."

"We're rising fast, Jake."

"Flood the centerline tanks."

"I'm flooding centerline tanks," Henri said. "I need more. I need speed and down angles to keep us under."

"All ahead one-third."

"Coming to ahead one-third. We're at sixty meters and rising at five meters per second. We're a cork, Jake."

"Full dive on the stern planes."

The deck angled ten, then twenty degrees down. Jake pressed his palms into the railing and shifted his weight to his shoulders.

"Fifty meters and rising at two meters per second," Henri said. "And our stern is even higher than that."

"All ahead standard."

"Coming to all ahead standard."

"You have full dive on the fairwater planes?"

"Yes, of course," Henri said. "We're still struggling. Forty-two meters and rising at half a meter per second."

Jake ran the numbers through his mind. Speed of nine knots, accelerating to fifteen, an angle of twenty degrees forcing the ship downward, the hydroplaning of the fairwater planes pressing against the ship, and the rate of influx of the trim and drain pumps against the *Specter's* lightness.

His mental equation resolved as favorable on the *Specter's* ascent.

"We're fine," he said.

"Thirty-seven meters," Henri said.

"And?"

"And steady. Now descending."

"Reduce the ship's angle to ten degrees down. Slow to all ahead one-third. Left full rudder, steady course south."

The deck became less taxing on Jake's shoulders, but it lifted him sideways.

"How's your depth control now, Henri?"

"Good. I can manage it with pumps."

"All stop."

"Coming to all stop. Are we drifting to the bottom?"

"Yes. Rig the ship for ultra-quiet. Everyone's going to hold their breath for a while."

"How hard do you want to hit the bottom?" Henri asked.

"Gentle. I don't want to give away the noise. A quarter meter per second?"

"I can do that. I'm pumping water off now."

"Very well, Henri. Bottom the ship."

"May I have the fathometer?"

"It may not help much on this steep bottom, but go ahead."

Remy interjected his report.

"I've lost the wires to both weapons," he said. "The maneuvering was too much."

"I understand. How did they line up against your last solution of the *Kilo*?"

"I don't have any new data on the *Kilo*. It stopped sending commands to the dolphins."

"But the dolphins are still pinging on us?"

"Yes, the dolphins know where we are, but I imagine that they can't tell the *Kilo* with enough accuracy to shoot us. Look at the data Pierre sent about using dolphins in undersea tactics."

"Sorry, Antoine, I've been busy. I'll trust you for now."

"Yes, trust me. It's good to be far from the dolphins."

"Let's keep it that way."

"I think they'll follow the *Goliath* because of its speed and noise. It's a far more interesting target."

"Has Terry shot yet?"

"Yes. He's porpoising. He's shot his cannon three times."

"Any sign yet of a hit?"

"I can't tell if they damage a helicopter unless they splash it."

"But the *Goliath* hasn't been hit?"

Jake avoided appending the word 'yet' to his question, refusing to utter the negative thought.

"No, absolutely not. That I would hear."

"No need to listen," Jake said. "Let Julien listen to the *Goliath's* battle. I want you to track the incoming torpedo."

As Jake looked to his display and saw the *Kilo's* weapon approaching his port flank, an alarm whined.

"Silence that."

"Active torpedo seeker alarm," Remy said. "The *Kilo's* weapon just went active."

"Are we in its acquisition cone?"

"Marginal. It's hard to tell. We'll know in about fifteen seconds as it hopefully crosses our stern."

"Brace for impact," Henri said. "Bottoming the ship."

"Perfect timing," Jake said.

With the torpedo having energized its active acoustic seeker, he decided that minimizing the *Specter's* reflective surfaces offered his best hope of survival. He eliminated his ship's entire bottom as a liability.

He held the railing as his knees buckled and the hull scraped the sediments.

"We're still moving at quarter of a knot," Henri said. "But we're slowing."

"Let friction stop us."

"The torpedo has passed through our baffles," Remy said. "It's following the *Goliath*."

Julien, a young sailor who had earned Jake's respect during the rescue of a South Korean submarine, turned his head and pulled back an ear piece.

"Something just splashed into the water, bearing two-six-eight. I think it's a helicopter."

"It could be any of the vampires running out of fuel," Jake said. "Make sure you got it right."

"He's got it right," Remy said. "I heard it, too. And I hear the first vampires splashing as they run out of fuel."

"I thought I told you to listen for the torpedo."

"You did, but you didn't say I couldn't listen for anything else. You know me. I like to listen, and I'm surprised I don't hear Terry pumping his fists in the air for shooting down his targets."

"How could you possibly hear that?"

"I can't. But what I can hear is that he's either out of range of my hearing, or he's stopped shooting."

"Nothing's out of range of your hearing."

"That's why I know he's done shooting. I think he shot down all the helicopters."

CHAPTER 11

Volkov released the railing, looked down, and watched the color return to his knuckles.

"We've escaped the second torpedo," the sonar operator said. "There are no remaining threats to our ship."

"Are the weapons a threat to any friendly assets?"

"No, sir. They'll run out of fuel before reaching the coast."

He studied the display by his side and eyeballed the worst-case scenario. The luckiest steering command to the closest torpedo would exhaust its fuel before acquiring the *Krasnodar*, provided he continued southwest–the direction of his adversary's escape.

Glancing at the latest data update, he digested his fleet's status. The stranded and impotent *Muromets* fought fires and flooding, three anti-submarine helicopters were downed, and the salvo of anti-ship missiles had splashed.

His new enemy, which the fleet had identified as the mercenary transport vessel, *Goliath*, working in tandem with its *Scorpène*-class submarine, *Specter*, had broken the bridge and pipeline under his guard. Redemption meant revenge, and revenge meant redemption. For his sanity and self-respect, he had to bring the assailants to justice.

And he would have help. The sizeable surface fleet sprang to action, the huge *Slava* cruiser leading the high-speed chase. The *Goliath* may have surprised and overpowered a *Grisha* corvette, but against the rest of the Black Sea Fleet, it and the *Specter* would succumb.

Long-range, long-endurance, anti-submarine aircraft zipped ahead of the enemy with the intent of dropping hardware to block the exit through the Bosporus. His sister *Kilo*-class submarines lagged behind him–one trapped in the Sea of Azov behind the bridge's cleanup effort, the rest getting underway from Novorossiysk. That suited him. If the *Goliath-Specter* tandem dared to remain submerged, the battle was his.

The Black Sea provided the bulwarks that penned in his prey, and he would track them down. But the sick suspicion that an adversary smart enough to launch a sneak attack of guarded assets was also smart enough to escape from the Black Sea worried him.

"I've received the new submerged threat signal, again," the trainer said. "This battle is confusing them."

"Just ignore it. Keep them chasing the *Goliath-Specter*."

Volkov found the dolphins' repeated reports of submerged contacts annoying as downed helicopters and splashing missiles had taxed their ability to report data.

"I'll do my best. They lost a lot of ground when the *Goliath-Specter* surfaced. I don't know if they're catching up or falling behind now with the *Goliath-Specter* submerged."

Volkov's request to fleet headquarters for damage reports of the *Goliath* revealed that the transport ship's port cannon had failed. The helicopter crews had been obsessed with survival at the expense of gathering additional useful data, and without evidence to the contrary, he estimated that the dolphins had planted their explosives over a free-flooding tank or other area of minimal impact.

"All ahead standard," he said. "Make turns for fifteen knots."

The gray-bearded veteran seated at the ship's control panel acknowledged the order.

"Time on the battery is three hours at that speed, while the fuel-cell system remains online," the veteran said. "It's one hour, twenty minutes without the fuel-cell system."

"Very well. Chart me a course to the Bosporus, minimum transit time, assuming the fuel-cell system stays online, and assuming maximum speed when snorkeling."

After the veteran acknowledged and turned to begin his calculation, Volkov realized that his opponent needed to follow a random zigzagging course to reach the Bosporus. Otherwise, a direct course would simplify the search for the new wave of helicopters that would seek the *Goliath-Specter* tandem.

"I estimate that we'll get there three to five hours before the *Goliath-Specter*," the veteran said. "It depends on the assumptions of the course it takes, but I've modeled them in the system for you."

Volkov reviewed and approved the assumptions.

He then noticed a new rhythm in an incoming mammalian signal.

"What's that?" he asked. "I noticed something different."

The trainer nodded.

"Andrei reports that the *Goliath-Specter* is now a medium-range target. It's a good estimate that the *Goliath-Specter* is less than ten nautical miles from him."

"Verify the bearing from him."

The trainer sent and received chirps.

"Four o'clock."

"Four? It turned toward the south. That explains why my torpedo hasn't acquired yet."

"I still have the wire, sir," the weapons operator said. "With this new update, I recommend a forty-five-degree steer to the left."

"Do it," Volkov said.

"My babies are useful, are they not?" the trainer asked.

"They could do even better if they close the distance to the *Goliath-Specter* on an intercept course."

"I never taught them the concept of an intercept course. They will just do their best to catch up, based upon whatever geometry plays out in their minds. It might be an intercept course, or they may follow the wake."

"So be it," Volkov said. "Send the data to the plot."

The sonar operator obeyed, and the icon representing a hostile submarine, Volkov's best image for the *Goliath-Specter* tandem, shifted in space to its updated location.

"Nineteen thousand yards, and opening distance slowly."

"It's within weapons range, sir, if you want to shoot again with a medium search speed," the weapons operator said. "There's little margin, and you'd have to act fast."

"How's my present torpedo doing?"

"Its low fuel makes a hit questionable."

"Assign tube one to the *Goliath-Specter*."

"Tube one is ready."

"Shoot tube one."

The pneumatic torpedo impulse system in the ship's forward compartment pushed out the weapon. The rapid pressure change popped Volkov's ears.

"Tube one away, normal launch," the weapons operator said.

"I'm going to let the *Goliath-Specter* drift to the south while I maintain course. Let it take its roundabout path towards the Bosporus while I take the direct route."

"It may be a moot point, sir," the weapons operator said. "Our second weapon may take care of the problem."

"Perhaps, but I must think two steps ahead."

Looking to his tactical display, he tapped a stylus over the location where the *Goliath* submerged, and then he moved the stylus to his target's present position. The speed averaged twelve and a half knots. He aimed his nose at the trainer.

"Let's force the dolphins to a better position. They're giving up a knot and a half and can't maintain a tail chase."

"Where do you want them?"

"Let's see if they can intercept the *Goliath* on its way back toward the west. Send them to the southwest."

"Six o'clock?"

"Yes. Send them."

"I'm sending them to six o'clock," the trainer said. "I also need to inform you that they'll need to sleep soon."

The warning reminded Volkov that his living tactical assets suffered multiple limitations. Having become a student of their skills after his last deployment, he recalled that they rested half their brains, keeping one eye open in alert defense, prior to resting the other half. But they were useless in their semi-alert sleeping state. And though they broached and breathed freely, they needed to eat.

"I understand," he said. "Can you produce a predictable sleeping and eating schedule?"

The trainer shifted his weight and appeared energized with

pride.

"Yes. It will take some coaxing, but I've conditioned them to work on half their normal sleep for days. I've also taught them to feed in their most efficient hunting formation. Andrei encircles a school of fish while Mikhail feeds, and then they switch. They are warriors, after all."

"How does that add up in hours?"

"An hour of feeding followed by four hours of sleep."

"Five hours total. I see. What's my absolute limit from now until they need to rest and eat again?"

"Probably two hours. I can't be sure and neither can they know or tell me. They can't reckon time."

"If I command their sleep and feeding now, how long will they be able to endure until they need another break?"

"I can guarantee you twelve hours of operations, but I believe they can go longer if I push them."

"Let's continue to use them now," Volkov said. "They might be able to tell me which way the *Goliath-Specter* runs as it evades my torpedo."

He looked to his sonar operator to get an update on his weapon, but the sailor's stiffness worried him.

"What's wrong?" he asked.

"Torpedo in the water!"

The terror in the sailor's eyes told Volkov all he needed. He had been ambushed, and his adversary's aim was true.

"All ahead flank!"

The *Krasnodar* shook, and mortal terror consumed Volkov as he forced his voice calm.

"Where is it?"

"In our baffles. Close."

"Launch countermeasures!"

The click and thud of the release and jettison of gas-generating canisters silenced the room with the inescapability of the desperation.

"Do you hear any sign of the submarine that shot us?"

"No, sir."

Volkov cleared his mind. Standing, he rested his hands on the elevated conning platform's railing and bowed his head. He needed to accept and understand his failure to give himself a chance of overcoming it.

He had chased the *Goliath-Specter* tandem, but given that an unknown assailant had attacked him, he concluded that the *Goliath* and *Specter* had split. The opposing submarine had become a ghost, and he had driven his ship by it, showing the *Specter* a high bearing rate. He had gifted his adversary an easy target.

The intelligence report about his mercenary opponents and the torpedo strike on the *Muromets* suggested that the incoming weapon would cripple his ship while sparing his crew's lives. But given his shame, he found himself wishing instead for a heavyweight torpedo to send him to oblivion.

"Torpedo is range-gating!" the sonar operator said. "It ignored our countermeasures completely."

"That's because it's wire-guided, and it's a perfect shot. It will hit us. Blow the main ballast tanks and emergency surface the ship. Pump water overboard from all tanks and make us as light as possible."

As the deck angled upward, he reached for a microphone to speak to the entire crew.

"We will take a torpedo hit soon," he said. "There's a high probability that the weapon will attach small explosives to our hull and create multiple holes in the ship. Close all watertight doors and prepare to fight the flooding in each compartment. However, if the weapon is indeed a heavyweight torpedo, all who survive the blast are ordered to abandon ship immediately."

The ship bobbed and rocked on the surface, and an idea inspired Volkov. If the weapon were to attach limpets, he could minimize the number of attachments if he presented the warhead the challenging, moving geometry of a tight circle.

"Left full rudder. Continue in a circle at flank speed until I say otherwise."

The ship rolled out of the turn.

"Impact imminent!" the sonar operator said.

While Volkov lifted the microphone to his lips, the incoming seeker's transmissions became audible in his hull. A chill consumed him, and he stared at ashen faces in the compartment.

"Brace for impact."

The benign detonation teased him with its less-than-lethal pop. He feared it might be a precursor to a heavyweight yield, but then he heard the thump and clamp of limpets snatching his hull.

The first explosion echoed in the surrounding steel, sending a spike of terror up his spine. Then multiple blasts hammered his hull, and he felt the metal below him shudder.

Red emergency diodes supplanted overhead lights as the room went dark, and after a minute of silence, he believed that the final limpet had exploded.

"Rudder amidships," he said. "Maintain all ahead flank."

The reports that flew into the control room tallied the damage. The gray-bearded veteran shouted over the room's buzz.

"The battery's offline. The shaft is coasting to a stop for lack of propulsion. The engineer recommends snorkeling and says he can bypass the battery to give you propulsion directly off the diesels."

"Very well. Raise the induction mast. Prepare to snorkel."

Hydraulic servos clicked over his head.

"Flooding is reported in the battery wells," the veteran said. "There's also flooding reported in the auxiliary machinery room. No other compartments report flooding. The ship is ready to snorkel."

"Commence snorkeling."

The twin diesel engines hummed to life.

"All ahead two-thirds. Make turns for ten knots."

"What course would you like, sir?"

"Due south. Get us out of here."

The veteran acknowledged the order and turned the ship. Volkov stepped to his sonar operator.

"We're still alive, and we're still in combat. Listen for the

Specter. It's out there, and its captain may be second-guessing his decision to use a gentle weapon against a double-hulled submarine. Keep listening as if your life depended on it."

CHAPTER 12

Jake watched the wide toad-head shake.

"Our slow-kill weapon punctured the *Kilo's* outer hull," Remy said. "I'm sure it killed the battery, and I hear flooding. But it's a double-hulled ship with six watertight compartments. I can't yet guarantee that you punctured the inner hull. It's surfaced for now, but it still may be able to submerge and fight."

"With a battery soaked in seawater?" Jake asked.

"It has a fuel cell air-independent propulsion system."

"That allows it to crawl underwater. That's not a concern, since we're racing for the exit."

"I still recommend putting an Exocet into its conning tower for good measure."

"I can't risk it. It would be a tracer bullet working the wrong way for their surface fleet. We need to get out of here before they overrun us."

"The closest active sonar system is about twenty-five miles away, and that's a guess at that range. But they're getting closer, and we can't outrun them."

"Not unless we slow them down. That's what the mines are for. I'd be surprised if Pierre hasn't already announced the mine-field. The problem is, I doubt the Russians will believe him until I blow something up."

Jake glanced at the fathometer, which showed two meters below the *Specter's* keel. He then looked at the tactical display to surmise the enormity of the problem. Renard's feed showed at least a half dozen ships pursuing him.

"I need to launch a heavyweight torpedo," he said.

"You're sure about a heavyweight?"

"It's the only thing that can simulate a mine. A slow-kill would have the reverse effect and confirm that we're in the vicinity of their hunting party. But I need them to think they're in a minefield and running into a mine."

"We're off the bottom and ready to maneuver," Henri said. "I recommend heading southwest and putting twenty-five meters under our keel before you shoot. The weapon will have to climb up the slope back to shallow water."

"Agreed. I'll give it the room it needs. All ahead one third, right full rudder, steer course two-three-five."

The deck assumed a gentle sideways slope.

"I need a target, Antoine. Find me something."

"They're all taking anti-submarine zigzag legs," Remy said. "That makes target selection at this range impossible. I can't assure you a target."

"Can you hear any merchant shipping in the way?"

"Of course. I hear all kinds of vessels along our threat axis. They're driving away from the Russian fleet and from the minefield I hope that Pierre has declared, but I can't guarantee you not hitting a merchant vessel."

"Then we'll let the geometry play out before I shoot. That means it's time to start laying this minefield. Henri, you remember the procedure, right?"

"You made me rehearse it enough times that I could do it in my sleep."

"Prepare mine one."

The Frenchman tapped icons.

"Mine one is ready. Awaiting mode."

"Anti-surface only," Jake said.

"Mine one is ready in anti-surface mode."

"Arm mine one."

"Mine one is armed."

"Deploy mine one."

Henri touched a monitor, and Jake watched the icon of a mine strapped to one of the belts around the *Specter* shift from a filled-in green image to a dotted outline.

"Mine one is deployed," Henri said.

"Very well," Jake said. "I didn't hear anything."

"Pierre said it was a quiet system." Henri said. "As usual, he was right. It's just a simple set of latches that release."

"I heard it," Remy said. "The latches released, and I hear the mine floating up."

"How can you possibly hear that? Never mind. All ahead standard, Henri. Make turns for fourteen knots."

Jake felt the *Specter* shudder while accelerating.

Two miles later, he slowed, deployed his second of eighteen mines, and returned to his evasion pace.

"Antoine, can you identify a target for me yet?"

"I'm starting to see separation between distinct ships, but I can't yet promise you to hit a chosen target. Their zigzagging is still a factor."

"How close is the closest surface combatant?"

"I have blade rate on the *Kashin*-class destroyer placing it at flank speed, thirty-eight knots. It's twenty-five thousand yards away. That's the closest vessel."

"Find me a smaller target."

"Smaller?" Remy asked. "You mean a more modern target with a more dangerous sonar system?"

"No, I mean smaller, as in I don't want to kill three hundred men when I can get my message across sinking a ship with only fifty. But you have a point. Find me a *Grisha* since it has a more dangerous sonar system."

Remy touched his display, seeking a direction to listen to one of the many threats.

"I have blade rate on the closest *Grisha*. It's moving at its flank speed, thirty-four knots. Range, twenty-eight thousand yards."

"Assign tube four to the closest *Grisha*."

"Tube four is assigned."

Jake studied the geometry and realized that the *Grisha's* next anti-submarine turn would nullify his attack.

"Check your fire, Antoine. I need better data. Henri, slow to all ahead two-thirds."

"Slowing to all ahead two-thirds," Henri said.

"Bring us to periscope depth."

The deck rose.

"Shall I prepare to snorkel?" Henri asked.

"We won't be up there long enough. I'm looking for a download from Pierre. That's it."

The ship rocked in the swells.

"Raise the radio mast," Jake said. "Get me a download of whatever you can from Pierre, Terry, or whoever's broadcasting from our satellite."

"Raising the radio mast," Henri said. "Shall I listen for other frequency bands as well?"

"Download everything you can, even the Russians. We'll store it and see if it's useful later. But let me know immediately if you have anything from the satellite."

He heard hydraulic valves click above him, and then a young sailor seated beside Henri garnered the elder Frenchman's attention with his triage of broadcast headers.

"We've got something from Pierre," Henri said.

"Live or delayed?"

"Delayed. The header says it's a direct tactical data feed to the Subtics system and a video message. It's coming slowly due to the jamming, but the frequency hopping is getting it across in broken pieces we can patch together."

As icons on the chart shifted the Russian hunting party to its truer positions, Jake noticed that the movement was slight for the closer ships. Antoine had nailed their locations independent of Renard's update from Ukrainian radar support. But the sonar guru's ability fell short in creating the tracking history beyond his hearing, and that information caught Jake's attention.

"The *Grisha's* zigzags are centered around a base course of two-eight-three," he said. "It's going to have to turn back towards us to maintain that course. Is tube four still ready?"

"Tube four is ready," Remy said.

"Shoot tube four."

Jake's ears popped with the pneumatic whine.

"Tube four, normal launch," Henri said.

"Do you have the broadcast?"

"I have all that's available from friendly sources."

"Lower the radio mast. Make your depth one hundred meters. All ahead standard, make turns for fourteen knots."

His weapon sent, Jake gave the chart a second review and noticed fewer ships chasing him than his imagination had entertained. More ships warmed up their engines tied to their piers than sought him at sea.

"We may get out of this alive," he said. "The plan is working. Pierre's plans always work."

"Excuse me, Jake?" Henri asked. "Was that an order?"

"No, I was talking to myself. But set flags in the system. I want to continue laying a mine every two miles."

"I'm setting flags to remind us to lay a mine at two-mile intervals."

Henri tapped his screen, and Jake looked at the silent priest seated to the side of the compartment. Andrew seemed calm as Jake waved him to the elevated conning platform.

"Any comments?" he asked. "Don't be shy."

"I sense that your decision to use a heavyweight torpedo bothers you, but I can see that you have to do it."

"Straight to the point. Yeah, it feels like a slaughter."

"Remember that your mission is the right thing, even though it must take a toll on human life. Many righteous causes bring unfortunate deaths. You can't blame yourself."

"I'm too busy surviving to worry about it."

"Then perhaps we should talk about it once we're safe."

"Speaking of safe, I need to figure out something. I feel too safe, like I have too much time and I'm missing something. The most dangerous threat out there, isn't really out there."

"Helicopters?" Andrew asked.

"You've been learning."

The priest nodded.

"I learn a lot from just watching, and your sailors are patient enough to explain their jobs when they have time. The team's a model of efficiency, even though they make it look easy."

"The core group has been together for a decade. Pierre, Henri, Antoine, Claude, and me."

"Claude never leaves the engineering spaces, does he?"

"Pretty much only for bodily necessities, and I doubt even for that sometimes."

"But you've got a team of thirty. You've grown since the beginning and have held a good team together."

"It's been constant growth until recently. We started small and by accident. It was just me and Pierre when I stole my Trident Missile submarine twelve years ago."

The words sounded matter of fact, the trauma and the rage of those days feeling distant.

"After that theft, which was technically our first mission, I was financially well off, which led to a boring life of luxury. Fortunately, the Taiwanese government forced Pierre and me back into business. They lent us a submarine much like this one and made us beat back the Chinese for them. That's when we met Olivia."

"The lady who's about to become the head of the CIA?"

Jake surveyed the control room for signs of a crisis, but he deduced that he had the freedom to talk. He considered the walk through history with the priest an acceptable way to fill time.

"But back then, she was just a field officer. Her job was to use me to get to Pierre and uncover his entire operations. That's not quite how it worked out, and she ended up joining us on the Taiwan trip. She also figured out that a Pakistani submarine had gone rogue so that we could stop it from nuking an aircraft carrier in Hawaii."

"That story alone is enough adventure for one lifetime."

"True, but the thrill became addicting, and we all wanted it. Some of the younger guys took the money and ran, but the core group stuck with it and grew. We moved to a *Scorpène*-class submarine on our next mission. My friend bought it."

The priest's eyes popped open.

"He bought it? The submarine?"

"It was more of a lease, sort of. I paid him ten million to help with stealing the Trident, and he turned that into an empire in South America. So he had the money."

"Amazing."

"We ended up losing that ship to save an American destroyer, but we stopped terrorists from crippling the United States with electromagnetic pulses from high-altitude nuclear air bursts. You remember the burst we couldn't stop. It took down the east coast."

"Everyone remembers that. I can't believe that was you."

"Well, it was technically the United States Navy. We just helped protect the destroyer that did most of the work."

"Still, that's of epic importance."

"After that mission, we started to retain crew members. About half the guys you see now joined us in pushing the Chinese back from their blockade on Taiwan. You might remember the low-intensity nuclear exchanges at sea. That was all Pierre's planning and arming."

"He seems to be behind anything interesting that happens in the ocean."

"We then helped with the latest power shift in the Falkland Islands, though I'm not sure the outcome matched anything we intended. But it did get Olivia close to the Argentine president."

"She gets a lot of good press out of that."

"She has us to thank, at least for the introduction. But the last piece of this team you see now wasn't formed until we helped the Philippines establish a defensive structure on one of their Spratly Island land masses. We helped slow the Chinese there."

"I don't remember reading about that."

Jake shook his head.

"No, there wasn't a lot of press. You probably read about our next mission, though, and didn't know it. We had the *Goliath* for the first time on that one. Pierre had it built to transport his submarines at high speed, but it had the extra benefit of being able to rescue a trapped South Korean submarine."

"I remember reading about some huge North Korean naval exercise that had people worried a few months ago."

"That's the one. That's where we picked up that young ace. I expect him to be as good as Antoine someday, if not better."

He aimed his head at Julien, who sat beside Remy.

"This is all news to me. You'd only spoken about your life in generalities, but this paints a picture. You don't have to tell me, but I'm curious if you ever shared any of this with Bishop Francis."

"A lot of it, yes. Most of it, actually, until he got too busy trying to prevent Christians from being slaughtered. I can't say that I blame him for putting his attentions where a bishop should."

Like a ghost, Henri appeared beside Jake, a step below him and separated from him by the elevated conning platform's railing. The Frenchman glared.

"You need to watch Pierre's message."

Jake moved to his display, invoked Renard's face on the video, and raised the volume.

"It's unfortunate that I cannot speak to you directly, but the jamming interference is strong," Renard said. "I hope you get this download. If not, the relevant information is in the tactical data feed, but I wanted to explain things myself."

As Jake glanced at the tactical chart beside the screen displaying his mentor's face, he noticed the grave danger he had missed. The icons of a massive sonobuoy field awaiting him were no longer a sonobuoy field.

His heart sank in rhythm with the Frenchman's annunciation of the news.

"As you've probably noticed, there's been a wrinkle in our plans. I underestimated the audacity of the Russians. The aircraft that we thought would lay sonobuoys are instead laying a minefield. The Kremlin has announced it and has justified it in retaliation for the act of terror against their sovereign state."

"Shit," Jake said.

"This is indeed a serious matter," Renard said. "But it is not insurmountable. In fact, it has unintended benefits. For example, you'll notice that your hunters have relaxed or soon will relax their chase for you. They see no need to barrel through the minefield I declared when you're trapped behind one of theirs."

Jake hit the pause icon.

"Antoine, are any of the ships zigging away from us?

"I was just going to mention that a few of them were breaking away to the southeast, but I was staying focused on our targeted

Grisha. Wait, it's turning towards the west now."

Jake saw Remy whispering with his apprentice.

"Julien says the ships behind the *Grisha* are turning west as well," Remy said. "It appears that they respect our minefield's declared borders as Pierre announced them."

On the display, Jake saw the arrows representing the Russian ships' directions turn from the rhombus that outlined the claimed boundary of doom. He touched the play icon.

"The minefield also explains why Russian air assets have been timid after Terry shot down the first wave of helicopters," Renard said. "I feared that with only one cannon, Terry would struggle to defend the sky, but the Russian minefield appears to have reduced the need for heroism from Russian pilots."

"So what the hell do I do?" Jake asked. "We're trapped."

As if hearing the question, Renard's image answered.

"Your escape now hinges on continued hiding as negotiations take place. I am seeking safe harbor for you with several nations in the Black Sea, but unfortunately, that may take days to achieve."

"You'd think someone would make a stink about having the Bosporus shut," Jake said.

Again, Renard's image answered as if listening.

"In parallel, Turkey is leading a protest to have the minefield removed. It's a strain on their commerce and on that of all nations of the Black Sea. The Russians can't hold that minefield forever. They're gambling that they can hold it long enough to find you and Terry. I'm betting that you and Terry can outwit them."

Jake tapped the pause icon.

"What does this mean to us?"

"I don't know," Henri said. "I haven't watched the video this far yet. He's almost done, though."

Jake noticed the timing bar resting near the end of the track as he tapped the play icon.

"I've communicated with Terry and have tasked him with neutralizing the remaining submarines," Renard said. "He's on the surface and outrunning all torpedoes that were shot at him."

"Terry's on the surface," Jake said. "Not for long, I hope."

"Until I can negotiate a safer harbor for you, your best option is still to hide in Turkish national waters. But instead of our planned coordinates, you and Terry will instead head for waters ten miles west of the minefield. I also recommend radio silence until you're in cluttered waters and can blend in with local radio traffic. Listen for me when you can, and good luck my friend."

"This changes things significantly," Henri said.

Jake verified on the display that the surface ships avoided the rhombus that his minefield carved in the center of the Black Sea.

"Yeah, it does. First, we stop laying mines. There's no need to create a minefield for deterrence when our hunters have already honored it."

"I agree."

"Second, I stop killing what I don't need to kill."

"The *Grisha*?" Henri asked.

"Yes."

"If you shut down the weapon, you'll be allowing one more ship to hunt us. They won't show us the same mercy if they find us."

"Isn't this odd? Me wanting to show mercy, and you trying to talk me out of it."

"I'm not trying to talk you out of it."

He looked at the Frenchman. Knowing the difference between Henri's passionate pleas and his neutral advice, he agreed.

"No, you're not. You're just making me think it through. Let's first see if it's possible. Antoine?"

"Yes, Jake, I still have wire control of the torpedo. What do you want me to do?"

Jake forced himself to avoid looking to the priest for guidance and tried to listen to his moral voice. The answer seemed murky or nonexistent, but he forced himself to decide.

"Shut it down," he said. "Spare the *Grisha*."

CHAPTER 13

Cahill watched a gust force Walker's eyes shut, making his colleague appear like a bug under his hearing protection muffs. The tiny camera on his executive officer's bridge-to-bridge radio caught sharp shadows shaped by halogen lights. Wave crests foamed behind the ship's stern as the transport ship churned water at flank speed.

"Say that again, Liam."

"The last bolt is removed. No more stanchions and no more temporary weapons. I'm sending the work team below."

"Very well. How's the port weapons bay?"

The starboard cannon fired.

"Dear God, Terry," Walker said. "You don't realize how loud that is from the inside."

"Try to stay focused."

"The port induction mast is beyond repair."

"Very well. We'll continue without it and rely on the starboard mast in a cross-connected feed."

"We've deployed and stowed the port cannon in manual mode as a test. It works. We've got fifty-two rounds staged in the bay for manual loading. It looks like we can salvage about forty more from the damaged magazine. Any other rounds for the port cannon will have to come from the backup stores."

"Stay up there and load the rest from the magazine."

The cannon erupted again.

"How are you doing against the *Kilos*?" Walker asked.

"The first rounds should land soon. I'll let you know."

Cahill looked at the display that showed the trajectories of his railgun's rounds. The speed leaders on the projectiles showed them slowing to six times the speed of sound from their faster muzzle velocities, yielding a travel time of fifty seconds to reach targets fifty miles away.

Green halos around the rounds indicated that Global Positioning Satellites guided them toward their targets–three surfaced *Kilo* submarines scrambling from their base at Novorossiysk to reach safe submergence depths.

To the north, Ukrainian helicopters provided radar support, painting his targets. He felt helpless in his reliance on airborne and orbiting sensors to empower his attack, but the tactic was working.

Then the icons representing the *Kilo's* flashed and became hollow outlines.

"We've lost the *Kilos*," his weapons controller said.

"Jamming?"

"I think so."

"It won't matter. The first round arrives in ten seconds. The *Kilos* are moving too slow for it to matter. We may not hit them in their diesels, but we've got enough metal raining down on them to make them think twice before submerging."

The halos then disappeared.

"We've lost GPS guidance," the weapons controller said.

"Very well," Cahill said. "Ballistic flight will be good enough. Keep raining metal on them."

The starboard cannon's rhythmic eruptions continued as the *Goliath* spat rounds towards the *Kilos*.

"Send satellite imagery to the main screen for battle damage assessment," Cahill said.

His target, the lead *Kilo*, issued billows of soft turquoise from its diesel engines. A ray of light blue extended towards it, spread its claws of buckshot, and drew streaks whizzing by the surfaced hull.

"Is that a miss?"

"I'm not sure. It looks like our shot skipped off the hull. The angle of attack is shallow."

"We may need to shift to explosive rounds, or at least non-splintering rounds."

"Give it a chance," Cahill said.

The next flash of blue missed wide, but the third punctured his enemy, and small plumes of azure wounds grew in the submarine's engine room.

"It's a hit!" he said.

The next two rounds missed, but the sixth hit.

"Those are hits on target," Cahill said. "That's enough for that submarine. I hope Pierre realizes it and shifts the guidance of rounds to the next *Kilo*."

"Incoming data shows an update to our rounds' guidance. He's shifting guidance now."

"Great work on Pierre's part."

The next twelve rounds punctured hobbling holes in the trailing *Kilos*.

"Let Pierre figure out what to do with the rounds that are in flight," Cahill said. "He can keep hitting the damaged *Kilos* or show mercy. It's his call. Shift your fire to the last *Kilo* that's trapped behind the bridge. It won't be trapped forever. Send forty-five non-splintering rounds."

"Non-splintering?"

"We need deep penetration into the water."

"Shifting fire to the last *Kilo*, forty-five non-splintering rounds."

Distant from the jamming electronics of surface warships and shore installations, the final undamaged Russian submarine in the Black Sea Fleet appeared helpless except for its ability to hide below the waves. But the shallowness of the Sea of Azov made Cahill optimistic.

Walker's voice distracted him.

"We're ready up here."

"Go ahead, Liam. Report."

"Ninety-four rounds are ready for use in manual mode on the port cannon. We'll need two men in the compartment, and they'll be isolated while we're submerged, but we've repaired the electronics and communications to the port weapons bay. The hydraulics were beyond repair."

"Very well, Liam. Good work. Get back inside. We've damaged the first three *Kilos*. I'm attacking the one in the Sea of Azov now."

"We're coming in."

Cahill watched the projectiles trace an arc for more than a

minute to the edge of his cannon's range.

"I'm in the port engine room now," Walker said. "The ship is rigged for dive."

"Very well. We'll stay surfaced and sprinting until we take out that final *Kilo*."

Rounds started splashing in the Sea of Azov, kicking up splashes of deep blue.

"Bring the port cannon online."

"Port weapons bay acknowledges," the weapons controller said. "They're raising the cannon manually."

"That should take thirty seconds to crank it."

The starboard cannon continued its periodic cracks.

"They're done, sir. It took them only twenty-six seconds."

"Send fifteen non-splintering rounds from the port cannon to the final *Kilo*."

The rounds from the port cannon joined the forty-five from the starboard in targeting the final *Kilo*. As the first ten rounds missed, Cahill watched their bright blue trajectories slice the air and splatter water around the submarine's last known position.

Then the rounds started spiraling out, tracing a search pattern for the elusive target.

"Cease fire," Cahill said.

As he watched the final rounds on the display follow their arc to the Sea of Azov, Walker joined him.

"Look on the bright side," He said. "Jake crippled the first *Kilo*, and you took out three more. The one on the other side of the bridge is the least threatening."

"They'll let it pass through the cleanup effort soon enough."

Walker's face lit up, and he pointed at the display. Cahill looked, and the final *Kilo* appeared on the surface, a white hot puncture wound atop its torpedo room.

"Maybe I spoke too soon," Walker said.

"Let's see what Pierre can do with the remaining rounds."

Five rounds sliced through the engine room, and Cahill sighed and fell back into a chair.

"Let's shift gears and start taking out engine rooms on the surface combatants."

"Why?" Walker asked. "All the Russian ships are honoring the minefield. Shouldn't we meet Jake and get out of here?"

"I need to catch you up on something while you were outside. The sonobuoy field is really a minefield."

"Bloody hell. We're trapped."

"Pierre's working on it. The Russians can't keep it there forever. He thinks they set the mines to deactivate at a preset time, probably three days. But it's all a guessing game at this point."

"So what do we do?"

Cahill stood and rapped his sonar supervisor's shoulder.

"Are we clear of the final torpedo yet?"

"I can't hear it anymore, but it's hard to be sure without a towed array. If you slow, I'll confirm on the hull array."

"Liam, man the ship's controls and slow us to five knots."

"Slowing us to five knots," Walker said.

"What can you hear?" Cahill asked.

The sonar supervisor reached over the shoulder of one of his operators and grabbed a headset. He placed it over his ears.

"Nothing," he said.

The operators confirmed the lack of evidence of a torpedo.

"With the active *Kilo* limited to eleven to twelve knots snorkeling, four to five knots submerged, we're well out of its weapons range," Cahill said. "I'm going to stay away from it, but I'll keep us in cannon range of the ships on the east side of Jake's minefield."

"Let's do it," Walker said.

"All ahead standard, make turns for fifteen knots. Right full rudder, steady on course two-five-five."

"The ship is at all ahead standard, making turns for fifteen knots," Walker said. "My rudder is right full, coming to course two-five-five."

"Aim the starboard cannon at the *Kashin*-class destroyer. Target the engine room with twenty splintering rounds."

"Aiming the starboard cannon at the *Kashin's* engine room,"

Walker said. "May I ask why the *Kashin*?"

"It has fewer Vympel systems to knock down our incoming rounds. In fact, if I believe the intelligence, it has zero Vympels."

"I like when you think like a surface warrior. The starboard cannon is ready."

"Fire twenty splintering rounds."

The railgun's clap reverberated throughout the room.

"Have you ever seen a close-in weapon system take down a railgun round? I know of nothing that's been designed for targets so small and so fast."

"You weren't with us yet when we last used railguns against modern targets. A Chinese task force in the Spratlys had good luck jamming the terminal guidance and avoiding the rounds. They used their close-in weapon systems towards the end of the battle, but things were so hectic that our boys didn't have a chance to gather any data. So the Vympels will be the first measurable test."

"Unless the ship doesn't have one, like the *Kashin*."

"It's old, but it packs a wallop. I'd like to remove it from the equation if this becomes an old fashioned gunfight."

"I hope Pierre is watching and attentive on the targeting."

"Let's see if we can get through," Cahill said. "Send him a note that I want to target the *Kashin's* engine room."

"The radio operator is attempting to transmit," Walker said. "No confirmation of receipt from the satellite yet. The Russians are still jamming us."

Cahill watched his first rounds shift direction a degree.

"That correction proves that he knows to hit the engine room of whatever we shoot at. Cease transmitting."

"The *Kashin* is taking evasive maneuvers," Walker said. "It's coming hard left."

The icon of the Russian destroyer blinked and then shifted from opaque to a hollow dotted outline.

"We've lost the *Kashin* on radar," Walker said. "The Russians are concentrating their jamming to protect it."

"Look on the satellite infrared."

Cahill watched Walker toggle his screen's pages and then back out to a larger field of view. White plumes billowed from the warship's four gas turbines."

"There it is," Walker said. "And here come our rounds."

"Pierre can use the infrared to guide our rounds."

"Here it comes," Walker said.

Cahill watched the first ballistic strip of bright blue splinter into smaller streaks. The hailstorm of buckshot sliced through the destroyer's hull but missed the sensitive propulsion equipment.

"Damn," Walker said. "A wasted round."

The next round missed wide as the warship shifted its rudder hard right and whipped its stern clear.

"Give Pierre a few rounds to adjust."

The next four rounds missed wide, and the following four rounds cut benign holes in the side of the destroyer's engine room.

"Do you want to send more rounds into the *Kashin*? You didn't even use the port cannon."

"I'm reserving rounds in the port cannon for defense, should we need to use our maximum rate of fire. And let's first see what Pierre can do with this salvo."

Blue buckshot landed between a pair of gas turbines, but the engines continued to burn in bright white.

"Close, but no effect," Walker said.

"Give it time. He's adjusting his satellite targeting."

The next round sent two shards of buckshot through a gas turbine. Whiteness receded to a pale blue as the machine rolled to a stop and its hot metal began to cool.

"There's your hit, Liam!"

"One engine down, three to go."

The next two rounds pounded the engine room but missed the vital machines.

"Damn it," Walker said.

A round of buckshot hit dead center on the damaged turbine's twin attached to the same shaft.

"That's better," Cahill said. "No chance of even dreaming about repairing that one."

The final rounds walked across the ship towards the other engines but missed.

"We need to get more rounds ready," Walker said. "It still has a fully functional shaft."

"Hold on, mate. Look closer."

"Good lord. I don't believe it."

"There's no way Pierre can say he did that on purpose, and if he does, I'll refuse to believe him. But I'll take being lucky."

Though undamaged, the final two turbines spun towards a stop. The gearbox that connected them glowed with a half dozen puncture wounds and the heat of grinding, mangled metal.

"Let's move on to the next target," Cahill said. "The *Kashin* is out of our way."

CHAPTER 14

Volkov shouted at his executive officer, who stared back with the smugness of knowing his political connections protected him from the repercussions of insubordination.

"I won't say it a third time. Get your ass back there before I confine you to your stateroom for cowardice!"

Volkov knew that he could motivate the lowest creature on his ship through shame.

"Am I clear?" he asked.

The man's face shifted, as if a spark had ignited the recognition of his need for self-respect.

"Yes, sir. I'll take care of it."

The executive officer headed aft to the watertight door. After the metal plate returned to its latches, Volkov let half a minute elapse and then gestured to his third-in-command, his operations officer.

"Get back there and help him out."

"Help out the executive officer, sir? Or did you mean the engineer, since he's leading the team in the auxiliary machinery compartment."

"I mean relieve the engineer as the executive officer's assistant. I want the engineer to get back to working on propulsion."

The operations officer turned, but Volkov called him back, leaned into him, and spoke into his ear.

"What I really mean is, relieve the engineer and keep an eye on the executive officer. Stall him and contact me if you see him screwing anything up."

As the officer departed, Volkov slid behind the backs of his seated control room team and reached his gray-bearded sailor. The veteran looked at him with tight crow's feet.

"Do you want the good news first, sir, or the bad news?"

"Bad. Always the bad news first."

"The battery is useless. Too many cells are damaged to use the remaining cells. They add up in series, and there's not enough voltage in the remaining cells, even if we could manage to connect the good cells together around the bad ones."

"I anticipated that. It's bad, but it's not really news."

"The good news is that your battery cells aren't going to blow up. The battery is disconnected from the electrical bus, and the damaged cells are completely immersed in water. So there's no hydrogen gas accumulating. The engineer has checked it."

"I guess that's good news."

"Given the situation, it's the best news you'll get."

The ship dipped in the swells, and Volkov grabbed a railing on the veteran's console for support. Above, he heard the head valve clank shut, silencing his diesels until the induction mast returned above the water to let the engines breathe.

"I see that our diesels are handling the load at five knots," he said. "That's easy. But do you have a calculation yet of our maximum attainable speed?"

"I have the numbers, but the engineer still needs to route the fuel cell and diesel outputs together with the battery disconnected."

"Tell me what you have."

"The engineer says he can give you twelve knots with the diesels and the fuel cell system while bypassing the battery. It's up to you if you want to put that much flow stress on the induction mast."

"Twelve knots will be acceptable. If the mast bends, I'll find a way to survive until we can return to port."

"Of course, we'll be slower on the surface, if you need to surface to reduce seawater pressure for the damage control teams."

"You've seen the same status reports I have about what the *Goliath* is doing on the surface. I won't become its next target."

"I understand, sir. But are you concerned about keeping our induction mast exposed? The attacks on our surfaced ships suggest that our enemy is getting high-altitude imaging support."

"I've asked fleet headquarters for an infrared view of our location, and it's very difficult to distinguish us from the ambient seas. Our intake isn't hot enough to make us easy to detect, and we'd be traceable by satellite or aircraft only once found."

A sound-powered phone chirped by the veteran's hand.

"May I, sir?"

"Of course."

The veteran lifted the receiver.

"Control room," he said.

Volkov watched the man's face relax.

"That's great news. I'll tell the captain."

"What news?"

"The executive officer reports that watertight integrity is restored to the berthing compartment down to fifty meters by having sealed the battery compartment."

"Good."

"Shoring is in place in auxiliary machinery, not watertight, but the drain pump can keep pace with the flooding down to fifty meters. He also reports that holes in auxiliary machinery can be sealed with welding, if you're willing to risk the noise. Estimated time to repair the auxiliary machinery room is eight hours."

"That's a fine report from him. It sounds like the operations officer and engineer coached him through some damage control."

"I know you don't like him, sir."

"He's useless because he doesn't care. He doesn't need to care, since his connections are strong."

"May I speak frankly?"

Volkov furrowed his brow.

"You? Always."

"I think you've rattled him enough already. He's going to command a submarine someday, whether he deserves it or not. Perhaps you can consider being more of a mentor for the rest of this mission. You've got his attention and have earned his respect."

Volkov grunted.

"What do I care about earning his respect?"

"You already said it, sir. Because his connections are strong."

"I'll consider it."

"What about our orders, sir? The crew is concerned about

what's next for us."

"Nothing yet. The fleet is awaiting my updated damage report before assigning me a new task."

"We've been through a big scare, sir. There were a lot of crosses in hands and praying before that torpedo hit us, and I also know embarrassing details about some men's reactions that are best kept to myself."

"The rumors will spread. They always do. Tears, sobbing, and soiling of undergarments, I'm sure. But how's the crew now?"

"They have resolve, sir. They saw your courage and coolness under fire, and they would follow you anywhere."

"I suppose that now's the time to have a look at the damage myself. Once I've confirmed the reports, I'll inform the fleet that we're ready for battle. In fact, have that message queued up to broadcast, and include the battery damage so they know our limits."

He walked across the control room and passed through the watertight door. The scullery and dining areas appeared unperturbed, except for the humidity created by evaporated and trapped seawater vapor. He walked down a stairway to the sleeping quarters, where he found a junior officer and two enlisted sailors.

"I had expected more people," he said.

"The battery well is sealed, sir," the officer said. "It's designed to be airtight against hydrogen gas. So it's watertight, too, but only to a limited depth. The executive officer stationed us here to react in case we lose watertight containment."

"What would you do if we lost watertight containment?"

The young officer's confident and quick reaction suggested that he had foreseen the question, or perhaps that the executive officer had come to life and coached him.

"First, I'd grab this phone and announce the flooding so that the ship could come shallow. Then, I'd await orders to proceed, but I'd be ready with these tools to cut open the air pipes and reseal them with the wooden shoring plugs you see next to the tool. It's the valves on those air pipes that are most likely to fail under pressure if we go deep, and that's how I'd take care of them. We'd have a leak around the plugs, but we wouldn't have flooding."

"Impressive. How long are you going to be standing watch here? Do you have a relief planned?"

"All three of us will stay here until whatever end, sir, unless you need us somewhere else. The toilets are right there, and people will bring us food and water as needed. You can count on us."

Volkov excused himself and returned up the stairs. At the top, he turned sternward and continued to the auxiliary machinery compartment.

He passed electronic cabinets and then descended rungs to the lower level. There, he saw men hunched over the floor, holding lanterns and passing tools to sailors hidden under the deck plates. The executive officer stooped among them and stood when he noticed Volkov.

"Sir, we have two holes in the compartment. The larger one is here, below the refrigeration unit. It took some ingenuity, but the engineer had a team remove the covers off some lockers, spot weld them together, and bend them to conform to the hull's shape. It's far from perfect, but it's slowing the flooding."

Volkov grabbed a small flashlight from his hip and then crawled on his belly to the edge of the deck plating. Wiggling his head and arm between the weight-bearing plates and the hull's insulating lagging, he gained an inverted view of the crawlspace under the refrigeration unit.

The salty humidity and musty scent convinced him that his ship would begin rusting.

Two men lying on their shoulders with drenched jumpsuits lifted their heads. He recognized a senior engineering sailor who tapped a hammer against the final block to press a wooden peg between the underside of the deck and the repurposed locker doors. Water sprayed from the edges of the flat, trapped metal.

"How bad is it?" Volkov asked.

"Captain? Is that you, sir?"

"It's me."

"It's not as bad as it looks. These pegs will hold until we can get some proper welding done. The water flows forward from here, and the smaller hole in the back corner of the compartment has a lesser flow rate. Both streams will flow forward if you keep the ship level, and the operations officer is stationing a bilge pump to route the streams to the trim and drain system. Our pumps will keep up."

"Great job."

"Thank you, sir. We're still a fighting ship."

Volkov retracted his head from the crawlspace and pushed himself to his knees. He then felt lightheaded as he stood, and he grabbed the executive officer's shoulder for balance and to get the man's attention.

"Yes, sir?"

"Good work," Volkov said. "Keep it up."

"Thank you, sir."

Something had transformed his second-in-command from a wart to a leader. He wondered if he should credit the fear of combat, the desire for self-preservation, or perhaps his own tough leadership. Delaying judgment for future consideration, he climbed the ladder and continued his sternward trek to the engineering space.

He passed the storage tanks carrying oxygen and hydrogen, the energy sources for the giant machine of fuel cells that combined the elements to create water and the electricity.

After shutting another watertight door behind him, he passed between the ship's twin diesels. They hummed and chattered atop rubberized mounts that trapped their acoustic emanations.

A few steps deeper into the compartment placed him at the propulsion control panel. The last man he expected to see stood in a small crowd of men with damp jumpsuits.

"Captain," the trainer said.

"I'm impressed," Volkov said. "It appears that you've been

supporting the damage control teams."

"Indeed he has, sir," the engineer said.

Volkov turned to see a short man looking back at him through thick glasses. The engineer had opened the sleeves of his jumpsuit and had tied them around his rotund belly. Seawater had darkened his clothes and had set white saltwater stains into them.

"He was one of the first to show up in auxiliary machinery, ready for action. I agree, sir. I, too, was impressed."

"If all dolphin trainers were to show such zeal, I assure you that the program would begin to flourish. You've more than carried your own weight. I commend you."

"Thank you, sir. Just one thing, though."

"Yes. What is it?"

"The dolphins will be awake in two hours. I'd like you to keep them within communications range, if you can. I know you may have orders that say otherwise, but I'm asking you to see what you can do to keep them with us. Otherwise, they'll wake up and head for home, and I'd rather use them, sir."

Volkov squinted and heightened his alertness to the trainer's demeanor. He sensed that the engineering staff around him shared his newfound respect for the man and his mammals.

"Use them for what?"

"I assume we have more hunting to do. Aren't the ships that attacked us still out there and waiting for us to deliver justice?"

"They may be," Volkov said. "If the fleet doesn't take care of them before we can, we may still have the opportunity open to us."

"How fast can we move, sir?"

"You mean, how fast can I verify our orders?"

"No, I mean the ship, sir."

"Four knots submerged on the fuel cell. Twelve knots at snorkel depth with the diesels and full cell combined."

The trainer's brow furrowed.

"They'll need time to get ahead of us."

"It's possible. Time is on our side, now that the Bosporus is mined. I consider your dolphins a valued asset, and I will plan our tactics accordingly. Let them finish resting and then have them swim ahead while I let my crew rest. We'll then seek justice as a team."

"Thank you, sir."

Volkov accompanied the engineer on a tour of the engineering spaces, verifying that the inner hull remained intact and that the equipment remained operational. However, he ignored the engineer's routine reports and played with a thought that teased him.

His crew had made it clear that they were ready to fight. Dismissing the engineer, he grabbed a sound-powered phone, whipped it, and awaited his veteran's voice.

"Control room."

"This is the captain."

"What can I do for you, sir?"

"I have an update for the message in the radio queue. Tell fleet headquarters that we're in a complete battle-readiness condition except for our speed and depth limitations."

"I will, sir. Anything else?"

"Yes," Volkov said. "Instead of asking the fleet for orders, tell them that I want twenty-four hours to handle this myself."

"Would you like to tell them our future positioning?"

"Yes. Tell the fleet that I'm thoroughly impressed with the abilities of the dolphins, and that I'm going wait eight hours right here to let them move ahead while I rest my crew. Then I'm going after my target during the following sixteen hours."

"Of course, sir, but which target?"

Volkov wavered inwardly about the answer. The first ship had attacked the assets he defended, but the other had attacked him, cracking his self-worth harder than the first.

"Tell them," he said, "that I'm going to sink the *Specter*."

CHAPTER 15

Cahill watched another round splinter and pelt the propulsion train of a *Grisha*-class corvette.

"That's it for that *Grisha*," he said.

"That's our last easy target," Walker said.

Cahill looked at the display that showed the positions of his stranded victims. He had crippled a *Kashin*-class destroyer and two *Grisha*-class corvettes, but he knew that every remaining ship within his range possessed a close-in weapon system.

"Let's test a Vympel system. Target the *Nanuchka* missile boat with twenty splintering rounds from the starboard cannon."

"The *Nanuchka* is targeted with twenty splintering rounds from the starboard cannon."

"Get a message out to Pierre that we're targeting the *Nanuchka*, just in case he can hear us."

As the radio operator seated next to Walker nodded his understanding, Cahill viewed his targets' positions. They appeared to be converging upon each other, optimizing their defense.

"Hold your fire," he said. "Check out the update on their positions. We missed it while we were attacking that *Grisha*."

"They're forming a tight formation," Walker said. "They can't be fifty meters from each other. They're converging around that huge *Slava* and its six Vympels. The *Buyan* missile boats are also moving to intersect our incoming rounds with two Vympels each."

"The *Nanuchka* is still out of reach of the pack. It went too far ahead of the rest and now has to scramble back, but it's not going to make it. Are you ready to fire?"

"Yes. The starboard cannon is ready."

"Did you send the message to Pierre?"

"Yes."

"Fire twenty splintering rounds."

The railgun announced its first shot. As the noise repeated every five seconds, Cahill watched the icons of his rounds streak towards the *Nanuchka.*

"Thirty-three knots," he said. "Running for all it's worth, but I'm going to make its speed fall to zero."

"The first round is arriving," Walker said.

Bright blue bulleted streaks raced from the *Nanuchka,* and the trace of the incoming railgun round broke into misty pieces on the infrared imagery.

"Damn," Cahill said. "Count one for the Vympel."

"There's your first documented test of a close-in weapon system against our railgun."

Blue streaks revealed that the missile boat defended itself against the next round.

"And that *Nanuchka* has no jamming protection since it's so far from the pack," Cahill said. "That says a lot about the Vympel."

"At least now we're learning about their defenses."

"This is being recorded, right?"

"Sure. Why?"

The Vympel took down the third round.

"Simple math. We know how many rounds we have left for our railguns, and we know how many rounds the Russian Vympel systems hold. The first one to run out of bullets loses."

As the *Nanuchka's* automated point-defense system destroyed the railgun's fourth incoming round, he had one of his sailors review the ongoing attack in slow motion to count the defensive rounds.

As the minute-long, twenty-projectile attack ended, Cahill saw the defiant, unscathed missile boat continue to flee.

"It's still making thirty-three knots," he said.

A sailor handed him a sheet with a scribbled tally of the Vympel's efficacy.

"I've got the analysis. It uses forty rounds per defensive shot. With two thousand rounds of storage per Vympel, that means we can bleed it dry with fifty total cannon rounds."

"Thirty to go until it's exhausted, then."

"We've got three-hundred and sixty rounds left in the starboard cannon, and seventy-nine in the port cannon. Including the one on the *Nanuchka,* that leaves us enough ammunition to bleed nine Vympels dry."

"That *Slava* cruiser has six," Walker said. "Then four more with the *Buyan* missile boats. Then another six when you add the rest of the ships. They can defend themselves with just half their arsenal."

"Half is all they'd get while they're running north. They'd only be able to bring half the Vympels to bear. But I see your point, especially since we need to keep rounds in reserve to avoid becoming fodder to aircraft."

"We've got the five hundred rounds of reloads in each engine room. We could replenish the starboard cannon as fast as we bleed it. The port cannon can be reloaded, too, with a larger work team and some athleticism, but it would be trickier and slower."

The math and the assumptions behind the possible scenarios danced in Cahill's head as Walker continued his assessment.

"But they can reload, too. If we give them breathing room, they'll reload their expended Vympels to keep pace, and I imagine that with all their ships, we'd run out before they would. Our long-range weapon advantage is questionable at best from here on out."

A new idea took root in Cahill's mind.

"Let's add a wrinkle," he said. "Let's test the Vympel against two simultaneous targets. Target the *Nanuchka* with ten splintering rounds from each cannon, synchronize fire manually."

Walker appeared to suppress a smile as he tapped his screen.

"That's what I was just thinking. Both cannons are ready with ten splintering rounds each. The gunners are on the phone with each other and will manually synchronize firing. Our rate of fire will be slowed in half with the manual count."

"Very well. I'm okay with that. From each cannon, fire ten synchronized splintering rounds."

The railguns sounded within milliseconds of each other, and they continued firing every ten seconds until the room fell silent during the rounds' ballistic flights.

"Here it comes," Walker said.

Ripping bursts of azure intersected with the twin traces of incoming streaks.

"The Vympel took down the first pair," Walker said. "It apparently can shift its arc of fire to the second round in time."

"Let's see if our luck improves," Cahill said.

The missile boat knocked down the second pair, but the third duet of projectiles drew a different outcome.

Cahill gasped as he watched bullets shatter one railgun round, but then the point-defense system erupted with insanity, sending a full one-second stream into the sky, followed by another long burst, and yet another.

"It didn't reach the second round before it splintered!" he said. "It attacked the buckshot. Perfect!"

"It's a hit!" Walker said.

"Another misfire like that from the Vympel, and that ship will be helpless. How'd our round do?"

"No effect on propulsion. Still thirty-three knots."

Cahill watched the Vympel take down two more pairs before the sixth and seventh duets confounded its guidance system, bled it dry of bullets, and landed half their ordnance. Then the eighth through tenth pairs punctured steel.

"There we go," Walker said. "We've hit the propulsion train. I see heat in reduction gears and at least one diesel spinning down."

"Make that two. The middle diesel appears to be cooling."

Cahill glared at the satellite infrared, hoping to see the third and final engine go dark. But it stayed bright, pushing the ship forward at fifteen knots.

"Prepare five more splintering rounds from the starboard cannon for that last diesel."

Two minutes and five rounds later, Cahill stranded the *Nanuchka* dead in the water. He turned his attention to the ships that protected each other east of Jake's rhomboid boundary. The icons merged and then yielded to hollow outlines.

"Chaff," Walker said. "They must have placed a ship upwind of the formation and are covering the entire group with chaff."

"We observed the Chinese doing that in the Spratlys."

"The Russians didn't need long to figure it out."

"They probably have enough chaff to hide from radar until they drive out of our weapons range."

"That's what they appear to be doing. They're heading north to skirt the edge of Jake's minefield."

"Check out the infrared satellite coverage."

"Shit, Terry. It's a cloud."

Cahill saw that the Russian fleet's heat signatures of white-hot propulsion equipment had transformed into a murky azure fog.

"How'd they accomplish that? A smoke screen?"

"It's got to be," Walker said. "The same ship that's shooting chaff is probably burning oil. The Russians know how to create smoke to hide."

Cahill felt his situational superiority over the Russian fleet waning. He had surprised them and forced them into reactionary action. But he knew they were smart and cool under pressure, and if he gave them enough time, he expected them to craft a deadly counterstrike.

And with the Bosporus mined shut, trapping him in the Black Sea, they had enough time.

"If they escape, they'll be back with a vengeance," he said.

"Do you want to try an earlier splintering time? We could expand our circle of buckshot and rain down hell over them, and there would be nothing the Vympels could do about it."

"We'd just be shooting tiny bullets blindly at big ships. I'd consider it a waste of ammo. If I'm going to shoot them, I'm going to need to paint them with our own phased array. We'll need to get within twenty miles to power through their chaff and jamming."

"That *Slava*-class cruiser has cannons that can reach forty nautical miles. And it's built to trade punches with ships bigger than us. Then you have to consider that we'd be well within range of every anti-ship missile they have. We need to strike from a distance, or we don't strike at all."

Cahill grasped for a solution, but it eluded him.

"Then there's nothing more we can do to them from here. They've found the right defensive tactics."

"They'll run out of chaff before they run out of smoke."

"Right," Cahill said. "We could shadow them at the same course and speed until that happens and then take our chances against their jamming. But to do that, we'd have to trace our steps back towards the *Kilo* that shot at us."

"Then we'd be inviting a torpedo."

"I know."

"So what's our next move, Terry?"

"Let's play a little defense now. We'll slow down, deploy our towed array sonar, and search for that *Kilo*."

Cahill ordered the railguns stowed as he slowed the *Goliath* and shifted the burden of his ship's electric propulsion motors to the six MESMA systems. He then ordered the ship to dive.

After escaping the rocking waves and slipping into the gentle bosom of the undersea world, he leaned toward his sonar supervisor's ear.

"Remember that you have a lot of unusual things to listen for. The diesels need to be running for that *Kilo* to be moving faster than a crawl. Listen for flow noise, too, since Jake's slow-kill weapon put at least a dozen holes in it."

"I already briefed the team on it."

Cahill looked at the tops of heads seated at the consoles of the Subtics tactical system. He recognized them as competent sonar technicians recruited from the Australian Navy, but he found himself wishing for an elite guru like Remy.

"Also listen for repetitive dolphin calls."

He stepped away and leaned back into his chair as the sonar team settled into their search. The banter among them suggested they had information worth sharing, but he let them analyze the incoming sounds before prying for insight.

When he turned to face Cahill, the supervisor's demeanor suggested hesitance.

"Nothing definitive yet," he said.

"What do you have?"

"We hear over a dozen contacts running diesels. All sorts of merchant ships are crossing this sea and avoiding Jake's minefield. And you have fishing ships starting and stopping."

"One of the contacts could be the *Kilo*."

"Agreed. But we don't hear anything definitive enough yet to declare one as the *Kilo*. Once we can correlate the *Kilo* with its diesels, we can track it by its diesels, but we need to find it by other means first."

"You understand that it needs to make dolphin noises once in a while to communicate with its dolphin friends."

"Yes, but that's highly random, if it's going to happen at all. For all we know, the dolphins swam home after they attacked us."

"Possibly. But have the team stay attentive to dolphin sounds on the bearings of all the diesels you hear."

A sonar technician rotated his head toward his supervisor, who leaned to him, chatted, and came back to Cahill.

"He found another one out there," the supervisor said. "That's fourteen contacts running diesels."

"I'll give you a course change soon to drive the geometry and help you resolve course and speed estimates to the contacts."

"That will help. I'll have them start identifying each contact and ruling out the ones that aren't the *Kilo*."

Cahill calculated that the Russian surface fleet sprinted a mile farther from his cannons for every two minutes he spent searching for the elusive submarine.

"We'll have to patient," he said. "I'll turn us north to drive geometry."

Fifteen minutes later, his sonar team had discerned the noisy imperfections of civilian propellers on most of the contacts. His sailors identified the other contacts as fishermen running diesels for electric power while drifting.

"None of them are the *Kilo*?" he asked.

"None," the supervisor said.

Then a young sailor heard a dolphin. The supervisor donned a headset and helped his technician listen in the direction of the mammal. Together, they discerned the faint rumble of quiet diesel engines.

"I never would have heard that engine if I didn't know where to listen," the supervisor said. "It's quiet."

"I'll make another turn to drive geometry on the new contact," Cahill said.

Two minutes later, the *Goliath* steadied on a new course, and the tactical data on the latest contact unfolded.

"You've got a contact moving at twelve knots," he said. "You can't hear any propeller blades yet, but it's fifteen miles away and within ten miles of where we last solved for the *Kilo's* position."

"I think we found it," the supervisor said. "It's moving to the southwest, towards the Bosporus."

"And towards Jake," Cahill said. "Are you ready for some old school submarine work?"

"You mean to trail it?"

"Maybe. Let's make sure it's the *Kilo*, first. Dolphin noise plus a diesel engine doesn't quite prove it. I'll get you closer."

"How close? Remember that you're on a hybrid ship that's not the type of hunter we're used to working on in the old navy."

"But the *Kilo's* badly wounded. I just want to get you close enough to hear it bleeding."

The supervisor frowned.

"We're not quite in a tail chase, but it's opening from us on a shallow angle. We can only get two knots of closure at our best submerged speed, and we'd be abnormally loud with our damage to the port weapons bay. Plus, its sonar techs know where we are since we were just shooting at their colleagues. This could easily backfire."

"You're right. I'm thinking of this like the captain of the *Rankin*, when I need to think like the captain of the *Goliath*. I'm going to the surface and see what's on our surface radar."

Five minutes later, his commercial search radar saw nothing

where his sonar team heard the suspected submarine. With the tactics shifted above the waves, Walker became vocal.

"We could send a few rounds that way and see if we can force an error," he said.

"No, that would reveal the secret that we know where the *Kilo* is. Let's share that secret with Pierre while it's still a secret."

"You're not going to let it get away, though, are you?"

Cahill looked at the displays that showed the incoming radar and infrared data on the Russian surface fleet. His former targets had pushed beyond railgun range, escaping at a speed equal to that of his ship's maximum sprint.

He toyed with the idea of giving chase, but he opted to stay on the *Kilo* that headed towards Jake.

"No," he said. "We have the *Goliath's* first chance to trail an advanced Russian submarine. I'd find that worthy of bragging about if I pulled it off while commanding the *Rankin*. Doing it in this beautiful beast will make it all the more sweet."

CHAPTER 16

Jake sent the *Specter's* periscope into a circular sweep of the Turkish waters off the coast of the northern city of Amarsa. As servomotors whirred and retracted the optical mast into the conning tower, he looked at his display to see the panorama of the seas above him.

"I count six visual contacts," he said.

Remy joined him on the conning platform and leaned by his shoulder.

"These all correlate to sonar contacts except that one," he said. "But you can't blame me for missing it. It looks like a small fishing boat. It's probably just drifting."

"Let's risk the time for a download," Jake said.

"Fair enough."

As Remy returned to his seat, Jake saw Henri glance at him.

"I'm ready for the radio download," the Frenchman said.

"Raise the radio mast and download the satellite broadcast."

Far from Russian jamming interference, Jake expected clean reception. Five minutes after giving the order, he had his data.

"Let's get below this mess of traffic. Henri, make your depth fifty meters."

During the slow descent, he played his mentor's video. The Frenchman's face sagged with fatigue and concern.

"I'll start with the bad news, which is sadly the bulk of this video report," Renard said. "I've run into bad luck finding you safe harbors. No country has agreed to take you in. I fear that the urgency of our timing has placed me in a weak negotiating position, but I promise to keep working on it."

The news irked Jake, and he shifted his weight in his seat.

"The Russians have developed sound tactics against Terry's cannons," Renard said. "He could cripple only one *Kashin*, one *Nanuchka*, and two *Grishas*. This is reflected in my update to your tactical data feed. If you're trying to determine what's consistent among those four ships and different from the others, don't bother. The link is imperfect, since the *Kashin* and the *Grishas* lack Vympel defense systems, but the *Nanuncka* has one."

Jake frowned. He blamed combat fatigue for having assumed that Cahill attacked random Russians. His mentor's report revealed deeper tactical considerations.

"The *Nanuchka's* Vympel worked at the expense of forty bullets per incoming round. But when Terry sent two rounds simultaneously, the Vympel missed the second round more often than it hit. So he has a counter-tactic to their counter-tactic. But the remaining Russian ships have converged to synergize their Vympels, along with employing chaff and smoke screens to blind our infrared satellite, effectively nullifying Terry's long-range attack."

Jake rested his forehead in his hand, awaiting whatever good news he dared to hope to hear.

"The Russian fleet is now together and moving around your declared minefield," Renard said. "They're shuttling helicopters from shore to replenish Vympel rounds, chaff canisters, and even sand bags, which I believe they'll use as armor around their propulsion systems and Vympels. Terry didn't attack the Vympel itself, but that's a tactic they need to defend against."

Looking to the tactical display, Jake saw two dozen Russian ships to the west of his minefield. They approached the imaginary line extending from the border between Romania and Bulgaria.

"You'll notice that the Russian fleet is moving slowly," Renard said. "I assume they're using the time to erect sand bag defenses, verify their plans, and let the *Kilo* you damaged approach you. Unfortunately, that *Kilo* is still behaving like a warship and is coming for you. Terry has found it and is trailing it."

Feeling trapped, Jake felt an urge to lash out at his closest potential victim and destroy the *Kilo*.

"I have little to report on the removal of the minefield," Renard said. "The Russians are standing firm. And though the Turks are mobilizing their mine clearing units, the duration of their work will be too long to help you. You remain trapped, and your present location is your best hiding place. I received your quick burst transmission of your coordinates. I've sent Terry instructions to join you there."

"So where's the good news?" Jake asked.

The Frenchman's image responded as if it heard him.

"The upside is that the surface fleet is the least of your worries," Renard said. "They appear to be in stasis, awaiting the outcome of something, and I believe that something is the *Kilo*, which I know you can handle. However, once you defeat the *Kilo*, I believe the Russians will strike from the air. I estimate that you have six hours until a strike could be organized with enough ordnance to overrun Terry's defenses."

"That's the good news?"

"I've also leaked a story to the international news agencies that a renegade band of human rights activists is responsible for the attack on the Russians," Renard said. "With a little luck, this Robin Hood story will add pressure to the Russians to remove the minefield."

"If that's all you've got, we're screwed."

The Frenchman's face darkened.

"There's one thing I want to make perfectly clear," Renard said. "This is an order. If I can't get through to you again, and if you're overwhelmed, you and Terry will save yourselves and your crews. Abandon your ships, make for shore, and turn yourselves over to the Turkish Navy. I've spoken to my admiral on the inside. He's stationing a security detachment near your present location."

Jake examined the icon on the nearby coast that represented ground troops, and he noticed the annotation identifying it as a Turkish Naval detachment.

"If you're thinking about scuttling the ships, don't," Renard said. "Leave them intact in Turkish waters. Since they're valuable assets, they have bargaining value. That's all for now. Good luck my friend, and listen for me when you can."

The screen went dark, and Jake committed several minutes to brooding in silence. Trying to force himself to accept a probable defeat sent him into a downward spiral of negativity, and he slammed his fist into the console.

He glanced to Henri, who looked away, deferring to Jake's new therapist. The priest appeared by his side.

"May I join you, Jake?" Andrew asked.

Jake kept his voice low.

"Yeah."

"Whatever burden you feel, you might want to share."

"Yeah."

"Do you want to talk?"

He sensed himself shutting down. His anger swelled, and the surging dark energy became a volcano suppressed under cracking rock. His vocal chords tightened, and the words choked behind them rose and stirred the cauldron of his mind. He had to squeeze out his one-word answer.

"Yeah."

"Did Pierre give you bad news?" Andrew asked.

"Yeah."

"Are we about to die?"

The innocent bluntness circumvented Jake's anger.

"No, it's not that bad. Not yet, anyway."

"Well, what was the worst of it?"

"An air strike. He thinks that's how they'll come for us. Terry can hold off small reactionary forces but not coordinated air strikes."

"I see," Andrew said. "So we're in danger of being defeated by superior numbers from the sky."

"That's pretty much it. The surface fleet is slowing down since they're probably becoming a backup plan to the air forces, and that *Kilo* is limping after us. I can handle that *Kilo*, but it's the crap that I can't fight that's pissing me off."

"Nobody likes feeling helpless."

The statement triggered Jake's pessimism.

"Helpless. Arrogant. Stupid. Who was I to think I could beat the Russians? I've always won with Pierre, and I thought I'd never lose. But we missed the play where they mined the strait.

It's so obvious in retrospect. I'm an idiot."

"This is tough for you because you're used to success. When success comes easily to someone, it's actually a sort of curse. It makes the simple, normal, human failures seem bigger."

"This isn't a normal failure."

"Of course, it isn't. The result could be catastrophic, but I mean the analysis and planning behind this is a simple miscalculation. You made a mistake, and you weren't alone. In fact, this is Pierre's mistake. You just bought into it."

The priest's words were placating his temper, and he nodded while reflecting upon the insights.

"This is almost funny," he said. "We're all at risk of getting blown up, and it took you about two minutes to figure out that I'm having a meltdown because of my pride."

"For what it's worth, it happens a lot. It's easy for the ego to drive us in the wrong direction."

Jake let the holy man's final words swim in his mind. Something about them piqued his thoughts.

"Are you feeling better?" Andrew asked.

"Hold on. I'm thinking."

"Of course."

"Okay. I've got a question. You said the ego can drive men in wrong directions. When I go into battle, I usually ignore my enemy's emotional flaws. I have to think that I'm fighting against a rational actor that's going against me on his best day."

"That's a good conservative estimate."

"Especially with the Russians. They like to plan to win and to be disciplined enough to make their plans work."

"I understand why that could stress you out, given that they're likely planning an air strike against us."

"You're right, but that's not what I mean, specifically. I mean that *Kilo* that's coming after us. It doesn't seem right. In fact, it seems terribly wrong. Why would a limping submarine come after me, when the air attack is gearing up to crush us?"

"I didn't know enough about combat to think of it."

Jake pointed to his position on the tactical display.

"We're here," he said. "The surface fleet blocks our movement to the west. The Turkish coast and the minefield by the Bosporus block our escape to the south. They think I won't risk going north because they believe I laid a minefield there."

"Okay. I see that."

"The *Kilo* is coming from the east. Even though we're hidden for now, the Russians have us pinned down within twenty miles in any direction. I think that *Kilo* isn't coming to play as a team member of the Russian fleet. I think it's coming for me, one on one."

He stared at the screen as the situation's geometric constraints shaped his theory.

"The Russians are allowing a mission of vengeance?"

"It's possible," Jake said. "They know they'll lose pilots and aircraft to Terry with an air strike, but a submarine can beat us with no further loss."

"I see."

"But maybe it's a renegade commanding officer. Authorized or not, I think that's where ego comes into it. I bruised the ego of that ship's captain and crew badly, and they're afraid to spend the rest of their lives with their lasting memory of me being mortal terror and humiliation."

"How could they hope to win? You damaged their ship."

"They don't know that Terry found them. They think that I'm completely distracted by the surface fleet and the threat of the air attack. They probably think I wrote them off hours ago and forgot about them, too. And to be honest, I did, until Terry found them."

The priest frowned.

"I imagine that you'll use this knowledge to our advantage to defeat the *Kilo*," he said. "But that doesn't solve the seemingly insurmountable challenge from the sky."

"No, it doesn't. And it wouldn't get us out of the Black Sea, either, now would it?"

"This sounds dire. Why do you look like you just received divine inspiration?"

Jake smiled.

"Because I just received divine inspiration. There's a plan taking root in my mind, and you need to remind me to thank you if it gets us out of here alive with our ships."

"Okay, I'm glad I helped, whatever I did."

"I'll explain later. Just keep our conversation and especially Pierre's video confidential."

He dismissed the priest, walked to the central navigation chart, and summoned Henri and Remy to his side.

"What is it?" Henri asked.

"I'm going to draw out a plan on the chart. While I do that, I need you guys to watch Pierre's video to understand the background. I've just released it for both of you to watch with your login identities. I don't want anyone else watching, and I want you guys to keep the information confidential."

"You looked ghastly ten minutes ago," Henri said. "Now you're almost giddy. What happened?"

"Watch the video to know why I was upset."

"We will, but what about your plan? Give me something to keep my spirits up while I'm watching this depressing video."

"Terry's trailing the *Kilo* and has determined that it's coming for us."

"That *Kilo* has enough of a head start on Terry that he can't help," Henri said. "If that *Kilo's* coming for us, we'll need to deal with it ourselves. I'm not seeing anything yet to support your enthusiasm."

"I know it sounds bad. Call me crazy, but I think I can turn this to our advantage."

"You mean to buy us time to survive through the night?"

"No," Jake said. "I mean to save the day and get us the hell out of here."

CHAPTER 17

Jake tapped the icon that started the tactical system's depiction of his plan. Images of ships moved around the display, demonstrating his intent with the *Kilo*.

"It might work," Henri said.

"It adds danger that we don't need," Remy said. "I don't like that we're trying this with damage to our conning tower from the *Grisha's* guns. I still haven't had a chance to analyze the impact of that to our acoustic signature."

"And that *Kilo* has a dozen holes punched into it from my torpedo," Jake said. "We have the advantage. I don't want the usual conservative Antoine for this. I want the superhero, gutsy Antoine."

"I don't recall having a twin. Where have you ever seen that fictional version of me?"

"I dream of him from time to time."

"I can't promise you an especially brave version of myself."

Henri tapped his fingernail against the icon of the *Goliath*.

"This fails if Terry doesn't learn of it," he said. "Without his confirmation of support, we won't know if we're wasting our time. And if he transmits to confirm his support, he risks ruining everything by revealing his position. It's a self-defeating proposition, unless you want to work on blind faith that Terry will do his part."

"He might be able to respond with a delayed communications buoy," Jake said. "Worst case, if this doesn't work out, I'll just put another torpedo into that *Kilo*."

"What type?" Henri asked.

The question surprised Jake.

"Are you going to make me decide now?"

"I think it's best that you do. Decide now so that you don't have to under stress later."

Jake wanted to avoid turning the *Kilo* into a mass grave, but the slow-kill weapon had demonstrated its limits.

"Heavyweight," he said. "Decision made."

"It's good to make a decision," Remy said. "But be careful that you don't send a heavyweight into Terry."

"You'd never let me do that," Jake said. "You can tell the *Goliath* from the *Kilo*."

"No matter how good your teams are, two friendly submarines in the same water hunting a hostile boat is dangerous."

"We'll have satellite coverage of the *Kilo's* snorkel mast."

"Provided we're both at snorkel depth."

"You saw Pierre's video, right?"

"Yes."

"Do you see anything else we can do? Would you prefer to wait and see what happens with negotiations and then, you know, do what Pierre suggested?"

Jake scanned the control room and verified that the cramped confines prevented him from a conversation of complete privacy.

"I know his final order was extreme," Remy said. "Of course, I don't want it to come to that."

"Extreme, but necessary if the world falls apart like he thinks it will. But if my idea with the *Kilo* works out, we can avoid it."

"There are so many unpredictable factors that have to be resolved favorably for this to work," Henri said. "And the required precision pushes the limits of feasibility."

"But consider if my plan breaks down," Jake said. "We could still fight our way out of it and proceed as Pierre ordered. I'm giving us a fighting chance for something better."

The Frenchmen fell silent, and their hesitance bothered him.

"I don't promise a democratic outcome, but I invite your votes, to know where you stand," he said. "Antoine?"

The toad-head shook.

"No. I don't like the chances of us shooting Terry by accident or vice versa. It's too dangerous for a supposed upside that might even get us into more trouble."

"I figured," Jake said. "That's why I asked you first. Henri?"

"May vote neutral? I see a balance of positives and negatives. It's one of those scenarios where I'm grateful that the burden of the decision is yours."

"Neutral is fine. I obviously vote yes, which makes it a deadlock, at least in this theoretical exercise."

"But it's not a theoretical exercise," Henri said. "Your decision is final."

"Right. So start driving us due north at twelve knots. We're doing it."

"We've followed you into danger in every ocean, and you've never led us astray," Henri said.

Jake reflected upon his history with the French mercenaries.

"You've never been in the Arctic with me."

"But I feel like I was there with you, based upon the amount of times Pierre's told me the story. My point stands. You are truly charmed like he says, and I have to believe that. I'll put us on ordered course and speed."

Henri stepped to his control station, and the toad-head shook.

"I still don't like it," Remy said.

"I understand. It goes against everything you hold sacred in submarining."

"Not quite everything, but close enough."

Remy returned to his console, and Jake went to his elevated conning platform.

"Henri, bring the ship to periscope depth. Prepare to snorkel. I want to add whatever juice I can to the batteries."

The deck angled upward and rocked. When shallow, Jake pressed the icon that raised his periscope for a panoramic view of ships crossing his path. After lowering the periscope, he had Henri raise the snorkel mast.

"Commence snorkeling."

The hull rumbled with the gentle vibrations of the sound-isolated diesels, and air rushed through ventilation ducts.

"Raise the radio mast," he said.

"The radio mast is raised," Henri said.

"Download the satellite broadcast."

A minute later, Henri reported that he had the update of tactical data but nothing personal from Renard. The icons slid to their new positions on the display.

"That's it," Henri said. "There's nothing else."

"That means no progress with negotiations," Jake said. "It's time."

"I'm ready."

"Link with the satellite, transmit a hail to Pierre."

"I'm transmitting a hail to Pierre."

Jake angled a microphone from his console towards his mouth as the speakers carried the Frechman's surprise.

"Jake?" Renard asked.

"It's me."

"It's good to hear from you, though surprising."

"I broke radio silence for a good reason. I'm sending you a data feed with a plan I want to run by you."

"Go ahead."

"Here it comes."

He tapped an image that sent the ideas captured in the *Specter's* tactical system to Renard's makeshift command post, buried within a Ukrainian naval base.

"Shall I digest it now?" Renard asked.

"Yes. I'm okay being exposed by my masts. I want to be found as part of my plan."

"You jest."

"I'm dead serious."

"Well then, shall we indulge in a video discussion?"

"Sure."

After watching Henri and his radio operator work their panels, Jake accepted a popup window's prompt for a video feed. Gray ovals underscored his mentor's eyes, and frayed silver strands formed mats atop his crown.

"God, you look tired, Pierre. Aren't you sleeping?"

"Not really. I'm more anxious in command centers than when at sea commanding submarines. There's something energizing about the proximity to the action. Speaking of which, you appear thrilled to be alive."

"I guess that's what happens when I have an idea I like."

"May I have a moment to review it?"

"Sure."

Renard angled his nose to a side monitor, frowned, and then raised an eyebrow.

"Do you really expect me to approve this?"

"Yeah. What's wrong? You already said you're willing to give up your ships. I'm giving you a chance to keep them."

"It's not them I'm worried about."

The Frenchman blinked and shrugged.

"Well, alright, I am worried about them," he said. "They cost more than my net worth and would take years to replace. In all candor, if I lose them, I'd be forced into retirement, and our operations would shut down forever."

Jake tipped his head and glared.

"Is that what you want?"

His mentor's hesitance worried him.

"No. I'm not quite ready for that. But I wouldn't find it completely deplorable either. I am getting on in years."

"You're barely past fifty-five. Stop whining."

"Tell me how you feel in twenty years."

"I will. But back to right now. I want to win this mission, and I don't consider it a win unless we get out of here with our ships."

"I won't condone your suicides."

Renard's pessimism stung, but he expected it and countered.

"Leave it up to Terry, then. Let him decide."

"Though he lacks your jaded edge, he's an adventurous young man. I fear that you're formulating an ongoing subconscious duel of bravery and one-upmanship."

"Huh. Good insight. I can't say I deny it."

The Frenchman turned his head.

"For God's sake."

"What?"

"I'm sending you a satellite feed. Look at yourself."

Jake beheld the feather-like wakes that his radio mast and snorkel mast combined to generate.

"I told you, I want to be found."

"You look like a training video on how to fail in commanding a submarine. How fast are you moving?"

"Twelve knots."

"Shall I order you a new radio mast now, or would you like me to wait until a particularly rough wave snaps it off?"

"Just wait. What I'd really like is for you to approve this plan and get Terry acting on it."

He watched the Frenchman lift a Marlboro to his lips and whip a gold-plated Zippo lighter underneath it. Smoke rose from the amber, and then his mentor blew a cloud.

"I imagine that if I say no, you'll attempt to contact Terry yourself directly, despite the possible consequences."

"I thought about it. But I figured you'd say yes. So I haven't decided yet if I have the balls to collude with him and override you."

Renard sucked two lungs full of apparent calmness from his cigarette and pushed gray wisps from his nostrils.

"I know you have the balls, so to speak. So I may as well display mine and give you my approval. You have it."

"I knew you'd love the idea."

"I accept it. I'll hail him now. Keep your masts up."

"I'll wait, masts up."

The video stopped, and Jake waited in solitude as his team kept the ship moving forward on course, at speed, and at depth.

Even the priest contributed, having learned to track ships on one of the rudimentary, anti-collision plots. Jake called up Andrew's plot, noticed a ship on his right that moved to his left, suggesting a possible intersection.

Before he could query Andrew, the holy man leaned toward the sonar technician seated beside him. Jake watched the men nod to each other in apparent confirmation of safety. Seconds later, the bearing to the incoming sound passed in front of the *Specter*, continuing on the left and away from a possible collision.

After what felt like eternity, his mentor's face reappeared.

"I've sent a message to Terry," Renard said. "I cannot verify his receipt yet, but I am hopeful that he'll acknowledge."

"It's pointless without him."

"Keep faith in me to connect with him, and I will keep faith in you to do your part. Take your ship deep now. You don't want to behave like an idiot and make it obvious."

Jake ordered the masts lowered and the submarine taken deep. He pushed forward at fifteen knots.

An hour later, he came shallow and slowed to twelve knots. He raised his masts to snorkel and to reach Renard.

"Good news," the Frenchman said. "Terry dropped a delayed communication buoy and has acknowledged his compliance with your plan. He's broken trail and is altering course."

"Good. Any sign of the *Kilo* changing course yet?"

"It altered course to intercept you twenty minutes ago. It's still at snorkel depth and being tracked on satellite–as you are most assuredly being tracked by satellites and radar while you expose your masts."

"The surface fleet isn't reacting?"

"No, as expected. Any hunt they could mount would now include the risk of attacking their own submarine.

"Then my job is pretty simple. It's up to Terry now. Did his message have anything in it about his confidence?"

Renard smirked.

"Of course. It's from Terry. He said to tell you that your idea was bloody brilliant and that your faith in his abilities is grossly overinflated, despite his assurances that he'll somehow manage to impress you and succeed."

"I'm not surprised."

"That's enough bravado. Get deep again before the Russians see through your ploy."

Another hour later, Jake reached the edge of his declared minefield. He slowed the *Specter* to five knots, came shallow, and raised his masts. His mentor's face appeared.

"Nothing new to report, I'm afraid," Renard said.

"That's good news."

"For your plan, yes. For my negotiations, no. There's been no movement on the minefield, and the entire squadron of Fencer attack aircraft at Sevastapol is on the runway being fueled. The pilots aren't in their cockpits yet, though, which makes me think they're being trained on tactics to deal with Terry's defenses."

"An entire squadron for us?"

"They'll make sure they succeed, and I suspect political games are being played between admirals trying to claim the ultimate victory against you."

"Too bad politics can't delay them forever."

"They can't."

"So it's time for me to play my last move. Hold on."

"I'll wait."

Jake moved between the shoulders of Antoine and his apprentice, Julien, who served as his expert on drone operations.

"Are you ready?" Jake asked.

"Yes," Julien said. "Drone one is ready in tube five, programmed to swim on course zero-four-zero, speed five knots."

"Very well. Launch drone one."

"Drone one is swimming out of tube five. Drone one is clear of our hull and deployed. I have wire connectivity and confirmation of propulsion."

Jake returned to his screen.

"The drone is deployed. I'm going to head below and become a ghost."

"I pray that your drone fools your enemy," Renard said.

"It will. But if it doesn't, we'll make it work somehow."

"I know you will. I appreciate your plan. It is indeed genius, and I must admit jealousy for not having thought of it myself. You're setting the right trap, and I believe in your ability to execute it."

"Thank you, Pierre."

"But don't become arrogant. Your intended victim has super-cavitating torpedoes, drones as good as yours, and the entirety of a fleet and naval air station behind it. Keep your wits about you, or you'll get everyone killed."

CHAPTER 18

Volkov stared at his chart.

"The *Specter's* last known position was here," he said. "At that point, two hours ago, it snorkeled and conducted radio communications."

With catalyzed zeal, his executive officer bounded from the sonar operator's side to the charting table.

"It started with its masts raised in the Turkish waters, where you thought it would be. From there it's drawn a straight line by raising its masts again an hour later, and yet another hour later. It's a simple pattern."

"The simplicity alarms me," Volkov said. "Its commanding officer may have suffered a tactical setback that forces him to snorkel every hour, or he may have suffered a short-term memory lapse and forgotten how to command a submarine."

"Either scenario is unlikely, sir."

"The more likely option is that he's intentionally going out of his way to demonstrate his location, course, and speed to us."

"That would mean that he's trying to send us a message."

The executive officer lifted a stylus and traced the *Specter's* path forward.

"If he stays on course, then he's heading into his own mine-field. We need to analyze the probability of that happening before we can interpret his message."

"Agreed. The declaration stated that he laid drifting mines with a time limit of twenty-four hours. We're still within that timeframe, and the drifting mines means that his map of their locations is imperfect. Even if he adjusts for currents, he's undertaking a fool's journey unless he can command the mines."

"I assume that he can turn his mines on and off with the proper sequence from his sonar system, just as we can with our mines."

Volkov granted that the *Specter* could navigate its own mine-field, but the reality of one mistake leading to oblivion made him challenge the practicality of the theory.

"Would you run through your own minefield if you were commanding the *Specter*?" he asked.

"I would for lack of other options. It's the only place where our ships cannot follow. And for all we know, he may be resetting timers on the mines within his reach to extend their lethality for days. He'd need only stay submerged and hide from aircraft while he hopes that diplomatic pressure shifts in his favor."

"I don't understand diplomacy as you do, but I don't expect that he'll be breathing long enough for it to matter, if I have an opportunity to influence his fate."

"You don't mean to pursue him into the minefield."

Volkov looked for signs of renewed cowardice but saw hardened resolve.

"No, but I believe that's his message," he said. "It's an invitation. He's taunting the fleet to follow him in."

"But why, sir? Why not just slip away and hide and use the minefield for defense?"

"There are many possibilities. One of which is that he's trying to distract us from the *Goliath*."

"The *Goliath*, sir? I don't see what help the *Goliath* could need, since it escaped our torpedoes without harm."

"I agree that the *Goliath* has no need of his help, but given the absurdity of his actions, we need to consider all cases."

The executive officer nodded in apparent deference to Volkov's lead in the analysis.

"I understand, sir."

"The second possibility is that he thinks one or more of us will take the bait and follow him in."

"He's a fool if he expects rash impatience from a navy that knows discipline and rigor."

"If he's really sending us a message, there must be more options to consider," Volkov said. "For example, he may be informing us of his ability and commitment to extend the duration of his minefield to match that which we created in the Bosporus."

"That's logical, sir. It's possible that he's sending several messages. I could see him announcing his commitment to hiding in his minefield, threatening to extend it beyond twenty-four hours, and daring us to follow him in. He's desperate and groping at all his possibilities, however remote they are to help him."

After a year and a half of watching his second-in-command flounder in arrogant incompetence, Volkov appreciated exchanging ideas with an awoken mind.

"Of course," he said. "You see the picture now. What other option might you suggest?"

"Well, sir, it could be a ploy. He could want us to think he's running to his minefield while he in fact turned from his minefield right at its border."

"True," he said. "But where he might truly be going in that case, is the difficult next question."

"I can't answer that, sir. No country in this sea would dare harbor him, though some may look the other way if he hides in their waters."

"He was already in Turkey's territorial waters when he began his fool's journey. There's no place safer for him than where he started his errant behavior. That's what doesn't make sense."

"Could this be a trap?"

"It could be, but why go to the trouble? He shouldn't even know that we're still battle-worthy, much less coming for him. But if he does, he could have easily ambushed us by staying where he was. There's no trap he can create that could make us easier targets."

A shadow consumed the executive officer's face as he fell into deep thought. Then his eyes narrowed.

"Maybe he's just taunting us to boost his crew's morale—to give them something to do other than wait."

"Perhaps. But we need more information beyond that which he's told us. I'm going to have a chat with our trainer to see where our prized hunters are to see if they can help."

The lithe man seated beside the sonar operator kept his eyes on the screen that showed incoming sounds.

"Where are they?" Volkov asked.

"Their last update was four minutes ago," the trainer said. "They're already in the minefield."

"And we're almost five miles from the boundary, allowing for positional uncertainty. "

Volkov glared at the trainer.

"What's wrong, sir?"

"I just realized that we should have found the *Specter* by now–if not with our sonar system, then with the dolphins."

"They're trying their lowest frequency whistles to extend the range of their echolocation. Though we've seen it work, that's unnatural for them. They prefer higher frequencies to find closer contacts."

Moving his eyes to the chart, Volkov saw the whale icon representing his bottlenose dolphins lurking five miles ahead of the *Specter's* future position within the rhomboid minefield.

"They should be within detection range already."

"There's no guarantee they'll see the *Specter* that far away."

"Ironically, I've developed stronger faith in your dolphins than you, based upon their recent performances."

Minutes passed, and Volkov grew impatient.

"Less than three miles between them and the *Specter*."

"Yes," the trainer said. "I admit this is problematic, but if it's out there, they'll find it."

The loudspeaker played a burst of chirps and whistles. Adrenaline flooded Volkov's body, and he grabbed a railing for balance against the rocking deck.

"That's them," he said. "What's their report?"

"Submerged contact," the trainer said.

"Verify their location and find out what they know about the contact. You're free to communicate without my intervention."

"Thank you."

"You've proven yourself, and so have they. There's no further need for me to approve your communications."

During an exchange of dolphin sounds, Volkov learned that

the mammals swam on the bearing where he expected to see the *Specter*. His prey's track followed its northerly course and held the speed of five knots it had undertaken outside the mine-field.

"Here comes the range from them to the *Specter*," he said.

The *Krasnodar's* control room fell silent except for the dolphin's incoming sound.

"The distance is near," the trainer said.

"Less than a mile?"

"Yes."

"You're sure?"

"Absolutely."

The sonar operator raised his hand and yelled.

"Metallic transient noise from the bearing of the *Specter*."

"Can you identify the cause of the transient?" Volkov asked.

"A dropped tool hitting the deck, perhaps. It's something blatant–a horrible mistake by one of the crewmen."

Volkov felt himself divided. Part of him indulged in the belief that fate had gifted him his vengeance while part of him sensed deception.

His response to his inner split covered the extremes of possibility as he projected his voice to announce it.

"Get the dolphins away from the *Specter*. Assign the *Specter* a location one mile south of the dolphins. Prepare the Shkval underwater rocket in tube six for the *Specter*."

His crew hustled to react and had the *Krasnodar* ready to launch within thirty seconds.

"Shoot tube six."

The rapid pressure change popped his ears.

"I hear our weapon clearing the ship," the sonar operator said. "Its rocket is igniting, and I hear the exhaust bubbles coming from the nose cone. The rocket is now at full thrust, and our weapon is turning towards the *Specter*."

Volkov expected his super-cavitating underwater rocket to accelerate to two-hundred and fifty knots, and his rapid calculation gave the weapon three minutes to run its eight-mile course. As he attacked, his instincts toyed with him, telling him to turn from a potential retaliatory torpedo while also telling him to do the opposite.

He chose the opposite.

"Secure snorkeling," he said. "We're going deep and slow."

His gray-bearded veteran ordered the submarine's diesels silenced, and as the rumble subsided, Volkov heard the induction mast slide into his ship.

"The ship is secured from snorkeling," the veteran said. "We're slowing to four knots, the maximum speed we can make on the fuel cell."

"Very well," Volkov said. "Make your depth fifty meters, left full rudder, steady course two-two-zero."

"Coming to fifty meters, course two-two-zero, sir."

"Reload tube six with a drone."

"A drone, sir?" the veteran asked.

"I'll explain later. See to it."

As the deck dipped and rolled, he watched his executive officer walk around the chart to his side.

"May I ask why you wish to go deep, sir?"

"One of two outcomes will be known within minutes. Either we'll be rid of the *Specter*, or we'll be certain of a ruse. If it's indeed the ruse, we'll be facing a newfound and alarming uncertainty of the *Specter's* location."

"You would then counter by going deep and depriving the *Specter* of the easy knowledge of our position."

"Yes, and also deprive the *Goliath*."

The executive officer pursed his lips.

"The *Goliath* could hardly keep pace with us while submerged, and it's remained undetected for half a day," he said. "To overtake us, it would practically need to have predicted our path and maneuvered ahead of us."

The executive officer's comment deepened Volkov's concern about the complexity of a possible trap. He flagged the combat transport ship as a danger greater than that of its long-range cannons. Against his ship's damage-limited ability, the *Goliath* posed the additional threat of a credible hunting submarine.

"Perhaps," he said. "But let's await the outcome of our Shkval before bogging ourselves down in speculation."

He rejected good luck as a valid tactic, but a tiny spark of optimism made him hope for pending victory as his rocket reached the would-be *Specter's* hull.

"The Shkval is within detection range of the target," the sonar operator said. "I hear the terminal guidance sonar."

"Very well."

Seconds ticked away without a hit.

"The weapon isn't veering toward the target," the sonar operator said. "It's not picking it up."

"Let it run its course," Volkov said.

"The weapon should now be passing the location of the *Specter*," the sonar operator said.

"Very well. Do you hear any evidence of the *Specter* attempting to evade our weapon?"

"No, sir. Nothing."

"So be it," Volkov said. "I've determined that the target is not the *Specter* but a decoy. I want you to keep tracking the decoy to verify this conclusion."

"Of course, sir," the sonar operator said.

"We've been drawn to this decoy and duped into shooting a weapon at it," Volkov said. "I conclude that the *Specter's* captain wanted me to head north towards his minefield and to attack his decoy. I still see no rationale for this, but the reasoning behind whatever trick he's playing lies in a different direction."

He looked at the tactical chart showing the *Krasnodar* driving away from the line drawn by his Shkval.

"I'm going to keep us submerged and hidden while this puzzle unfolds," he said.

"It's difficult to hunt our enemy while limited to four knots, sir," the executive officer said. "While we're deep, we're also limited in what the fleet can share with us."

"The fleet will hail us to come shallow if there's something worth sharing."

"Agreed, sir, but we've also exhausted half of our allotted time to hunt the *Specter*. We're racing the clock."

"I know," Volkov said. "But we have several assets that can search the waters faster than our own ship."

"You mean to deploy drones."

"Three of them. I want one sent to the northeast, one to the southeast, and one to the southwest."

"I see your vision now, sir. If we're close enough to find and engage the *Specter* before we run out of time, then we're close enough to use drones."

"Yes, and we're also going to have another asset working on our behalf."

On cue, the trainer looked to Volkov.

"Where to, sir?"

"Send the dolphins towards Amarsa, Turkey, right back down the track of the *Specter*. If its captain has gone out of his way to make me think he traveled north, let the dolphins see if he fled in the complete opposite direction."

CHAPTER 19

A strange thought danced in Cahill's mind.

The dolphins that had inundated his bridge had also nudged him closer to his submariner's nature. Operating submerged and encased in steel suited him. Despite them being his enemy, he found it impossible to hold a grudge against animals that the Russians had turned into warriors against him.

Since the deviations from a standard *Scorpène* submarine's control room deprived him of an elevated conning platform, he stood in the room's center and pressed his palms into the tactical table. A downward scan confirmed the history of the *Kilo* having veered north after Jake, giving the *Goliath* time to outpace its prey's westerly advance.

The aging data also showed the Russian surface fleet remaining disengaged while the *Specter* transited south in hopes of enticing the wounded submarine to follow.

"It's been an hour since our last update," he said. "By now I'm only guessing where that *Kilo* is. Slow to three knots and take us shallow for an update."

"Slowing to three knots and coming to periscope depth," Walker said.

The deck angled as the *Goliath's* momentum became an upward glide. With the ship slow at periscope depth, Walker raised the periscope, grabbed a visual sweep, and then lowered the optics. Cahill found the waters north of the heavier Turkish coastal traffic unpopulated.

"There are no close contacts," he said. "Raise the radio mast and download the broadcast from the satellite."

With the masts mounted in the rear of his ship, he heard distant echoes of the hydraulic valves clicking to raise his antenna above the waves. The deck rose in a rogue swell and then steadied into a rhythmic rocking during the download.

He looked to his sonar supervisor.

"See what new contacts you can find while we're slow and shallow."

"We are. We passed an acoustic layer on the way up, and we're hearing a bunch of surfaced contacts we couldn't hear below the layer."

"Anything unusual or alarming?"

"Not that we notice. Most of it's to the south, near the coast, as you'd expect. There are a few contacts in shipping lanes, but nothing sounds like a warship or a shallow submarine."

"Analyze what you can while we're up here, which won't be long," Cahill said.

"We've got the download," Walker said.

"Make your depth fifty meters. All ahead standard, make turns for fourteen knots."

Free of the *Specter's* drag, Cahill felt comfortable coaxing the *Goliath* to sustain the extra knot submerged.

Keeping fourteen knots pulled electrons from his undersized batteries, and he honored the inefficiency of a double conversion from direct current, to alternating current, and back to direct current required to account for the small numbers of cells. But with his MESMA units shouldering the overwhelming majority of the burden, he expected that he could hold the speed for days.

The world tilted downward as icons shifted around the plot.

"Nothing from Pierre other than the tactical update?"

"Nothing," Walker said.

"The tactical update will have to do, then. It looks like the *Kilo* took the bait and attacked Jake's drone."

"That's expected. Our sonar team heard that fake transient noise from here. It was practically impossible to tell the difference between the drone's recording and the sound of real metal."

"That was all according to plan," Cahill said.

"But then the *Kilo* didn't stay at snorkel depth," Walker said. "It was last seen going under, and our satellite has no sign of it for the last half hour. That's a concern."

"You're still thinking like a surface warrior. I concede that it's now harder to find, but it's stuck at four knots, and we know it's running its trim and drain pumps to get rid of its water. Our sonar team will hear it."

"If it's indeed heading after Jake."

Cahill noted the *Specter's* location on the plot.

"It is. Jake's dead in the water with two masts exposed while charging his batteries. The Russians will find him."

"Maybe you're right, Terry. Maybe I still underestimate what we can do underwater. I notice that the four-knot speed limit guarantees that we'll be ahead of the *Kilo*. We'll get to Jake before it does."

"Let me set the course," Cahill said.

He tapped an icon that showed him the direction to travel to reach Jake's submarine.

"Left standard rudder, steer course two-six-one."

An hour later, he ordered the *Goliath* shallow for another update. Renard had remained silent, other than his tactical feed, which lacked information on the *Kilo* but showed the need for a modest course correction to reach Jake.

"Come left to course two-five-nine."

Forty minutes later, a sonar operator stirred, earning the supervisor's attention and a brief chat.

"We picked up the *Specter's* diesels," the supervisor said. "We're within two miles of it."

"What bearing?"

"Two-five-five."

"Shall I steer us to two-five-five?" Walker asked.

"Yes, come left to course two-five-five."

Walker tapped an icon to nudge and then center the ship's rudder. Cahill found the catamaran's movement imperceptible.

"Shall I slow us?" Walker asked.

"Not yet. Energize the side-scan sonar, full power."

Cahill faced the array of displays behind him that showed camera views of the darkness outside the *Goliath*. One screen shifted from blackness to the monochromatic return of the high-precision side-scan sonar.

"Energize the laser communication system."

"The laser communication system is energized," Walker said.

Minutes later, an oblong shape took form on the side-scan sonar display.

"There's Jake," Cahill said. "Right where he's supposed to be. All stop."

"The ship's at all stop," Walker said.

"Energize external lights," Cahill said.

"External lights are energized."

As the *Goliath* drifted towards motionlessness, the underside of the *Specter's* hull appeared in a forward-facing camera.

"Secure the side-scan sonar."

"The side scan-sonar is secured," Walker said.

"Deploy all four outboards. Steady us under the *Specter*."

Walker tapped keys, and four small outboard motors with propellers located under each corner of the *Goliath* nudged the ship's mass to motionlessness underneath the submarine. The transport ship's cameras showed the *Specter's* hull above it on a skewed angle.

"We have laser lock," Walker said.

"Run our audio connection through our main speakers. Run the video on console seven."

"I'm sending the audio to the main speakers. Video is coming up on console seven. Do you want me to use the outboards to keep us under Jake?"

"Yes."

Cahill spun towards the screen behind him, and Jake's face appeared while his voice filled the room.

"You found me."

"It was easy. I hope the Russians know where you are, too."

"The helicopters above their surface task force have been painting me with radar for hours. They know where I am."

"Then the question is if they've been able to inform the *Kilo*. Any sign of it coming to periscope depth?"

A French accent filled the space.

"None," Renard said.

The Frenchman's image appeared on the console next to Jake's. Cahill thought he looked more tired than during their last encounter, but he withheld his comments about his boss' appearance.

"I see you have a real-time link with Pierre."

"Of course," Jake said. "There's no sense in pretending that I'm hidden. So I may as well get full use out of being up here."

"I hate to spoil the reunion, but we're racing a clock," Renard said. "The Russians must be losing patience with their *Kilo's* failure to engage Jake, and you have limited time to trap it."

"So how does our plan change, if at all?" Cahill asked.

"Jake increases the bait while you go hunting."

"I'm going to fake a flooding casualty in a few minutes to make sure the *Kilo* knows where I am," Jake said. "I'll flood water into my tanks and run my pumps to push water right back out. I'll have a few guys banging on pipes to simulate damage control."

"Isn't that too obvious?" Cahill asked.

"I don't see that we have an option given the timing," Jake said. "It may be obvious, but the *Kilo's* commander has to respect my flooding casualty as a real possibility."

"He's hungry," Renard said. "He wants vengeance, and he's racing the same clock as you. He'll come for Jake. You just need to remember that you're in hunter submarine mode until you're close enough to him to preclude him attacking you. Then and only then can you shift back to using the full force of the *Goliath*."

"Got it, mate."

"I'm updating your tactical plots with my latest analysis," Renard said.

Cahill called up the plot on a console. The icons remained unchanged, but new lines and arcs came to life.

"The red line shows the most direct route the *Kilo* could be taking towards Jake," Renard said. "It has just over two hours before it can be at the edge of its torpedo range, which is indicated by the red arc I've drawn around the *Specter*."

"What happens if I can't get the mission done before the *Kilo's* within the arc?"

"That's what the next, inner arc is for," Renard said.

Consistent with his flare for drama, his boss invoked the curved line as he spoke.

"That's the limit of the Russian Shkval. I won't subject Jake and the crew of the *Specter* to an underwater rocket. If you track the *Kilo* to within ten miles of Jake, or if you can't find it before the timer runs out on the *Kilo's* direct run to Jake, the mission is over."

"Over?" Cahill asked.

"Yes. You'll flee towards the coast and prepare to abandon your ships in Turkish waters."

"That can't happen," Cahill said. "The Turks can't protect us from the Russians."

"Yeah, isn't that like chasing a bank robber over county lines?" Jake asked. "Aren't the Russians free to pursue us all over the world, after what we did to them?"

"The Turks may not have the force to equal the Russians, and international maritime law is murky," Renard said. "But the complexity of invading a sovereign nation's waters to hunt you would at least cause the Russians to hesitate."

Cahill's optimism lagged that of the Frenchman. He wondered if Renard embellished the safety of Turkish waters.

"There's no progress on removing the minefield or finding us a safe harbor?" he asked.

"Unfortunately not," Renard said.

"Then I need to get moving."

The Frenchman's sagging features darkened.

"Unless you care to retreat now," he said. "This is your last chance to back out of your pending heroic deed. Even knowing your abilities and that of the *Goliath*, I'm hesitant to see you do this."

"No, mate. I'm doing it."

"I own your ship, Terry. My word is final."

"But you wouldn't say no. I know you too well by now."

Renard looked away as he worked a fresh cigarette to his lips and lighted it. Despite noting the intended dramatic pause, Cahill found it soothing. His boss knew how to instill confidence.

"I could decide either way," Renard said. "But I've deferred to your confidence, just as I would with Jake. I can only hope to learn that you are as charmed as he."

"I've heard all his stories, mate. I know he's gifted, but I plan to prove that I'm your worthy commander as well."

"You already have. That's my concern. I don't want to lose you, especially when I see a safer way out."

"But you don't want to abandon your ships."

The Frenchman blew smoke and focused his gaze above the camera that faced him.

"No, I do not."

"Then the time for talking is over."

"Wait!" Jake said.

"What's wrong?" Cahill asked.

"Dolphins."

Cahill felt a dark pang of anxiety at the mention of his aquatic nemeses.

"Are you sure it's them?"

"Antoine has been studying their communications pattern," Jake said. "It's distinct and repetitive. It's them."

"Do you know what they're saying?"

"Antoine's good but not that good."

Cahill heard the *Specter's* sonar guru speaking in the background. Jake excused himself for a quick chat and returned.

"Correction," Jake said. "Antoine thinks that dolphin noises sent in isolation concern information about their location and that exchanges with the *Kilo* are queries and responses about the behavior of a target the dolphins are tracking."

"Which type is he hearing now?"

"It's impossible to tell. The *Kilo's* still too far away to hear if it's responded back to them."

"I hear the dolphins now, too," the sonar operator said. "They just sent out a noise."

"We hear the dolphins on the *Goliath* now, too," Cahill said. "I think that indicates that the *Kilo* has a pretty good chance of knowing where you are. That's what we want."

"But it also means the dolphins are probably coming for me, which means they'll be between you and the *Kilo*. If they tell the *Kilo* about you, you're screwed."

"That's a problem."

"The dolphins will see you," Jake said. "There's no way around that. Nature has made them too good to fool."

"You're right, mate. You need to kill them."

The silence told Cahill he had challenged his colleagues' morality. He realized that nobody, including himself, had considered the dolphins an enemy worthy of destroying until now.

"Let me confer with Antoine," Jake said.

"A disheartening request," Renard said. "But appropriate."

"I know. I felt like a mongrel for saying it."

"You had no choice."

Jake reappeared.

"Antoine needs help solving the range."

"You're stuck where you are," Cahill said. "Let me drive out a few miles and see if we can triangulate the range."

"You won't have time to come back here and tell me what you found."

"Right. Listen for me on the radio for a short-range voice transmission. I'll send you a message when I've got them."

"And send it again as you hear my torpedo getting close to them. I'll need to detonate it by wire. So any real-time data you can give me will be useful."

"You should send two torpedoes–one long and one short, just to be sure."

"Roger that," Jake said. "With what we know now about the dolphins, I see no need to fake my flooding casualty."

"Agreed. Cancel it," Renard said.

"I need to get moving," Cahill said.

"Indeed you do, my friend," Renard said "Remember not to engage the *Kilo* beyond five hundred yards. If you do, you'll be at risk of a torpedo. Within five hundred yards, you'll be protected by the same safeguards that prevent the *Kilo* from shooting itself."

"Don't worry, mate. I'm not getting anyone killed–except those bloody dolphins."

CHAPTER 20

Volkov checked his chart.

The dolphins had located the *Specter*, but so had the fleet. Though he remained below periscope depth, he received the coordinates of his enemy over the low-frequency bandwidth signals that tickled the antenna he floated near the surface.

As his executive officer typed in the fleet's data on the *Specter*, he watched the oval of uncertainty shrink to a singularity.

"The dolphins were accurate," Volkov said. "The limit is our ability to understand them. If you could teach them to communicate with more precision, I could use them to shoot weapons to the limit of my torpedoes."

"That would take months," the trainer said. "Maybe years."

"It's a moot point today," Volkov said. "The *Specter* is out of torpedo range. Eighteen miles.

"That's two hours of driving to reach nominal launch range," the executive officer said. "Alternatively, you could snorkel to achieve greater speed and get there in forty minutes."

"That would give away our position."

"I imagine that the commander of the *Specter* can estimate our exact position already, sir. If he's conservative, he's assumed that we're heading straight for him after shooting at his decoy."

Volkov glared at his chart, trying to surmise the tactics of the *Specter's* commanding officer. The permutations of his enemy's possible intent seemed tortuous.

"I don't want to spend undue time at snorkel depth," he said. "I'll make one rapid trip shallow to grab the updated tactical feed, and then I'll end this. Prepare tube six for the *Specter*."

"Torpedo in the water!" the sonar operator said.

"What bearing?"

"It's from the *Specter*. Zero bearing rate."

"Shooting at us? From that distance? He must be mad, even if he has the vaguest notion of where we are."

"He may have heard a transient noise from us and took a poor guess at our range," the sonar operator said.

"Did you hear any transients from our ship?" Volkov asked.

"No, sir."

"Regardless. I'll turn to verify that the torpedo is far away. Come left, steady course one-two-zero."

"There's a second torpedo, sir! It's from the same bearing."

"How loud?"

"Very faint. I suspect they're both far away, both launched from the *Specter*."

"Time will tell as I drive this new course."

"I could use more speed to drive the bearing and to be sure of the distance, sir."

"Very well. So be it."

He looked to his gray-bearded veteran.

"Bring us to snorkel depth and prepare to snorkel."

The room tilted upward, and the *Krasnodar* rocked. After the veteran raised the snorkel mast, he heard the gentle vibrations of his hungry diesels.

"Make turns for twelve knots," he said.

At his best speed, he watched the lines to the torpedoes fan out and pinpoint the incoming weapons.

"They're far away," he said. "They're from the *Specter*."

The explosion rumbled through his hull, tickling his naked ear. The next boom of thunder followed seconds later.

"This makes no sense," he said.

"I'm confirming," the sonar operator said. "I no longer hear the *Specter's* torpedoes. The detonations were from both its torpedoes. I hear no more torpedoes in the water."

"Mark the location of the detonations on the chart."

The intent and outcome of his adversary crystalized in his mind as red icons marking the exploded warheads appeared.

Glancing up from his console with sullen eyes, the trainer reaffirmed his suspicions.

"Andrei? Mikhail?"

"I am sorry," Volkov said. "The second weapon appears wellplaced."

"My babies?"

"Try to hail them."

The trainer tapped his keys, and the *Krasnodar's* pre-recorded dolphin sounds filled the room. During the sad moments of silence, Volkov looked to his display where the fleet's input to his tactical data feed adjusted the *Specter's* position.

He looked to his gray-bearded veteran.

"Tube six is ready, sir. Other than reaching optimum range, the ship is ready to launch the torpedo."

"If the *Specter* is going to stay at periscope depth and drift, my torpedo won't need to chase it. I can shoot from maximum range. How far are we from maximum range?"

"Half a mile, sir."

A second hail to the dolphins went unanswered.

"My babies."

"I cannot offer you solace," Volkov said. "But I can offer you revenge. I invite you to launch the torpedo. We'll be within range in minutes."

Holding back tears, the trainer looked to him.

"I will do it," the trainer said.

Volkov nodded, and the sonar operator tapped keys to send the launch authority to the trainer's console.

Tasting his vengeance for attacks against his homeland, his submarine, and the dolphins he had grown to respect, he counted the final seconds in his mind.

Then the shrill dissonance of ripping metal stopped him. The staccato spiking screeches resonated around him, and he discerned that the harsh discord arose in front of him.

His first instinct suggested that he had suffered a collision.

"Mother of God!" he said. "Hold your fire."

The trainer froze, and the sonar operator tapped keys to revoke the trigger. Volkok looked for his executive officer, but the man's newfound zeal had propelled him halfway to the forward door to investigate the problem.

Seconds later, the ripping repeated, and a report of flooding in the torpedo room rang through loudspeakers.

"All stop," he said. "Have damage control teams lay to the torpedo room. Raising the periscope."

While his gray-bearded veteran announced the unfolding casualty, he tapped keys to raise his optics and grab a panoramic sweep. As the next volley of shrieks hammered his hull, he ran his eyes over the image. With the lack of a visual object into which he had embedded his bow, he formed a quick theory.

The *Goliath's* cannons.

"Secure snorkeling," he said. "Make your depth thirty meters, smartly."

Another volley ripped metal.

"We're going deeper during a flooding casualty, sir?" the veteran asked.

"To evade cannon fire. Do it!"

The deck dipped, but a ship the size of the *Krasnodar* labored during three more volleys before the shredding subsided. Thinking the worst had passed, Volkov heard a new ripping from behind him.

With his stern pushing down his bow, his propeller rose before it could seek the safer depths. While shallow, the rear of his ship incurred four volleys of pounding before the depths protected it.

But the depths also brought increased water pressure to squeeze the seas into his submarine. The report came from his engineer officer

"Flooding in the engine room! Loss of propulsion!"

Volkov slapped his hand on the nearest officer he could find. The operations officer's young, frightened eyes faced him.

"Lay to the engine room and lead damage control for the flooding while the engineer restores propulsion. The holes will be numerous but small. You can handle this."

As the young officer headed sternward, a sailor entered the control room from the front and presented a mound of metal.

"The executive officer wanted me to show you this, sir."

"Come," Volkov said.

"It's an example of the rounds used against us. He believes they splintered before hitting the water and then hit us with a spreading pattern. We're lucky that most of these didn't penetrate the bilge and create two holes each. The water absorbed most of the energy."

Volkov held the metal and noted that friction had smoothed its edges.

"Thank the executive officer for bringing this to my attention. Return to the torpedo room and assist him."

As the sailor left, the trainer looked at him.

"Can I shoot now?"

Survival had pushed vengeance against the *Specter* from Volkov's mind. His first instinct allowed him retaliation, but wisdom precluded shooting with possible damage to the tube.

"Wait," he said.

The gray-bearded veteran raised a sound-powered phone.

"The executive officer has a status report."

"On the speakers," Volkov said.

The electronic amplification of the bandwidth-limited sound-powered phones made his second-in-command sound a world away.

"Multiple tubes are damaged, including tube six. Do not attempt to launch the weapon in tube six. I repeat–tube six is damaged. Hold your fire from tube six!"

Volkov reached for a microphone.

"Understand tube six is damaged. Holding fire on tube six. Report status of flooding in the torpedo room."

"Water is building in the bilge and appears to be rising slowly. I can't tell yet if the pumps will keep pace. Shoring will be difficult with the numerous holes. I'll need more men to bring towels, bed linen, anything to stuff into the holes."

"Approximately how many holes?"

"Fifty. Maybe sixty. Average diameter is two centimeters."

Volkov looked at the trainer.

"If you are to have your vengeance, we need to stop the flooding. You heard him. Grab ten men and take them to the torpedo room with towels and linen and knives to cut the cloths and to cut through lagging to get to the holes."

The trainer departed, and Volkov raised his microphone.

"Find me useful tubes," he said.

"The torpedo nest is damaged," the executive officer said. "It's obvious that the tubes were the target of the attack. I recommend cutting the wires to our drones and closing the muzzle doors so I can investigate all tubes."

"Cut the wires to all drones and close all muzzle doors. Report to me when you've assessed the tubes."

The veteran waved his phone for Volkov's attention.

"The engineer has a report, sir."

"Put him on the speakers."

"I heard the executive officer's report, sir. The same surgical attack happened back here on our motor. Propulsion is down, and I have approximately thirty holes. I've already sent for extra support from the crew to stuff the holes."

"Can you get me propulsion?"

"I need to open the reduction gears, sir. It's possible, but it will take time–at least an hour. The motor survived, but I've got two holes in the gears. They may have survived, but I can't tell until I'm inside the case. The gears locked up due to shrapnel."

"Is the outboard available?"

"Yes, sir. I can get you a knot and a half with it."

"I'll take it. Deploy the outboard."

He looked to the gray beard.

"Can you get us to twenty meters and hold us with a knot and a half?" Volkov asked.

"If anyone can do it, I can. We've still got enough momentum to come shallow and reduce the flooding. What happens once I've got us there is unknown."

"Make your depth twenty meters."

"New contact, bearing one-six-five," the sonar operator said.

"Submerged or surfaced?"

"Submerged. It just passed through the acoustic layer. I hear hull popping. It's definitely on the way up."

"Designate the new contact as the *Goliath*."

Volkov feared that the transport ship intended to finish him.

He pushed vengeance against the *Specter* behind his need for survival and lifted his microphone.

"Executive officer, I need a heavyweight torpedo ready in a tube now. The *Goliath* is coming for us."

"Tube one, sir! It's just been verified as usable. The hydraulic system's damaged, but we can load a torpedo manually."

"Load tube one with a heavyweight torpedo."

"It will take fifteen minutes. We need to set up the block and tackle system while the men are being sprayed by water."

"Do it in five. Your life depends upon it."

"The *Goliath* just broached, sir," the sonar operator said. "I hear its gas turbines spinning up."

"Its commanding officer thinks we're helpless. He's coming in to finish us off. He'll be surprised to learn that even with the beating we've taken, the *Krasnodar* is still fighting."

"The *Goliath's* gas turbines are online. Its screws are accelerating to flank speed, making turns for thirty-four knots based upon blade rate. Bearing rate is zero. It's coming right for us."

Reluctant to gift his enemy verification of his exact location, Volkov withheld his radio mast below the waves. He looked to his veteran in hopes of a low-frequency update from an attentive fleet.

"Anything yet from the fleet on the *Goliath*?" he asked.

"Yes, sir. Here it comes. *Goliath* is surfaced. Coordinates to follow. Air strike against the *Goliath* is launched, first weapons on target in fifteen minutes. The surface task force is moving in against the *Specter*."

Volkov leaned over a console and called up a screen for manual data entry.

"Read me the *Goliath's* coordinates."

The veteran dictated, and Volkov typed. The icon appeared and Volkov held his breath.

"Mother of God. It's less than five miles away. Has its commanding officer gone mad?"

"If he wanted to shoot a torpedo, he would have already," the veteran said. "We're well within range."

"Any sign of an incoming torpedo?" Volkov asked.

"No, sir," the sonar operator said.

"He can't possibly know that I'm unable to shoot back at him. He can't possibly trust that his aim was that good on my tubes. I'll even have a tube loaded soon."

"Still no sign of a torpedo, sir."

Having seen his adversaries minimize the lethality of their attacks, Volkov wondered if the *Goliath's* commanding officer had disabled but spared the *Krasnodar* out of chivalry. Such a sentiment seemed consistent for a battle in which excessive ordnance had been spent but less than two dozen men had perished.

The theory explained why he continued living, but it didn't explain the *Goliath's* sprint in his direction. Then he considered the air strike and realized that hiding near or under his ship served as an excellent defense for the transport ship.

Tapping his fingers on his console, he attempted to avoid the temptation of accepting the simple answer. His wisdom spurred him to seek something deeper.

An idea began to form but evaporated. Then it came again, survived for a fleeting moment, and then vanished.

Failing to put the idea into words or to frame it as a coherent construct, he found himself holding a fractional thought. Fueled by a combination of paranoia and uncertainty, he let the concept grow into a verbalized question that he hoped would lead to a command.

"How's your depth control?"

"I'm holding a neutral trim," the veteran said. "Just barely, but I'm holding it."

"Then you won't mind if I deprive you of the knot and a half of speed."

"I can manage, as long as you stay shallow."

"Very well. Have the engineer turn the outboard ninety degrees to port. I want him to spin the ship clockwise."

"May I ask why, sir?"

A pang of embarrassment agitated him while he considered

the possibility that the future would prove his suspicions ridiculous.

"The *Goliath* is a transport ship capable of carrying a vessel of our size. I want to complicate that for him, in case that idea is on its commanding officer's mind."

"I will see to it, sir."

"And once you're done," Volkov said. "Have every available man report to the gun locker. He may attempt to board us. Prepare to repel borders."

CHAPTER 21

The *Goliath's* radar data showed Cahill the inverse of his desires.

Where he hoped for clear skies to the north, a swarm of angry Fencer aircraft approached. Where he hoped to see helicopters from the surface fleet to the east, he saw clear skies.

"Have the men start moving backup rounds to the port weapons bay for manual loading."

Walker acknowledged and assigned a sailor to manage the task.

"What will we shoot?" he asked.

"We'll start with the Fencers," Cahill said. "I know we're unlikely to hit, but we might just slow them down."

"Splintering rounds from both cannons?"

"Yes. Prepare to fire one hundred splintering rounds from each cannon."

"The cannons are ready."

"Fire."

The railguns cracked.

"Incoming data feed from Pierre," Walker said. "Helicopters are heading for Jake. Our Ukrainian support crew has them on radar, but they're just over the horizon from our phased-array."

"I'm sure they got nervous after Jake submerged. They're looking for him, and time's his greatest asset. We need to buy him more of it with our cannons."

"But time's working against us. We need to get to the *Kilo* before the Fencers get to us. We need to slow them down."

"I'm more concerned about the *Kilo* if it finds a way to shoot us," Cahill said. "We rained down hell on its tubes, but there's no guarantee that we silenced its torpedoes."

"The fact that it didn't shoot at us yet is a good sign. Four minutes until we're within five hundred yards."

Cahill tapped his sonar supervisor's shoulder.

"Can you hear an incoming torpedo?"

"No, but we're moving so fast that I wouldn't hear one until it goes active."

"At that point it would be too late."

"I know. I'll feel better once we're under that *Kilo*."

"Or within five hundred yards," Cahill said. "I'll feel safe enough when we're protected by torpedo anti-circular run safeguards."

He turned and faced the console that showed Renard's face.

"Any new thoughts?"

"None," Renard said. "God speed. Sprinting towards the *Kilo* is your best tactic."

"I don't suppose now's a good time to lobby for stronger propulsion motors? I've got enough power in me turbines and MESMA system for at least two more knots, but it's wasted."

"Duly noted."

His boss' face froze in pixelated absurdity as Russian jamming took its toll. It then reappeared in its fatigued normalcy.

"What about Jake?" Cahill asked.

"When the helicopters started seeking him, he realized that he could no longer wait for you. He's decided to deviate from the escape plan and take on the Russian fleet himself."

The audacity fit with Cahill's perspective of his colleague.

"I feel bad for the Russian fleet."

"I share your optimism," Renard said. "And you can help him. I see that you now have a helicopter on your radar. I suggest that you divert one of your cannons to his cause."

"Liam, shift the port cannon to the helicopter."

As the railgun sought a new target, Cahill looked at his tactical display. The *Goliath* reached within a mile of his best estimate of the *Kilo*.

He respected the Russian commander's restraint in withholding his masts below the surface. Cahill's ship had no short-range returns on its radar, and he had to guess at his prey's precise location.

His radar did discern aircraft of the incoming strike force. As he tried to count the swarm, he saw one icon disappear.

"We hit a Fencer," Walker said. "But there's too many of them.

Most of them will get through."

"Forget the Fencers," Cahill said. "They're showing that they're not turning back no matter how much we shoot. Turn both cannons to the helicopter."

"I'm aiming both cannons at the helicopter."

The icons of the strike force seemed unstoppable.

"The Fencers are surely coming with anti-submarine weapons," Cahill said. "We need to submerge soon so they don't know where to drop them."

"Let me guide a few rounds into the helicopter for Jake."

"You have twenty seconds. Then we'll need to start defending ourselves below the waves."

The icon of a railgun round intersected with that of the helicopter, and the aircraft fell from radar.

"It's a hit!" Walker said.

"Secure the gas turbines, shift propulsion to the MESMA systems, and prepare to submerge."

The high-frequency whir ebbed.

"The ship is ready to submerge," Walker said.

Cahill offered a parting look to his boss.

"Got to go, Pierre."

"Good luck, my friend."

The Frenchman's face froze as the communications link attempted to frequency-hop around the Russian jamming.

"Submerge the ship," Cahill said. "Make your depth fifty meters. Make turns for fifteen knots."

He grabbed a console for balance during the down angle.

"How's fifteen knots possible submerged?" Walker asked.

"Strain the battery for the extra knot. Every second counts."

"Got it."

"Start listening for torpedoes and for the *Kilo*," Cahill said.

"No sign of torpedoes," the sonar supervisor said. "We're listening for the *Kilo*."

"Flooding? Damage control efforts? Pumps?"

"We'll hear it, Terry. Give us a few moments."

Unable to find patience, he snapped an order.

"Liam, energize the side-scan sonar, full power," he said. "Sweep it in all directions."

"Energizing the side-scan sonar."

"We've got the *Kilo*," the sonar supervisor said. "We hear its outboard motor and we're pinpointing its other sounds. Bearing is three-three-eight."

"Liam, come left to course three-three-eight. Focus the side-scan sonar dead ahead."

Cahill glared at the screen showing the three-dimensional sonic image of the water. His eyes burned.

"Nothing," he said. "We must still be over half a mile away."

"Maybe not," the sonar supervisor said. "We're getting a return from the side-scan sonar."

"Range?" Cahill asked.

"One thousand yards."

"That's our *Kilo*. We're close, but we're still in danger."

He counted seconds as the *Goliath* neared its victim, and the multiple cuts of sonic return created an oblong shape on his display.

"There it is," he said. "I would say the aspect is narrow, except that it's blurry."

"The sounds from the *Kilo* are shifting, too," the sonar operator said. "One second the pumps are loudest. Then the outboard. Then the broadband flooding noise."

Cahill surmised the nature of the oddities.

"I think that mongrel's figured us out."

"You mean that we're coming to grab him?" Walker asked.

"That captain has balls and brains. He's spinning himself in a circle to make it difficult for us."

"Our outboards can manage it though."

"Manually, yes," Cahill said. "But there's nothing automated in our system I know of to deal with this. Damn that bloody bastard. He's going to make us work for it."

"This means we can't take our usual lateral approach, either. We'll need to stop underneath and handle the orientation with the outboards exclusively."

Cahill brooded over the Russian's surprising twist.

"He's doubled the complexity," he said. "We need to get this right in six axes–three-dimensional positioning and three-dimensional rotation. This complicates matters."

"At least he won't kill us," Walker said. "We just crossed within five hundred yards. Torpedoes are no longer a threat."

"Right. Let the crew know where it is and have them prepare for loading operations. This may take some tricky manual work with the presses and multiple eyeballs on cameras."

After Walker spread the word through the primary loudspeaker, Cahill ordered him to slow the *Goliath* to a drift. The forward-scanning sonar placed the *Kilo* one hundred yards away.

"Deploy the outboards," he said. "Energize external lights."

The exterior lights turned the blackness in his unused monitors into ugly pale grays.

"Secure the side-scan sonar," he said. "Energize the upward-scanning sonar."

He was exhilarated when the tactical system's integration algorithms transformed the acoustic return from his scanning sonar into the form of the *Kilo's* stern.

"I'll take manual control from here," he said. "I'm stopping us right underneath that mongrel."

The upward-scanning sonar showed the blurred view of the submarine. Spinning above the *Goliath*, the *Kilo* appeared to leave a sonic trail like a comet. Cahill's quick glances at camera views showed the Russian ship sliding in and out of lights bathing the water above the cargo bed.

"Look at those holes," he said. "Jake's torpedo pounded a dozen wounds straight in, but that thing would still be fighting and running if we didn't hit it, too."

"Jake sure gave it a beating, but it kept fighting," Walker said.

Cahill looked down and tapped an icon.

"I'm shifting us towards the *Kilo's* center of mass."

The focal point of the submarine's rotation appeared to glide over the center of the *Goliath's* cargo bed. He tapped keys that commanded the outboards to flip direction in unison and bring the mighty ship to motionlessness.

"Good job," Walker said. "Not to be downer because I know you just made it look easy, but the hard part comes next."

"It's all a matter of perspective. Coming to forty meters."

"Terry, wait! You forgot to set us into a matching spin!"

"Oh, did I?"

"What are you doing?"

"Just wait."

Cahill watched the *Kilo's* outboard, extending two meters below its engine room, swing towards his rising ship. From the corner of his eye, he saw Walker blush.

"Okay, I understand now."

"And here it comes."

The *Kilo* spun atop the Goliath without incident.

"Damn," Cahill said. "Missed it. Coming to thirty-nine meters."

In a monitor, he saw the outboard clear the *Goliath's* port engine room by less than a foot.

"We'll get it on its next half rotation over the port bow. Coming to thirty-eight meters."

"Why doesn't he just surface?" Walker asked.

"The sea state is calm enough that it doesn't buy him anything, and he may be afraid of friendly fire."

"Here it comes," Walker said. "Turn up the sonar volume."

The distant crunching of metal against metal rang through the sonar loudspeaker as the outboard banged against the *Goliath*. What little remained of the small motor after its first impact snapped when it collided with the starboard bow.

"Why didn't I think of that?" Walker asked.

"You're still learning the art of undersea warfare," Cahill said. "And I have to admit that I didn't think of it until three seconds before I tried it."

"We still need to match the spin, but at least you've got it drifting to a stop."

Cahill tapped keys.

"I'm using all four outboards to twist us to the right. I'm manually matching the *Kilo*."

"High-pressure air," the sonar operator said. "It's blowing its ballast tanks."

"Very well," Cahill said. "So be it. The surface tension will stop his confounded rotating sooner."

The submarine slipped above the cameras' reach.

"You're not worried about aircraft?" Walker asked.

"Yes, I'm worried. But they can only attack with guns unless they're willing to sink their countrymen. And strafing runs are deadly for them, since our cannons will be above the water. Coming to twenty-five meters."

The depth gauge showed the *Goliath* ascending as gray yielded to the shallow sunlight.

"We're at twenty-five meters," Cahill said. "Get the cannons ready."

"They're ready," Walker said. "Just waiting until we're shallow to deploy them."

"The *Kilo's* rotation has stopped," Cahill said. "The loading system can now match its movements in the swells. I'm taking us up. Coming to twenty meters."

As the *Goliath* slipped upward, its cameras and sonar combined to feed data to its automated loading algorithms.

"System-calculated distance from the bed to the cargo's keel is ten meters," Cahill said. "I'm shifting trim control to automatic loading mode, verify a setting of two meters per minute rise rate."

He shot periodic glances at the display to double-check the ship's automation. He admired the *Goliath's* delicate computerized dance of shuffling water fore and aft to keep itself level while shedding water overboard to gain levity.

"I'm slowing the system to one-half meter per minute rise rate," he said.

"Depth is twelve meters," Walker said. "Our sterns are above water. May I attack?"

"Deploy the cannons. Take control of the air battle, and keep

Jake in mind."

"It's a swarm of Fencers out there," Walker said. "I need to start shooting to hold them back."

"Very well, damn it. Jake's on his own."

The railguns cracked as Cahill absorbed the illusion of the *Kilo* falling through shimmering rays into the *Goliath's* waiting cradle. Sensors registered pressure on the bed.

"Contact!" he said. "Engaging the presses."

Cameras caught the hydraulic arms rotating downward and pinning the submarine.

"We got one," Walker said. "Scratch one Fencer."

"Excellent! Secure the cannons. I'm submerging the ship."

"Terry," Walker said. "The hatch is opening. The Russians are trying to escape."

"I'm still submerging. I'm sure they'll figure it out and change their minds."

"They took the hint. They're closing the hatch. I suggest you try to get a message to Pierre."

"Connect me."

"Nothing. No real-time connection is possible. The Fencers are jamming us."

"I'm sure he's watching on satellite."

The *Goliath* dragged its cargo under the waves.

"I'm taking us to twenty meters," Cahill said.

"No deeper?" Walker asked.

"I don't want to drown our new guests, and I'm going to porpoise our way out of here to help Jake."

"The port cannon can't cycle fast enough."

"I know. We'll use the starboard cannon only."

"I'll ignore the Fencers then," Walker said. "I assume we won't be surfaced long enough at any given moment for them to shoot."

"Very well. I'm coming to fourteen knots and placing a ten-degree down angle on us to elevate our cannons."

While he braced against the dip, the pressure sensors registered increased force as water pushed the *Kilo* against the bed.

"Coming to course one-nine-zero," Cahill said. "We're making straight for the Bosporus. Liam, fire two splintering rounds from the starboard cannon at helicopters as I porpoise. Coming to twelve meters."

He elevated the *Goliath* to lift its railguns into the air.

"I've got a helicopter on radar," Walker said. "Shooting two rounds from the starboard cannon."

The railgun cracked twice.

"Securing the starboard cannon," Walker said. "It's stowed."

"Coming to twenty meters," Cahill said. "How long until our rounds will require terminal homing?"

"Twenty seconds."

"Coming to twelve meters. Guide the existing rounds in flight and send out two new rounds."

As the railgun fired, the phased-array radar picked up the distant rounds as they passed wide of the helicopter.

"Miss," Walker said. "You need to shorten this porpoising cycle."

"I will. Coming to eighteen meters."

Staccato puncturing sounds pelted the hull, and Cahill grabbed a microphone while the ship submerged.

"Damage report. What's been hit?"

Silence.

"Damage report," he said. "What's been hit?"

"Twenty seconds until the rounds require terminal guidance," Walker said.

"Damn it. Coming to twelve meters."

"This is starboard weapons bay. One of those Fencers made a run at me. The cannon took a beating. The barrel's got holes in it. The feed is torn up pretty bad. It's out of commission."

"Get out of there and seal the compartment behind you."

The icons of the distant rounds and the helicopter merged.

"Hit!" Walker said.

"Excellent!" Cahill said. "Coming to twenty meters."

"The Fencers are still following us," Walker said. "They may try to strafe us again if you keep giving them a predictable course. There's just too many of them."

"I need to head towards Jake to protect him. I've still got a cannon."

"You need to protect your crew. You were three yards away from losing a man instead of a cannon."

Cahill paused for several breaths to let the adrenaline subside.

"Let's stay submerged but change course before heading towards Jake to see if we can confuse these Fencers."

CHAPTER 22

As the low-frequency radio wire absorbed Renard's feed, Jake oversaw two French sailors typing coordinates of the Russian surface combatants. Updates entered the Subtics system, and he assigned weapons to the closest combatants.

"Assign tube one to the *Slava*."

Remy tapped keys.

"Tube one is assigned to the *Slava*. We're still out of torpedo range."

"It's coming for us, Antoine. Like every one of them, it's coming right for us because the Russians think we're trying to run. But we're going to surprise them."

"Perhaps we should instead be doing what they think we're doing. I see nothing wrong with trying to leave."

"No, Antoine," Henri said. "Jake's right. Pierre and I agree. His latest feed says a dozen helicopters are already at the Bosporus. We wouldn't be able to get by their screen even if Terry can coerce the *Kilo* into turning off the mines."

"A railgun and a Phalanx system pointed at your hull can make people behave as you would like them to," Remy said.

Jake drew a breath to reply, but his lead mechanic continued arguing in his defense.

"The decisions are final," Henri said. "We're not challenging an army of helicopters. Less than a handful is remaining close to the ships in defense."

"A handful, you say?" Remy asked. "Five torpedoes will kill us as quickly as would a dozen. What's going on with the negotiations? Shouldn't this be over now that Terry has that *Kilo*?"

"Julien, while Antoine whines, assign tube two to the *Krivak*," Jake said.

"I'm not whining. You know me better than that. You need me listening to the water anyway. Julien can handle our weapons."

"I meant no insult, Antoine. I'm just trying to make light of this. God willing, this will be the greatest standoff of all time."

"Or we'll all be punished for our collective arrogance."

Jake looked towards the priest and shrugged.

"Are we facing karma? Justice for our bravado?"

"Priests aren't oracles, and karma is outside my area of expertise," Andrew said. "I can't say what the outcome will be, other than to say that I believe you're of sound mind and temperament."

"You understand the magnitude of what I'm doing, right?"

"I think so. You're putting a thousand lives at risk."

Jake tallied the potential upcoming death toll. The *Slava* contained five hundred men, the *Krivak* had two hundred, and each missile boat contained sixty.

A dark voice within him reminded him to add the *Specter's* crew of thirty.

"More or less," he said. "You got a prayer for this?"

"I've been rolling through them for the last twenty minutes."

"Keep it up."

"Can I have a minute please?"

Jake walked around the table and crouched at the priest's knees.

"I would like to offer the sacrament of reconciliation to anyone who wants it. Can I do it in your stateroom?"

"You mean confession?"

"Yes."

The request struck Jake as incongruent with the situation, but he had brought the priest to let him exercise independent judgment.

"How long would it take?"

"A few minutes per person, unless they have a lot to confess."

"You'll have to make it fast so that my guys aren't busy confessing instead of fighting."

"I know ways to keep it short."

"Three minutes per man?"

"It will be tough, but yes."

"You don't mind if I ask why you're doing this now?"

"I'm offering a chance for absolution of sins. It could make the difference between entering God's Kingdom or not."

"This is just for my Catholic sailors?"

He knew he'd asked a good question when Andrew blushed.

"I'm wrestling with that."

"I didn't know you could give sacraments to non-Catholics."

"I can't, except in exceptional circumstances. When the circumstances are exceptional, I can expand the invitation."

"What defines 'exceptional'?"

The priest cleared his throat.

"In our case, it's the danger of imminent death. Maybe you can tell me how much danger we're in."

The discussion bothered Jake on multiple levels, but he knew the answer the priest needed.

"I'll expand the invitation for you."

He turned to walk back to the tactical chart.

"Jake?" Andrew asked.

"What?"

"Do you want the sacrament?"

"I wouldn't know what to confess, and now's not the time to muddle through it. If your god's really there, he's going to have to keep me alive a little longer if he gives a damn about me."

He returned to the table and stooped beside the sailors to verify that they entered the correct targeting data. Recognizing one as a Catholic, he shared Andrew's offer and told him to pass it on to all shipmates of Christian faith.

"Tube five has been reloaded with a heavyweight torpedo," Henri said. "The team is loading tube six. You'll have heavyweight torpedoes in all tubes within five minutes."

"Very well, Henri. Julien, assign tube three to the northern *Dergach*. Assign tube four to the southern *Dergach*."

As the young technician obeyed, Jake stepped beside Henri at his ship's control panel. The *Specter's* hydraulic, high-pressure air, mast controls, major electric indicators, and ballast systems sprawled before him like an anatomical chart.

"Do I need to slow down?"

"You can hold eighteen knots for thirty-two minutes," Henri said. "You'll have nothing left for evading weapons, though."

"I need speed now. I won't be evading anything later."

"You sound like a different man from the leader I've followed during the last decade."

"This is a different situation. It's the first time I've conceded that we can't win. I'm playing for a stalemate."

The swiveling toad-head in the corner of his eye caught his attention. He suspected that a helicopter's sonar pulse had bounced off his ship's hull, but his expert allayed his fear.

"The ships have begun anti-submarine evasion legs," Remy said. "I'm analyzing, but it looks like all of them are turning."

"Very well, Antoine. That complicates things, but it's expected. Keep track of which ship is which if they cross."

"Their sonar systems are shifting to short-range searches."

"They're hedging their bets that I decided to come for them. They've got all bases covered."

"I recommend going below the acoustic layer," Remy said.

"You'd have trouble tracking our targets."

"I'm barely tracking our targets now. We're at the limits of the data we can manage. Too many fast ships. Too much maneuvering. Too much guesswork on which torpedoes would hit which ships if launched."

"I get it that you're not starving for data, but you would be if we went below the layer."

"Pierre's data will guide us."

"It would be slow and delayed," Jake said.

"It beats being found above the layer and killed."

Jake walked to the charting table and noticed his proximity to the Russian fleet. The closest ship entered the edge of his torpedoes' reach.

"I agree. Henri, make your depth three hundred meters, smartly. Get us down there."

"Making my depth three hundred meters."

Jake braced against gravity.

"Tube six is loaded with a heavyweight torpedo," Henri said. "All tubes are flooded and equalized."

"Very well, Henri. Now prepare all remaining mines for deployment in surface mode, timers set to disarmed. I'll deploy them when we're steady below the layer."

Henri tapped a sequence of images.

"All mines are ready to deploy in surface mode, timers set to disarmed," he said. "You're sure you want them disarmed?"

"Yes."

"Your reach to arm them with our sonar system will be limited to six to seven miles."

"That's good enough. It's the threat that counts."

"You're the boss. Depth is two hundred meters on the way to three hundred meters."

"Very well. Keep us on this aggressive down angle. Level us off hard when you get us on depth."

A red diode shone on the Frenchman's panel.

"I've lost wire communications," Henri said.

"It will come back. Our floating antenna is adjusting to our depth excursion."

Jake summoned two young sailors from their seats at consoles back to the table.

"You're going to have to enter data and enter it fast when we get our communications back. We just passed below the layer, and even Antoine will be lucky to hear the ships."

His stomach fell as the deck leveled.

"Steady on three hundred meters," Henri said.

"We're below the layer," Remy said. "I still hear the variable depth sonar from the *Slava*. It's below the layer, too."

"How strong is it?"

"Low power level. It's still far away."

"By the time it could find us, this will be over," Jake said. "You can use the *Slava's* variable depth sonar to help target it."

"Communications are back," Henri said. "Data is coming."

Freeing his young sailors to enter the ships' locations into the Subtics system, Jake sat, submitted the *Specter's* coordinates, and invoked the icon of a deployed mine.

"Henri, deploy mine three."

The mechanic tapped a monitor, and Jake watched the representation of a mine strapped to one of the submarine's belts shift from a filled-in green form to a dotted outline.

"Mine three is deployed," Henri said.

"Helicopter dipping sonar," Remy said. "Bearing one-eight-eight. Medium signal strength, and it's below the layer."

"Stay cool, everyone," Jake said. "Helicopters can get really close without actually finding us, and there's no sense in trying to outmaneuver them. We're staying on course."

"We're passing the closest point of approach to the lead ship," a young sailor said. "It's a *Grisha* eight miles off our port side."

"Very well," Jake said. "Julien, assign tube five to the *Grisha*. Assign tube six to the *Buyan*."

"We're half a mile from mine three," Henri said.

"Very well, Henri. Deploy mine four."

"Mine four is deployed."

An icon on a digital belt around the *Specter* became a dotted outline, and Jake submitted the coordinates. He stood, turned, and surveyed the room. Remy's young apprentice announced his latest update.

"The *Buyan* is in torpedo range," Julien said.

"Helicopter dipping sonar," Remy said. "Bearing three-four-one. Medium signal strength, but stronger than last time."

"Can they detect us?" Jake asked.

"Less than fifty percent probability, but possible."

"Stay calm," Jake said.

"We're half a mile from mine four," Henri said.

"Very well, Henri. Deploy mine five."

"Mine five is deployed."

Jake tapped the ship's coordinates into the system to flag the location of his mine.

"The *Krivak* is within weapons range," Julien said.

Studying the chart, Jake saw a need to adjust his course to maximize the number of targets he could hit while making sure the huge *Slava* remained his primary prize.

"Henri, come right to course two-nine-five."

"Coming right to course two-nine-five."

"That should get you within eight miles of the *Slava* in two minutes if it doesn't change course," Remy said.

"We're half a mile from mine five," Henri said.

"Very well, Henri. Deploy mine six."

"Mine six is deployed. The first mine belt is empty."

"The southern *Dergach* is within torpedo range," Julien said.

Before Jake could acknowledge the young sailor, he heard a haunting, distant whistle ringing throughout the room.

"Helicopter dipping sonar," Remy said. "Bearing two-six-two. High signal strength. This is bad, Jake."

"That's what I just heard on the hull, right?"

"Yes. We're in danger."

Unsure if an air-dropped torpedo fell towards him, Jake assessed his options. He needed to reach the *Slava* to give his attack full teeth but knew that helicopters were unshakeable.

"Henri, all ahead flank, make your depth fifty meters, fast!"

The world tilted upward and rumbled.

"I'm taking us above the layer to buy time while the helicopter looks for us below the layer," Jake said.

"But you've just exposed us to every ship's bow sonar," Remy said. "There's at least three of them with high probabilities of detecting us."

"I understand, Antoine. Get the sonar system loaded with the order to arm the mines, maximum transmit power."

"I'm preparing the sonar system to arm the mines, maximum transmit power."

"We're in torpedo range of the *Slava*!" Julien said.

"We're also a blob of bright green dots on the *Slava's* sonar system," Remy said. "We are geo-located. We are an easy target. We are found. I'm sure of it!"

"Game over," Jake said. "Time for the final move. Henri, open the muzzle doors to all tubes. Prepare all weapons to swim out to their assigned targets."

The Frenchman tapped a sequence of icons.

"All weapons are ready. I can launch all of them with a single command upon your order."

"Not yet. Hold your fire. Surface the ship."

"Passing fifty meters towards the surface," Henri said. "Forty meters. Thirty meters."

"Raise the radio mast and snorkel masts."

"Raising the radio mast and snorkel masts. Passing ten meters."

"Hold on everyone!" Jake said.

He clinched himself over the back of a seat as the deck lurched, leveled, and bobbed. Recovering his balance, he tapped an icon to raise his periscope and grab a panoramic view.

Two small ships dotted the horizon, a veering helicopter appeared frozen in flight, and the huge hull of the *Slava* cruiser spanned five degrees of azimuth.

"Any incoming torpedoes?"

"No, thank God," Remy said. "I hope Pierre is watching us."

"He is," Jake said. "He knows what to do."

The loudspeaker delivered the Frenchman's voice.

"Indeed I do," Renard said. "Stand down, Jake."

Jake snapped his jaw towards a display and saw his mentor. Receiving a real-time feed in the midst of the Russian task force suggested the welcomed oddity of discontinued jamming.

"Pierre?"

"Stand down," Renard said. "I repeat–stand down."

Jake straightened his back, twisted his torso, and yelled.

"Check fire, all tubes! Check fire! Check fire! Everyone show me your hands in the air."

As he scanned the room to verify that his team had transformed into open-palmed statues, he heard hovering helicopters' rotor wash whipping water outside his hull.

"What's going on, Pierre?" he asked.

"It's over."

"You're sure?"

"You sought a standoff, and you found one. Well done."

"So now what? Am I going to die here, or did you manage to pull off your magic?"

The Frenchman blew smoke and squinted.

"Your lack of faith in my skills offends me."

Relief flooded Jake's tense body.

"So we're okay, then?"

"Jake," Renard said. "Shame on you, my friend, if you thought that I would ever fail you in a negotiation of this magnitude."

CHAPTER 23

Jake hunched over the console.

"You're sure?" he asked.

"Yes," Renard said. "The Russians have agreed to a ceasefire, and you're ordered to shut your outer doors immediately."

"Henri!" Jake said.

"Yes, I heard. I'm shutting all the outer doors."

"Get Doctor Tan up here, too."

"I understand your caution," Renard said. "But I don't think that will be necessary."

"I don't want to piss them off for lack of being able to talk to them."

"Don't be surprised if they never hail you," Renard said. "They'll likely avoid communicating with you. Consider it the proverbial cold shoulder, so to speak. And I'm sure they have English translators aboard in case they decide to give you orders."

Jake found the prediction odd, but it made sense as he digested it.

"Fine. But I still want my translator. What else are the terms of the ceasefire?"

"You must remain surfaced and head directly to the Bosporus. I recommend that you alter course now as a gesture of compliance."

He checked his chart.

"Henri, come right to course zero-five-five."

"Coming to course zero-five-five."

"Very well. Prepare to snorkel."

He heard the induction mast rise, and then he ordered the *Specter's* diesel engines to propel the submarine forward and recharge its batteries.

"All ahead two-thirds," he said.

"Coming to all ahead two-thirds," Henri said.

"Is ten knots okay?" Jake asked.

"It's fine," Renard said. "Your speed wasn't specified in the agreement, but faster is better since I'm sure they wish to be rid of you as much as you wish to leave."

"What's the plan once I'm at the Bosporus?"

"Terry will release the *Kilo* to be towed to Sevastopol. He'll then take you into his cargo bed and escort you out behind Russian minesweepers."

"Sounds too good to be true."

"Don't be fooled into thinking this is a goodwill exercise," Renard said. "This is a hastily designed business agreement that could crumble under a false move. In fact, I hate to consider the outcome had you surfaced outside of torpedo range of the *Slava*. The tangible threat to the flagship was vital."

Jake tried to picture the intricacies of give and take that his mentor had masterminded.

"I figured that my showing up with an itchy trigger finger counted for something."

"More than you care to know. It might have been the shortest ceasefire in modern history had you failed to deliver the threat of sinking the cruiser along with its escorts."

"I didn't plan on failing."

"Don't be surprised if a task force shadows you on your way out. In fact, you may need to remain extra vigilant to avoid colliding with the *Slava*. Don't let yourself be damaged by a spiteful maneuver that could be claimed as an accident."

"I won't."

He wondered how close he had come to death.

"So, when was this really over? When was I safe?"

"You mean when did the Russians agree to the ceasefire?"

"Yeah."

"Roughly about the time I saw a helicopter hovering over you while another joined it to finalize a tandem targeting solution."

"So, I was going to be dead in about ninety seconds?"

"You're not complaining, are you? I left you plenty of time."

"No, but I'm left wondering how you did it."

His mentor cleared his throat.

"This will be best discussed in private."

"Henri," Jake said. "Keep us on course and speed. Take periscope sweeps every five minutes. Call me if we're hailed or if you see anything you don't like."

In the solitude of his stateroom, Jake found the priest.

"I assume we're going to live?"

"Yeah. I figured the rumor had spread throughout the ship by now, but I see that you've been locked up in here."

"I finished taking confessions and decided to stay here."

"Can you do me a favor and make sure everyone knows what's going on? Henri's running the show in the control room so that I can talk to Pierre in private. He can give you the details."

"Sure. I'll make sure everyone is okay."

"Sounds like what a naval chaplain would do."

"We don't just read books and preach the Gospels."

Jake noticed his hands shaking and sat on them. He wondered if he would benefit from counseling.

"When you're done with the rest of the crew..."

"Yes?"

"Uh, never mind."

After Andrew departed, Jake opened his laptop and greeted his mentor.

"We're alone," he said.

"Good," Renard said.

"So, how'd you bail me out of this?"

"Miss McDonald came to our aid, through unofficial channels, of course. She used a mix of threats and enticements to secure your escape from the Black Sea."

"If I know you, you've had this move in your back pocket since the beginning."

The Frenchman smirked.

"I left it as an open possibility when I last saw her."

"She had a plan in her back pocket, then?"

"I'm sure she did."

Jake realized that his mastery of deadly warships seemed meaningless compared to the wielding of political clout.

"What did she do?" he asked.

"She offered cash as recompense for damages, cash as recompense to the families of the deceased, assurances to keep the United States out of the Crimea issue publicly, and the pulling back of the threat to the Russian fleet that you and Terry posed."

"Wow."

"She has growing power that's becoming hard to measure."

"She called up some guy in Russia and bought our way out?"

"It wasn't that simple. I believe she's communicating with a governor of rising power who runs the state in the region that controls the sea. She's positioning herself as an ally with him as a hedge in case he wins the next presidential election. But she's also working through the United Nations."

"Directly?"

"Doubtful. Between her growing power and her desire to exert control from a distance, she makes people work on her behalf. In this case, her agent positioned her as a neutral ombudsman to the United Nations. Her claim is that we, the unruly terrorists, approached her to broker the peace, hiding the fact that she has a longstanding relationship with us, of course."

Jake ran dollar values in his head, counting the cost of the damage he had inflicted.

"And supposedly the Russians believe that the group that just attacked them was willing to pay for the damages? There's no way. That had to cost more money than the value of the *Specter* and *Goliath* combined."

"They're not stupid," Renard said. "The money is coming from a mix of public and underground sources that Miss McDonald had lobbied prior to asking us to undertake this attack. The Russians can surmise this, but the local governor will play along because he needs the money. Crimea is a money pit."

"She must have really wanted this political win if she was willing to round up so much cash."

Renard blew smoke and tightened the crow's feet beside his steel blue eyes.

"She and I have learned to read each other over the years. I estimated three to four billion dollars total cost for this stand-off scenario when I first assessed this mission."

"So that's it? Money, promises, threats. Are there any rules of engagement, or disengagement, to be specific? There must be more rules to this that I need to follow in the next days and weeks."

"Indeed. You need to vanish after Terry loads you and stay vanished so that the Russians can claim victory. You'll pass through the Bosporus and Dardanelles submerged, but you'll have Russian minesweepers escorting you to protect you from interference."

"That's going to be tough, even with an escort."

"I have faith in you, my friend. Rather, I have faith in Terry, since he'll be driving."

"How's he doing?"

"Ask him yourself. I'll establish a communications bridge."

Renard rolled his shoulder in front of his face as he reached for an adjacent console. Ignoring Jake, he held a brief talk with the Australian and then aimed his nose at the screen.

"We're bridged," he said. "Go ahead and call him up."

"Okay. Give me a second."

Jake tapped keys, and Cahill's face appeared on the console beside that which held the Frenchman's visage.

"I heard you did great work, mate. Gutsy stuff."

"I was just about to update Jake on your work. Granted, you faced only one submarine as opposed to an entire fleet, but you managed to take it with you as a trophy."

"Right, but you're making me give it back," Cahill said. "I was just about to force it to escort me through the minefield."

"That would have been a battle of wills that I'm relieved you didn't need to face," Renard said. "I fear its commanding officer would have resisted you."

"But we don't have to worry about that, thanks to Jake."

"Thanks to Olivia, really, from what I hear," Jake said.

"Right, mate. How bad does this put us in her debt?"

Renard blew smoke out the side of his mouth.

"Not at all, per my reckoning," he said. "She knew that she was sending us into a sea with a solitary chokepoint blocking our exit. Though I doubted that the Russians would have the audacity to mine it shut, I considered the option."

"Without telling us about it," Jake said.

"Though it happened, it honestly wasn't a high enough probability in my mind prior to the mission. I had only directional thoughts about it, but grant me credit for having prepared Miss McDonald for the possibility."

As the room rocked in a deep swell, a rapid knock preceded the door swinging open, and the priest stuck his head in the room.

"Henri says that the *Slava* turned its cannon towards us. He thinks it's worth your attention."

"I'll be back, guys."

He darted from the stateroom and slid by the priest in the passageway. When he reached the control room, the mechanic met him on the elevated conning platform at the periscope control panel.

"Andrew tells me you've got a concern with a cannon?"

"It's not quite pointing at us, but it's close. Would you like to look for yourself? I've got the periscope pointed at it."

"Sure."

"The *Slava's* captain is just flexing his muscle."

Jake realized that he needed Renard's guidance. He reached for images on a screen and invoked the Frenchman's face.

"In case you didn't hear, the *Slava* just rotated its cannon about five to ten degrees in front of my bow."

"You're sure it's not pointing at you?"

"It's close, but not that close. I'm sure. I'm tempted to open an outer door and show that every action brings a reaction."

"Don't! You must remain meek."

"Then someone had better be speaking on my behalf. Who's talking to the Russians now?"

"One of Miss McDonald's officers, through a United Nations representative. I can tell you no more about the person's identity."

"Can you get him–or her–to deal with this?"

"Yes. A moment please. I must put you and Terry on hold."

Renard's screen went dark, and Jake shifted his conversation to his colleague.

"What's your status?" he asked.

"Just waiting for you and your entourage," Cahill said. "Tight lipped these mongrels are. I didn't try to hail me newest friends in the *Kilo*, but they haven't made the slightest peep either."

"How's your ship and the crew?"

"I had only the one bad injury when I took a shell in me port weapons bay. I just had him picked up in a Turkish helo that Pierre arranged."

"He's got clout, doesn't he?"

"He surely does."

"What about the *Goliath*?"

"In addition to the port weapons magazine and the damned dolphins flooding the bridge, they mangled me starboard cannon with a strafing run."

"If you'd ever figure out how to stop weapons other than by putting your ship in front of them, you'd stop bruising it."

From the corner of his eye, Jake saw the *Slava's* cannon rotate away. Renard then appeared.

"Your problem with the *Slava* should be handled," he said.

"It is. No more cannon threat. Thanks."

"You should also be nearing visual range of Terry."

"Are you that dot I see coming over the horizon on me radar?"

"Probably," Jake said.

"When do I let go of me *Kilo*?"

"After towing lines are made up to the *Krivak*," Renard said. "That's the ship that's towing it back."

"I'm really going to do this without talking to any of the Russians?" Cahill asked.

"Count your blessings," Renard said. "God willing, you'll suffer nothing but boredom until I meet you in Toulon."

"Toulon?" Jake asked.

Renard pressed a cigarette into an ashtray.

"You missed much of the dialogue while Terry and I were nervously awaiting your final confrontation with the Russians. As part of staying in hiding while the Russians spin the international story to their desires, you'll have to stay submerged even after the Bosporus. You're not going to be able to transit the Suez."

"I asked him if we could just keep going and pass through Gibraltar," Cahill said. "But he insisted on stopping in Toulon."

"I have strong connections there where I can hide both ships under covered wharves while tending to our repairs."

"Repairs and upgrades," Cahill said.

"Yes. Upgrades, too. I promised Terry stronger motors. He'll be pushing thirty-seven knots the next time you deploy."

Jake felt an urge to ask when that might be, but the exhaustion of the subsiding adrenaline left him uncaring.

"So we're submerged all the way to Toulon?"

"Indeed. But I will arrange for recreational activities when you get there. I'll fly in the wives, and we'll make a vacation of it."

"What about Terry and the other bachelors?"

"They'll enjoy the wine and the sun. Don't you worry, I've got one important activity planned that I know you'll like."

"What's that?"

"Team building. We're climbing Sainte Victoire."

CHAPTER 24

Oscillating between sullenness and anger, Volkov stood atop the *Krasnodar's* conning tower. Enclosed in its bridge, he and his executive officer stood with a conscripted lookout, using their elevated view to verify line handling between the submarine's crew and the sailors of the *Krivak* frigate.

A skiff from the surface combatant cut its engines and drifted between the *Goliath's* rakish catamaran hulls. A sailor perched on the watercraft's prow tossed a ball to sailors standing on his rounded bow. After fielding the throw, the handlers pulled the rope attached to the orb up the rounded hull, dragging a nylon line behind it.

Wrapping figure eights around the submarine's cleat, the sailors readied Volkov's vessel for towing. A report from the bridge-to-bridge radio reached his executive officer.

"We're ready, sir."

"Very well."

He turned and glared into one of the *Goliath's* external cameras, lifted his palms, and shrugged. The executive officer nodded towards the transport ship.

"Are you sure you don't want to hail him and tell him to wake up and release us?"

"I have orders to avoid radio contact with the commanding officers of both hostile vessels, and I don't feel like giving him the satisfaction of hearing my voice."

"There were no deaths on his ship or ours, sir. You'd think we could hold a civil conversation, submariner to submariner."

"He killed nearly thirty of our countrymen. We lost too many aviators and other good men who were simply doing their duty. And the disruption to the economy of Crimea is chaotic. There are already riots and rekindled separatist demonstrations. He's no saint."

"His impact on Crimea proves how important our mission was to protect its lifelines."

"The mission was my failure."

The executive officer gave an earnest stare.

"Our mission was a failure, but we were not failures. You were not a failure. You fought with skill and tenacity against a vicious ambush. The admiralty must see this."

"The admiralty will gloss over my actions and grade me upon the results."

"Not if I can help it. I don't know if my family's political reach can place your heroism in the proper perspective, but I will do everything in my power to help."

For the first time, Volkov appreciated his late-blooming executive officer's connections.

"I won't be so humble as to refuse," he said. "I thank you for your offer. But I suspect that my fate is my fate, and I expect to be relieved of command upon return to port."

"Sir?"

"I pushed my ship and crew too far into danger and made us a liability."

"The trap you fell into is only evident in hindsight. But when you review the clues you had at your disposal, it was unpredictable that we'd end up in that cargo bed. You can't blame yourself."

"I do, and they will."

"But even if you grant that, you were a mitigated liability. The aircraft were still able to strafe the *Goliath* without harming us. And you had me convinced that you would have never turned off the mines, no matter the threat."

Volkov checked his heart for a truth that remained unsettled.

"I'd like to think I would have remained stalwart against the threats of the *Goliath*, but I fear I would have conceded to spare the lives of my men."

"No, sir. You would have called his bluff. He and the captain of the *Specter* have armed their ships and formulated their tactics to minimize the loss of human life. They wouldn't have drowned us. They're not saints, but they're not monsters."

"Thankfully, we'll never have to find out how far he would have taken it."

He reflected upon the *Goliath's* commanding officer. Though he was a mercenary, Volkov believed that legitimate nations dictated and supported his actions, making him a fellow warrior. He doubted he would forgive him for destroying assets under his guard and for killing innocent men, but he respected his courage and skill.

"And I'm not going to hail him," he said. "He knows what to do. Let him do it."

"You're right. Take a look, sir."

As the hydraulic presses rolled back from his submarine, Volkov noticed the subtle creeping of the sea up the transport ship's side. The water lapped the *Krasnodar* with its undulations, and the *Goliath* became a semi-sunken vessel.

A small cauldron of churning whiteness formed behind the escort *Krivak*, raising the rope from the water. As tension wrung droplets from the nylon, he saw a laminar wake ripple from his waterline. The ship that had held him captive slipped behind him while the frigate pulled him towards the awaiting formation of the *Slava*-class cruiser and its entourage of missile boats.

"Good riddance," he said.

He gazed beyond his stern and saw the railguns of his former captor jutting through the waves. The *Specter* entered his field of view as it circled towards the empty cradle. A modern *Dergach*-class hovercraft lingered to supervise the eviction operation, and as he shifted his gaze to the west, he saw a pair of Fencers offering airborne eyes over the ships.

Beyond his departing enemies, three of his country's minesweepers marched in formation through the abandoned delta that gave way to the Bosporus. Becoming dots on the horizon, helicopters swept for mines ahead of the ships.

Since his country had deployed and mapped the field, he knew that the cleanup effort focused on retrieving the unused ordnance for future use. The slowness of forward progress indicated the added caution with which his nation's politicians had ordered the incident-free eviction of the tandem mercenary menace.

"Don't you hope that a stray mine blows them to hell, sir? I mean, accidents happen."

"I've already heard from three layers in of my chain of command that there will be no accidents during this eviction."

"This doesn't feel like justice. We're letting them leave after what they did?"

"I've been told that the settlement was lucrative."

"We're too great a nation for our compliance to be bought."

"True. But we're also too great a nation to ignore a generous gesture that is supported by multiple nations of significant power. There's careful politicking occurring beyond our comprehension."

"Perhaps my father will know. I'm sure he's been worried and inquiring."

"Call him. I'll send for the global satellite phone."

The executive officer's face brightened and then grew stern.

"I would love to, but I don't want to abuse my privilege of rank. If I call, I would like every man to call, and I will go last, unless you wish to."

Volkov narrowed his eyes.

"Where have you been for the last year and a half? Until we absorbed that torpedo hit, you presented yourself as a much less capable man."

"Mortal fear, sir. I was reborn when that torpedo hit us and we survived. I didn't plan this. It just happened."

"But you're exercising qualities I didn't know you had. You're showing judgment, courage, foresight, tactical ability... I gave up training you a year ago because you were unresponsive."

"I admit to being lazy because I didn't know any better, but that's changed now."

"I'm still stymied by how you've gained such experience without demonstrating it."

The executive officer shrugged.

"It was easy, sir. I may have been lazy, but I couldn't help myself from learning by watching you."

Unsure how to respond, Volkov nodded his head in a gesture of respect and appreciation. He lifted a microphone to his mouth.

"Control room, bridge," he said.

"Bridge, control room," the gray beard said.

"Have the satellite mobile phone sent to the bridge and set up a rotation for each man to have one minute of liberty to call home."

"Right away, sir!"

The echoing clang of a young sailor's boots against metal rungs rose from underneath the grate at Volkov's feet. He stepped back, opened the trap door, and pinned it against a latch. The crewman climbed through and offered the phone.

"No, I will go last," Volkov said. "Make your call. Mind you, the executive officer and I will be listening to make sure you share nothing confidential. Tell your loved ones that you are alright, but share nothing of the ship's location, actions, or condition."

"Yes, sir."

"You'll brief the next man on the rules of communication before he uses the phone?"

"Yes, sir."

"And so on and so forth."

"Yes, sir."

"Make your call."

While eager-eyed sailors paraded to the bridge, vented their emotions, and then scampered back into the *Krasnodar*, Volkov heard a crackling voice in a bridge-to-bridge radio. He recognized the frigate's commanding officer, a man with whom he had consumed respectable volumes of vodka and beer after training exercises.

"I have good news, Dmitri."

"You're buying the drinks tonight? I could benefit from ingesting my own body weight in alcohol."

"Well, it's true that I will buy, after what you've been through. It was a stressful mission for me, but I didn't take any damage. I can't imagine what it was like for you."

"I'll tell you about it tonight."

"I look forward to it. But that's not the news."

"What is it then?"

"My helicopter has found your dolphins."

"That's impressive."

"Right where you lost track of them."

"You're sure it's them?"

He likened himself to an idiot the moment after he asked.

"I'm quite sure they're the only dolphins wearing blue swim-suits with cameras mounted on their heads."

"Alive, I hope?"

"Yes, at least I think they both are. One of them isn't moving, but he is upright on the surface while the other swims around him. I'm sure medical attention is required."

"Can you get their trainer to them on a skiff?"

"Really? For dolphins, Dmitri?"

"Trust me, they've earned it."

He heard his friend sigh.

"Very well. Get your trainer ready and I'll have the skiff pick him up on your port side."

"I'll explain tonight why you're doing the right thing."

"Yes, you will. But as of now, I'm no longer paying for the drinks all night. You're buying the second round."

Volkov summoned his veteran on his microphone.

"Get the trainer on the phone."

"One moment, sir. He's right here."

"Yes, sir?" the trainer asked.

"A helicopter has found your dolphins. At least one is alive. The other is questionable, but I'm hopeful. I've arranged for you to board a skiff and retrieve them."

The line went silent.

"He's on his way up, sir," the gray beard said. "He took off into the conning tower like lightening."

The echoing ring of boots against rungs rose like staccato, and then the trainer materialized. Holding back tears, he trembled. Volkov shrugged and then raised his arms, conceding to the inevitable.

"Very well. Let's get this over with."

The trainer fell into his chest and embraced him.

"Thank you."

"It was my pleasure. You earned it."

Volkov pushed him back.

"Enough. You have work to do. They need your attention. Get out of here."

Forty-five minutes later, the frigate's skiff pulled away from the *Krasnodar*, and a sailor handed the satellite phone to the executive officer.

"That's it, sir. That's everyone except you and the captain."

The executive officer turned, lifted the phone, and hunched into an earnest conversation. When the minute elapsed, Volkov remained silent and let the man continue, wondering how he would deal with the uncomfortable situation of having nobody to call when his turn arrived.

His few friends were drinking buddies who commanded naval vessels and hid their loneliness together in alcohol. As for a wife, he stood atop her steel hull.

As he sought a clever way to hide his social solitude, he noticed the arm pushing the phone his way.

"My father wants to speak with you."

He accepted the phone and pressed it against his ear.

"This is Commander Volkov."

The voice carried the certainty of a man accustomed to people listening.

"Commander Volkov, is what my son said true? Did he show courage and skill during your battles?"

"Yes, sir. He showed great character under stress. I was impressed. His performance was exemplary."

"My son? I'd never seen any spark that could ignite him to his potential. But when he just talked to me, he sounded like a changed person. I thank you for turning my son into the man I wanted him to be. I am in your debt."

"It was my duty, sir. I was happy to do it."

"You know I have great wealth and political power within the region."

"Yes, sir. I don't claim to know the full extent, but I'm aware of your reputation."

"I am privy to information that's relevant to the forces around you. I know how each member of your admiralty will position himself in response to what just happened. Are you ready to hear what you will experience upon your return to port?"

Volkov swallowed and felt his heart pounding.

"Yes, sir. I'm ready."

"You may have already surmised what I'm about to tell you, but I regret to inform you that your submarine career in the Russian Navy is over. You'll be relieved of command."

The words were a lance in his sternum, and he forced a reply through his tight throat.

"I appreciate your candor."

"The truth is that all the admirals admire your efforts, regardless if they admit it or not. So you'll be allowed to have an administrative job until you're eligible to retire. But the power center of the flag officers will use you as the scapegoat."

"I'm sure I'll manage, sir. It's traumatic for anyone to leave behind command of a ship, whether it's to become a squadron commander or a scapegoat. I appreciate you warning me what sort of path I must now take."

"There is good news, however. It may not seem good now, but it will in time. People whose business it is to know things are aware of what you did. You have a fan base among select captains of industry who want to interview you for high-level positions."

The wind forced Volkov to yell into the mouthpiece.

"I haven't considered a career beyond a submarine. This is happening fast. I'm still commanding my ship as we speak."

"I understand. I don't mean to overwhelm you, but I do want you to know that you have a powerful ally in me. I will make sure that you have options. A man of your quality would be wasted behind an administrative naval desk."

"Thank you. I don't know what else to say."

"Say that you'll join me for dinner. There are many men eager to meet you. In fact, I'm enjoying an expansion of my network as word spreads that I've positioned myself as the gateway to you. There's one new name in particular that I'm dying to meet before making the introduction. You've created quite a following."

"I'm honored."

"May I count on you joining me for dinner tomorrow? I assume you'll want your privacy this evening."

"Yes."

"I look forward to it. My son will tell you when my car will pick you up at your quarters."

The line went silent, and Volkov handed the phone to his executive officer.

"We're having dinner with your father tomorrow night."

"We're not. You are. He doesn't mix family with business."

"I'm sorry. I didn't mean to exclude you."

"You didn't, sir. You included me in the most exclusive place I needed to belong but couldn't get to. I have my father back."

Volkov enjoyed the sentiment and then turned his attention to the water.

Placing binoculars to his face, he looked far beyond his rudder into the southern distance. Atop the *Goliath*, the *Specter* became a dot on the violet horizon, shrinking under the golden rays of the setting sun.

As the most thrilling episode of his life drifted away, the notion of never again seeing the tandem of mercenary ships filled him with relief–and sadness.

CHAPTER 25

Jake climbed the twisting earthen path up Montagne Saint Victoire, the peak he had seen glorified by the post-impressionist, Paul Cézanne. As uneven and jagged stones slowed his steps, an updraft from the valley lifted the scent of lilac into his nostrils.

Enjoying the risen sun's rays, he squatted against an olive tree and felt it bend. Hungry, he reached into his backpack for a baguette and wedge of Camembert before mashing the cheese into the bread. As he washed down a mouthful with a swig from his water bottle, he heard boots abrading rocks against rocks.

His wife, Linda, appeared in flannel hiking garb as she labored against the incline. She stood over him.

"You said this would be fun!"

"With those curves, I figured you'd have more power in your caboose."

She smacked his shoulder and issued a curse in Aramaic. Then she raised her pitch and added swears in the Iraqi dialect of Arabic. Recognizing the foul words, Jake laughed.

"Now say that all again in English."

"No."

"Yes."

"Fine, then. Divorce!"

"That's not what you said."

"It was close enough, you butt-head."

"Come on, it's not that bad. Rest with me and have a snack."

She sat beside him.

"It's embarrassing. I'm slowing everyone down."

"Only the young kids are ahead of us. The old dogs are still behind us."

"So what does that make us, if we're not the young kids or the old dogs?"

"I don't know about you, but I'd be with the young kids if you weren't my anchor."

She smacked him–repeatedly, and then she grabbed the

mashed cheese and bread from his hand.

"Give me that," she said.

Expecting a full meal with the team at the top of the mountain, he relinquished the food.

A group of Christians returning from a pilgrimage to the summit strolled by on their descent, and he greeted the two dozen people as they approached the end of their day's journey.

"They must have gotten up early," Linda said.

"That's how they do it."

He wanted to dart uphill, test his physical conditioning, and translate for the mix of young French and Australian sailors who he assumed struggled to bridge their language barrier. But he appreciated that his wife held him back because Renard had ordered him to keep pace with the bodyguards that protected his mentor's inner circle of irreplaceable men.

Looking ahead to the next switchback, he saw two muscular figures that scanned the trail, the adjacent escarpments, and the sky for threats to Renard's employees.

When he had met the guards, Jake recognized the unshakeable confidence of special forces personnel, and their oversized backpacks betrayed the existence of multiple firearms. Renard had justified the presence of the trained protectors by noting that his mercenary band had lost the luxury of anonymity.

Even the once-safe mountain required vigilance.

Jake heard crunching and looked to the trail below. Familiar people came into view as they rounded a bend, and Renard raised his voice.

"Good morning, Linda," he said. "You seem troubled, my lady."

"Jake said this would be fun, but I think he's crazy."

The woman beside the Frenchman, his wife, interjected.

"I agree with Linda," Marie said. "I do these climbs only when Pierre insists. These men view climbing the mountain as a challenge like a dragon to be slain. I'd be just as happy to rent a helicopter and enjoy the view from the top."

"The view is amazing so far," Linda said. "I can't wait to see the view from the top. I just don't like these jagged and crooked rocks. It's so hard to take a step."

"You'll get there," Marie said. "I know this is annoying, but you have to be patient and humor these egotistical pigs."

"I can't argue with being egotistical or a pig," Renard said. "But I take issue with the idea of a helicopter. The journey makes you appreciate the summit."

"Yeah, come on honey," Jake said. "It's worth it."

Walker and his wife rounded the bend with Cahill pacing himself behind them between the second pair of bodyguards. The Australians appeared invigorated with color in their faces.

"Okay. I'll be fine," Linda said. "Help me up."

Ninety minutes later, Jake held his wife's hand as they rounded a turn, and a chapel came into view. He crossed the doorstep and smelled stale oak. Except for a statue of Christ and a few rows of pews, the chapel was bare with a worn floor.

In the grassy yard outside the chapel, a dried-up well attracted his attention. He escorted his wife to it and peered between the bricks into a dirt-filled hole.

He walked her to a glass wall that blocked people from falling down the southern escarpment. The green plain spanned the horizon.

"It's beautiful," Linda said.

"Pierre tells me it used to be greener until a fire swept through almost thirty years ago."

"That's too bad."

"I guess it's recovered by now, but I'm no botanist."

Lifting his finger to the glass, he turned to verify Linda's attention.

"Toulon's in that direction. That's where our ships are hidden in a dry dock. On a clear day, you can see the town from up here."

After an eleven-day submerged voyage as Cahill's cargo, Jake had ridden the *Specter*–while still atop the *Goliath*–into an enclosed and covered wharf in the dark of night. He had handed his keys to his engineer officer, who missed the mountain voyage while tending to the ships' repairs with Cahill's engineer.

"Are you ever going to show me your ships?" Linda asked.

"What ships?"

"Oh yeah. I'm supposed to play dumb."

"You're not missing anything. Toulon's okay, but we'll be spending this vacation in nicer places. Come on."

He pulled her towards a structure that resembled a misplaced barn but which served as a gathering room for climbers resting below the summit. Inhaling, he smelled dampness and age.

Three young French sailors labored through an English description of their national navy's sonar training while two Australians listened. When Jake entered the room, they waved, and one said that the front-running climbers were waiting at the summit.

"If you're hungry, you'd better follow me," Jake said. "I'm going to hand out the food. First come, first served."

He retreated from the room and met a bodyguard ushering him and his wife to catch up with the rest. Rounding the cabin, he lost his balance as his foot slid across dirt. Slapping his palm against a rock, he steadied himself.

"Are you okay?" Linda asked.

"Yeah. Just watch your step. The last stretch is the hardest."

He stopped and let a young couple pass on their descent.

"They look happy," Linda said.

After turning a last corner, Jake saw the summit. Visitors stood and sat around the six-meter tall cross that graced the rock.

"It's not the highest point," he said. "That's over there to the left. But it's in a great spot to be seen from all over."

"I like it."

"Well, grab a sandwich from my back pack and check it out. I've seen it before, and I need to pass out the sandwiches."

He walked the upper section of the mountain, passing out lunch to the French and Australian sailors who comprised half of the mountaintop's guests. He passed a tiny living quarters that housed a single sentinel who watched for fires and tended to travelers in need, and he found the priest on a small observa-

John R Monteith

tory deck.

"You hungry, Father Andrew?"

"I'm starved. What do you have?"

As the party's strongest climber, Jake carried the bulk of its food. He had felt the weight lift from his shoulders as he had passed out a dozen sandwiches from his pack.

"I've got a few left."

"Roast beef?"

"I think so. You'll have to rummage through them."

He offered his back and let the priest withdraw his lunch.

"While you're back there, can you grab me turkey?"

"I don't see any turkey. How's ham?"

"That's fine. Can you zip me up when you're done? We're the last ones."

Jake turned, and Andrew handed him his sandwich.

"Thanks for hanging out with us."

"I'm glad you invited me. It's beautiful up here."

"That's why we come up here. When do I have to give you back to Bishop Francis?"

"I've got another week. I'm on vacation now."

"I didn't know priests got vacations."

"We're human like everyone else."

"You're welcome to hang out with the gang. We've got a few activities planned."

"I'm not sure everyone was happy about me being aboard. My guess is that they'll want you to reconsider before trying to bring me on a future deployment."

"I wasn't entirely sure I was happy about having you aboard, either. You spooked me out when you were offering confessions."

"Thankfully, it was an unnecessary gesture."

"What's your overall sense of things?"

Andrew collected his thoughts.

"Your anger was in check," he said. "You told me that was your worry, but I didn't see it except for rare moments."

"I surprised myself. Maybe I'm getting old and mellow."

"There's more to it than that. You can remain angry and bitter at any age. Something positive must have happened to you."

"I suppose."

"Did this experience help you gain any clarity on your personal philosophy?"

"Every time I flirt with death it makes me think about the value and purpose of life."

"I know what you mean about flirting with death. I couldn't understand it when you explained it in Michigan, but after living it, I get it. I'm curious, though, if you feel closer to God."

Jake felt calmer than he could remember as an alarm on his phone reminded him to take anti-retroviral drugs.

"I hadn't thought of it much, but I guess so."

"Linda has told me about your anger issues. So did some of your shipmates. So I know they've been real. But you seemed anything but driven by anger. You were driven by purpose."

"I can't argue. It just seems weird. I don't feel angry now, either, but I'm afraid I can erupt at any second."

"You said you stopped drinking. That could be a factor working in your favor."

Checking himself for an urge for inebriation, he found none.

"I used a drug called Naltrexone in the Sinclair Method, and I swear by it. I understand there are other processes and drugs interventions that work, but I know what worked for me."

By habit, he downed his medications with a swig of water.

"I suppose I'm also no longer living in fear of an early death from a virus that someone else gave me out of malice."

"You never mentioned that."

"I got the virus from an old captain during a blood transfusion. Then he tried to blame me for giving him HIV, and everyone sided with him. My career was over in a blaze of false accusations and shame, and that's pretty much the whole reason I went temporarily insane and stole a submarine in the first place."

"That's a good reason to be angry. I don't know about stealing a submarine, though."

"That's how angry I was. I obviously had issues before that, too, that made me an angry person. But now it's just a bad memory and a daily pill regimen."

"Maybe you can enjoy being less shackled by anger. That should help you focus on the positive things in your daily life and give you a new perspective."

"Just like that?"

"Not just like that. I think you've already started subconsciously. You can keep it going consciously now."

"I guess I can give it a shot. What are you talking about? Daily affirmations? Positive thinking exercises?"

"Sort of. Would you do me one favor for yourself?"

"That's a weird request, but probably."

"I'd like you to act Catholic for three months. You've had the catechism training. So why not come back to the Church and experience the full deposit of faith? I think you're in a place now where you can get out of crisis mode and explore and live your philosophy."

Jake tried to sidestep the commitment.

"I know it would make Linda happy," he said.

"I think it would help you, too. You don't have to lie or make pretenses. You can attend Mass as long as you are believing in Christ's message to the best of your ability."

He recalled the simplest pragmatic reason to favor Christ.

"Even if I'm just doing it for no greater reason than, say, Pascal's Wager?"

"That's fine as a starting point. If you reject Christ as your savior and you're wrong, you're in Hell for eternity. But it costs you nothing to seek to believe in God. So why not seek to believe?"

"It's not that simple," Jake said. "I know I brought up the wager, but you have to consider the other religions that would condemn me if I choose Christ. For example, if Islam is correct, then believing in Christ as the Son of God would condemn me, and Pascal's Wager is an incomplete statement."

"You've read the Bible and the Qur'an, haven't you? You're one of the best read laymen I know."

He reflected upon the encyclopedias of philosophy he had digested. With independent wealth, he enjoyed exploring mankind's ultimate question. He wanted to know the truth about why humankind existed.

"That's a good point. The historicity of the Qur'an doesn't stack up for me. To buy into Islam, you'd need to produce a book older than the Bible that denies Christ's divinity while upholding the parts about the miracles. Nobody can produce that evidence, and I'm only going as far as the evidence. On the other hand, there's a metric ton of it supporting the Bible's books."

"The historicity of the Bible in terms of ancient copies and corroboration with other sources is orders of magnitude greater than that of any other work of antiquity. It was a part of my decision to follow Christ, even before analyzing the content."

Jake reflected through the other religions that required deviations from Christian philosophy for salvation. The ancient document archive was lacking for all he had studied.

"I agree that Pascal's Wager is a good enough framework to make me seek to believe."

"So I'll see you in Mass?"

"Why can't I just go to a nondenominational church, or Lutheran, or Methodist, or Baptist, or Episcopal or et cetera et cetera? You and Bishop Francis have been great to Linda and me, but isn't Christ available pretty much anywhere?"

"I can guarantee you His presence in the Eucharist at Mass, but He's anywhere He wants to be."

"I'm not ready or even thinking that I want to go back to the Catholic Church. I heard the message there in my childhood, and it didn't stick. I want to hear the message from different sources."

"I'm happy as long as you get closer to Jesus."

"Okay. I'll make the effort."

He heard his boss' voice.

"Jake!" Renard said.

"Yes, sir?"

"Will you join us? I'm going to share my news. We're huddled together on the other side of the summit."

"I'll be right there."

He excused himself, walked by the cross, and then knelt with the *Goliath's* top two officers, Henri, Remy, and Renard. The bodyguards lingered outside the circle.

"No reading material?" Jake asked.

"We're not diving into any great detail. I just wanted to share some important high-level thoughts. I could have done this somewhere else, but I thought this would be a worthy venue for highlighting the bright outlook I see for us."

"What's going on?" Jake asked.

"Yeah, spit it out, mate," Cahill said.

"I have several items. The first is my recent conversation with Miss McDonald. She considers our mission to have been a success, even with having to buy our way out of it."

"Does she consider us in her debt?" Jake asked.

"No. That's perhaps the greatest news of all. And this isn't just my subjective read. She stated it clearly. I suspect that she enjoyed calling on her allies to pool the cash together for the Russians. I think it helped her flex her political muscle."

"So this was our most profitable mission yet?" Jake asked.

Renard raised a cigarette to his lips and then lowered it upon Jake's reminder.

"Pierre? The fire hazard?"

"Yes, I forgot. I should just keep these things in my pocket forever. I've lost track of the times I've tried to quit. Now, to your point. Yes, our mission was lucrative. We are out of Miss McDonald's debt, and I plan to use the proceeds for growth."

"Another ship?" Cahill asked.

"Exactly. The Taiwanese have been building the *Goliath's* twin, and with Miss McDonald's payment, I can accelerate the pace. I expect to see it complete within a year. Then we can pair it with the *Wraith*, and we'll have a presence in the Atlantic and the Pacific."

"That's great," Jake said. "But we're still low on talent. We barely have enough to staff the *Specter* and the *Goliath*."

"Agreed," Renard said. "That's why I'm happy to share another piece of potentially good news."

Lacking a cigarette, the Frenchman bit into his sandwich to gain his dramatic pause. Mirroring the cue, Jake bit off a mouthful of ham that he coughed up when Renard shared his climactic gem.

"I've made a job offer to a new commanding officer."

"You're kidding," Jake said.

"No, I am not. I can't say yet if he will accept, but I've met with him and made my pitch. I can only hope that he'll see the benefits of joining our merry band."

"Well, who is it?" Jake asked.

"Though you have yet to be introduced, I believe you all know him. His name is Dmitry Volkov."

THE END

About the Author

After graduating from the Naval Academy in 1991, John Monteith served on a nuclear ballistic missile submarine and as a top-rated instructor of combat tactics at the U.S. Naval Submarine School. He now works as an engineer when not writing.

Join the Rogue Submarine fleet to get news, free audiobook promo codes, discounts, and your FREE Rogue Avenger bonus chapter!

Rogue Submarine Series:

ROGUE AVENGER (2005)
ROGUE BETRAYER (2007)
ROGUE CRUSADER (2010)
ROGUE DEFENDER (2013)
ROGUE ENFORCER (2014)
ROGUE FORTRESS (2015)
ROGUE GOLIATH (2015)
ROGUE HUNTER (2016)
ROGUE INVADER (2017)
ROGUE JUSTICE (2017)
ROGUE KINGDOM (2018)

Wraith Hunter Chronicles:

PROPHECY OF ASHES (2018)
PROPHECY OF BLOOD (2018)
PROPHECY OF CHAOS (2018)
PROPHECY OF DUST (2018)

John Monteith recommends his talented colleagues:

Graham Brown, author of The Gods of War.

Jeff Edwards, author of Steel Wind.

Thomas Mays, author of A Sword into Darkness.

Kevin Miller, author of Declared Hostile.

Ted Nulty, author of The Locker.

ROGUE HUNTER

Copyright © 2016 by John R. Monteith

Stealth Books

www.steatlhbooks.com

The tactics described in this book do not represent actual U.S. Navy or NATO tactics past or present. Also, many of the code words and some of the equipment have been altered to prevent unauthorized disclosure of classified material.

ISBN-13: 978-1-939398-59-8
Published in the United States of America

Made in the USA
Columbia, SC
12 August 2019